Homesick

ROSHI FERNANDO

BLOOMSBURY
LONDON • NEW DELHI • NEW YORK • SYDNEY

First published in Great Britain 2012
This paperback edition published 2013

Bloomsbury Publishing, London, New Delhi, New York and Sydney

50 Bedford Square, London WC1B 3DP

A CIP catalogue record for this book is available from the British Library

ISBN 978 1 4088 3040 6
10 9 8 7 6 5 4 3 2 1

Typeset by Hewer Text UK Ltd, Edinburgh

Printed and bound in Great Britain by CPI (UK) Ltd, Croydon CR0 4YY

MIX
Paper from responsible sources
FSC® C020471

www.bloomsbury.com/roshifernando

For Tom

CONTENTS

HOMESICK

Victor is thinking of other parties, of his childhood: quiet, dignified, the productions of an excitable wife of a dour clergyman. Homemade marshmallows, he remembers, lightly coloured with cochineal, dusted with icing sugar. He stands in the hallway of his own home in south-east London, looking at the late afternoon sun colouring everything with a honey glaze. My, he thinks, he can even see his own pudgy hand, reaching up to the table to steal a sweet, and a servant clucking away behind him, shoo shooing him, as if he were an escaped hen. If his father had seen him, there would have been the nasty, damning words about thieves, about hell. He hears Preethi and Nandini in the kitchen, the pan lids banging, the murmured voices, one of them chopping at the table, a small laughter. I am rich, he thinks.

He walks into the sitting room, adjusts cushions on the plush cream sofas, a recent investment. The plastic covers have been removed for this evening, but will go back tomorrow: Nandini said that, once bought, this three-piece suite would be their last.

It must survive thirty years, then, he thinks, for we are so *young* still, barely fifty. The sun is setting. He stands by the window, looking out to the opposite houses. Already there is music from the end of the street: West Indians, their party will be raucous. Never mind, never mind. He takes his C. T. Fernando record out of its sleeve, holds it carefully by the edges, blowing the dust away gently into the last pink rays of the sunshine. When he places the needle on to the crack-crack of the outside lines, he can smell poppadoms frying, he can feel the warmth of other air, he can hear the voices of people long left behind. And Victor's eyes fill with tears, for there is no going back in his life. Only the moving forward to better things, there is only the climb up steep, green hills that signify this Britain. He sits gingerly on the sofa as if he were the guest and the sofa the host. '*Ma Bala Kale*', C.T. sings, and Victor hums along, remembering that the poppadoms will not be fried until the evening.

o

Preethi is angry. Nandini is again talking of money, of wasted opportunities. She is talking about resolutions, and Preethi is tired of saying – *yes, Ammi*, I will work harder, I will forget that under this skin, there is *me*. She wants to say – you know I'm slow, I'm not like Rohan and Gehan, I just can't *do* what you want me to *do*. But she changes the subject. Talks about Clare, her friend from school, coming to the party.

'She's got the whole of *Brideshead* on video. Sometimes we watch two episodes . . .'

'Watch? But I thought you studied together?'

'Yes. We do. But sometimes, we take a break and watch – and it is by Evelyn Waugh. And you used to watch it with me.'

Which wasn't true, she thought – Ammi was always asleep on the sofa.

They are silent.

'So, who is coming tonight, Ammi?'

'Wesley and Siro. This one, Gertie – she is bringing that foster child of hers. And her brother. He's done *very* well. He is here attending *Sandhurst*.'

'What's that?'

'Officer training.'

'What? For the army? Which army?'

'The Sri Lankan army, fool.'

Preethi pauses for effect. 'The Sri Lankan army who like to repress and murder Tamil people. You know, Tamil people like me and Dad?'

'Don't be clever, clever. We left that behind, all that talk. You're in England. Talk of English politics. How can you understand Sri Lanka? It is not ours to understand any more.'

'That's rubbish,' she starts, but her mother slaps her hand. It stings.

'Don't say "rubbish" to me. Do you think I would have said "rubbish" to *my* mother?'

Preethi washes her hands, and wiping them on her backside, edges around her mother's chair in order to leave.

'Where are you going? Come and chop the rest of these onions, then peel the carrots and grate them.'

She wants to call Clare. Tell her to bring a bottle of wine, which they can sneak to her room and enjoy by themselves. She sits back down at the table and starts to peel the carrots.

'Onions first!' her mother says. It is going to be a long New Year's Eve night, Preethi thinks. But tomorrow will be 1983, and something good should come of it.

Nandini finally in the shower, Victor takes another journey around the theatre of his house, imagining the characters who will be there shortly, seeing them stand with drinks in their hands, their colognes mixing with smoke, the perfumed silk-saried ladies perched on the chairs he has placed around the sitting room and dining room. The table is laid: Rohan and Gehan helped Preethi by lifting it and pushing it into the centre, so that people can travel around it, serving themselves from the various dishes Nandini has prepared. They had argued this morning, about the expense of a party. Nandini said he should have asked fewer people. But he knows that not everyone would come. Nandini is tired all the time, he reminds himself: he had been on Preethi's side. He would have let her go to college. She was happy at the local school. But Nandini took a second job, begged the private school to take Preethi on. Every penny is saved: no, he won't think about it now. He wears a Nehru shirt, khaki, and cream slacks. He looks into the hall mirror, combs his floppy straight hair back into the quiff he has worn since he was eighteen. All of his friends wear their hair this way.

The clock in the hall strikes seven. Gertie said she might come early, but the rest of the crowd are always late. Victor can hear the television upstairs in his bedroom. He helped Rohan carry it up there, in case the younger crowd got bored. He walks upstairs to see what they are watching. He looks around the door. His three children are lying on his double bed. Gehan holds the video buttons, and leans on his elbows, flat out on his tummy. He is still a baby, behind his glasses. Rohan and Preethi lie leisurely side by side, propped up by pillows. The tape finishes rewinding, and Gehan presses play.

The familiar trumpet solo, the white words, and then the fade into a single face, a stilted Italian accent: 'I believe in America.'

'*The Godfather, The Godfather* – it is all you watch,' he says from the doorway. They shush him. 'Hmm, hmm – that can wait. Your mother will need to get ready. Enough, enough. Go and put a change, Gehan. Rohan.'

'I'm changed, Papa,' Preethi says.

'I know you are, darling. You look lovely,' he says, as she walks past. He touches her face, pinches the burgundy satin of her dress. 'Come and choose some music with me,' he says gently, 'they will all be here soon.'

Preethi watches from her window for Clare. She managed to call, and Clare said to look out for her Dad's Mercedes. Clare is staying the night, as her parents are going to a party in a hotel in town. Down the road, there is laughter, reggae music, shouting. Preethi wishes she was there: all her friends at her old school were black. She misses Sonia and Marcia and Shanelle. She wonders if they are partying somewhere, maybe in that club in Peckham they used to go to.

She can see cars stopping on the street, and people getting out. Saris, men in suits. She turns to her door:

'Someone's here! They're here!'

Chitra and Richard don't arrive until nine-thirty. They have battled with public transport, pushed against the crowd on their way to Trafalgar Square, and now walk leisurely up to the door.

'Listen,' Chitra says. Richard pulls her to him and kisses her. 'Listen,' she says again.

'What?'

'Music. Baila music. And can you smell it? Can you smell the curry?'

She stands on the doorstep, but doesn't ring the bell. What will they say? The people who knew her before she left her husband for Richard will all be there, sitting as they always do, in vicious eyeing circles around the room. But she cannot resist, and Victor said he wanted her to come. He insisted that she come. And she is proud of Richard, this famous writer, this gorgeous god with his shoulder-length, greying, Byronesque hair. Suddenly, the door opens, and she peers in, as Preethi throws her arms wide.

'Aunty! Come, come!' and they are pulled in to the warm embrace of the party.

Victor knows they are expecting him to say something. Nandini has indicated with a nod that the food is ready to serve. He looks around him, from face to face. There are thirty or forty people there, talking, laughing, some kissing on either cheek. Mr Basit is sitting in the centre of the sofa, his wife Rita perched on the arm next to him; Jenny, their daughter, is upstairs. Nandini is not happy because Mr Basit brought a bottle of whisky, and insisted that Victor try some. Victor gave up drinking in the summer of '77, the same week Elvis died. But Victor respects Mr Basit, and it is an honour that he brought such a special bottle of whisky – old whisky, Basit says. Victor had opened the bottle, taken cut glass tumblers from the kitchen (Nandini specifically told him earlier that only plastic cups must be used), and poured a glass for Mr Basit, a glass for Wesley, a glass for Hugo, a glass for Mr Chatterjee and a glass for himself. He did not offer any to Kumar, Shamini's cousin, even though he slinked about the back door purring obsequiously at Victor. Nasty-looking fellow, drunk when he got here, Wesley said. They had stood together outside in the garden, five friends, toasting the New Year. It had been a quiet moment of clarity, filled with the resonance of the cold, bell-like clinking of their glasses. They had all knocked the drink back, in one, as they would have done with arrack in Sri Lanka. And the salt harshness of the spirit on his lips dances there still. He looks around at the party, and he sees them all in the swimmer's gaze of a whiskied moment. Nandini's eyes shine black and hard, as he raises his glass and shouts: 'Friends! A toast! Here is – I mean – *to US*!' and he stumbles a little, and laughs. 'Time to eat, time to eat . . .' Nandini turns, calls to Preethi, and Preethi and Nil, Siro and Chitra follow her to the kitchen to start bringing through the tureens of mutton, lentils, silver platters of yellow rice, glass bowls of salads and baskets of poppadoms.

Victor sits down next to Gertie. Her foster child May is with her.

'Hello, little girl,' he says, pinching her cheek lightly. 'There are a lot of other little girls upstairs. Why don't you go and play?'

She shakes her head.

'Shy, shy,' Gertie says. 'Talk to my brother, will you? He's another shy one, *nayther*?' she says, poking the young man sitting beside May. Victor nods to the man, an officer in the army.

'Come and eat,' he says to the fellow. The brother had been introduced but Victor cannot remember his name. The whisky has clouded his mind, and all he sees are colours now, around each person, greens, purples, golds, crimsons. Around this man, there is a yellow fire, an easy lion aggression: if the fellow were to open his mouth, a roar of the fire would belch out, and Victor realises he hates him, without reason. On impulse, he takes the man's hand, pulls him from his chair, and pushing his shoulder lightly, leads him to the dining room, where people are already loading their plates. Nandini stands watching the dishes empty, waiting to swoop down to refill them. He catches her eye: she smiles from the side of her mouth. Victor looks at her across the party, and a tenderness for her erupts from him, and to his embarrassment and surprise, he imagines their warmth in the dark, the smell of her neck, the soft flabby skin of her stomach, crushed and stretched and worn. And he sees around her a glow of pink and mauve, which takes his breath away.

⭘

Upstairs, *The Godfather* has got to the wedding night, and Rohan has stopped the video. There are too many little children wandering in and out of the room, and he is embarrassed by the actress's high pale breasts: so ugly to him, so unnatural, the way she turns to Michael and removes her slip. The older kids are annoyed, and he is ushering children down the stairs to go and eat. But there is a crush in the hallway, so children run up and down the stairs, trying to go further upstairs to see what Preethi is doing in her bedroom. Gehan has taken the boys his age into his own room, and they are playing Monopoly for real money they have rummaged from coats hanging on the banister.

Preethi calls down to Rohan: 'Get the ghettoblaster out! Clare brought some tapes.' He thinks this is not such a bad idea. Nil comes to help him.

'Where's Mo, tonight?' he asks her. Her brother is one of his good friends, and he is disappointed he didn't come.

'He's gone up to Trafalgar Square with some mates.' She seems shy; it is strange, for they have known each other since they were toddlers. Nil is beautiful now, with her long hair and her deep reddish skin, the high cheekbones like her father Wesley. Her eyes dance at him.

'You've got a secret,' he says. He knows her, he can read her.

'I've got engaged,' she says. He didn't expect it. It is a punch in the head.

'No,' he says. 'Who to?'

'Who do you think? Ian, for goodness' sake.'

'And Uncle's going to let you marry a white guy? Like hell!'

'Yes, he is.'

'You haven't told them, have you?'

'Yes. They won't stop us. They like him.'

'They've met him? Liar. You're making it up.'

'I brought him home.'

'What, for a curry feed and a quick sing-song?'

She slaps his back. 'Shut up,' she laughs. 'I'm hungry. Let's go and eat.'

But before they go down, he pulls her back to his parents' bedroom, and closes the door, and quite unexpectedly, they find they are kissing in the dark, the way they have often kissed before. He feels nothing sexual towards her. His dick nestles limp in its place, but there is comfort in their kiss. When they walk out, he knows there will be no more kissing Nil, and so he prolongs it, keeps her there, against the door, brushing her hair away from her face, and smiling at her closed eyes.

In the kitchen, Nandini and her friends are talking about relatives in Sri Lanka. Shamini's husband's family are cousins to Victor's father. Nandini pretends to be interested, but what she and Shamini have in common is something internal and unsaid. They had both defied their families and married Tamils. Shamini's husband had left her. Victor, her husband, her *husband* – there were no other words for the upstanding, beautiful man who lay next to her, who stood tall, who took her hand and held it, sometimes as if clinging on – he was here, and although Shamini felt their equality, they are not equal. Shamini is a sniping woman, silly with her children, the two little girls Deirdre and Lolly. If she talked of them, it was always about Deirdre, the clothes she has bought for Deirdre, the expense, Deirdre's shoes, Deirdre's beauty. And in fact, the child is a fat-faced thing, who uses both hands when she eats, smearing food down her lovely dresses, picking her nose too. Nandini hates the child: there is something like an animal about her open mouth. Lolly, they all like. She had been a charming baby, with big eyes and willing to go to anyone with her arms raised out for a hug. But even Lolly has seemed to become a wretch recently: like a beaten dog.

'And why did Gertie foster a black child, *chchiii* . . .' Shamini says, under her breath to Nandini.

'What do you mean?' Nandini says sharply. Chitra and Dorothy turn.

'The blacks,' Shamini says even more quietly, 'nasty . . .' but before she can continue, Nandini comes quickly to her and holds her arm.

'We are all the same, in this house. Who are you to say you are better? All are welcome. Sinhala, Tamil, Burger, Black.'

'I am just saying,' Shamini begins, but the other women stand behind Nandini.

Dorothy draws a breath. 'You know, Shamini – I have been here longer than most of you. Do you know, Hugo and I came in '62? And when we got here, it was the black people who made us feel welcome. Look at me – I am almost white. And Hugo, he *is* white, after all. But our accents, our clothes – people turned away. Even at church. And who became our friends? The black people we met in our building. That child is a lost child . . .' but she cannot go on. She does not understand Shamini's objections.

Gertie and May come into the kitchen to wash their hands, followed by Kumar, Shamini's cousin. He is holding Lolly by the hand.

'Lolly, come here, darling,' Nandini says. Chitra strokes her head as she walks past. Her hair is short, like a boy's, parted at the side with a diamante clip pushing it back behind her ear. A short yellow dress and tights, and strangely, as she approaches, she has to tug her hand away from the drunk cousin, and his hand trails down the dress, behind her. All the women but Shamini look at him, and Dorothy clucks him away. Renee Chatterjee calls down the corridor, 'They're trying to get Rita to play the piano! The singing! I love the singing!'

'Lolly,' Nandini says, 'this is May. Take her now and go and play upstairs with the others, darling.'

Lolly approaches May, and shrugs at her. May follows, and the party of women laugh, following Renee's voice into the corridor and to the sitting room, where already the chords are being played of the song about Surangini, and the fish man. Nandini can hear Victor's raised voice in the dining room, and the laughter that follows, and she smiles.

Preethi and Clare are drunk by eleven. But not too drunk, because Vita, Nil's sister, has joined them and so has Jenny, and they have shared the bottle of wine, giggled about boys and talked about sex, and Clare has told them what a blow job is, and they have all agreed that it is something that they will never do, not for all the money in the world.

'Imagine even holding one,' Preethi says, and they break into hysteria, but it is false. It is a party, and they are drunk. Clare has cigarettes, and offers them around. Preethi and Jenny refuse, but Vita takes one, and they all stick their heads out of Preethi's window to look up at the moon and continue talking. The party has slipped leisurely into the front garden, and men stand with drinks and cigarettes, and their smoke reaches Preethi and Jenny, Clare and Vita. They stay quiet to listen, because there is an urgency to the voices, and Preethi sees it is her father and a beautiful young man talking.

'There are other ways,' her father says.

'What do you suggest?'

'Killing, beating, all of this – it is not the answer. *Forgiveness* – that is the answer,' Victor says.

The young man throws his head back and laughs, then drinks down his drink. 'Forgiveness? What has your forgiveness done for you? You think the way things are in Sri Lanka is down to the Sinhalese? The Tamils didn't do so badly under the British, did they? Should we have forgiven after they left? Where would we be now? Still under Tamil rule, that is where, and no more Sri Lanka,' he says, clicking his fingers. 'And you here – what will your forgiveness do for you here? The whites hate you!'

Clare shouts down, '*I* don't hate you, Victor! I *love* you!' and Preethi elbows her, and Vita chokes as she tries to smother her cigarette puffs so her uncles don't see her.

'You see,' Victor laughs, pointing up at the window. 'It is nearly midnight. We don't want to argue now, do we?' He puts his hand out to the young man, and rests it on his shoulder. 'Come, come. I will get you another drink. Come and sing,' he says.

Preethi hates her father for this. She hates his appeasement and his gentility.

'Oi,' she shouts down, after they walk away, 'leave my dad alone!' and the four of them laugh again.

Chitra calls up. 'Silly girls! Wherefore art thou, silly girls?'

They giggle, and choke, and watch other people in the dark – Hugo kissing Dorothy's hand as he leads her back into the house; Richard and Chitra easing their way down the hill, arm in arm. 'Bye, Aunty!' Preethi shouts after them.

'D'you think she does?' Clare says, and they all squeal at the thought of Chitra and Richard going home to bed.

'Course she does.'

'What, blow jobs?'

'Err, don't,' Vita says.

Preethi hangs out of the window still. 'It's a beautiful night,' she says. 'On such a night as this, did fair Troilus . . . what is it?'

'Oh, I don't know, Preethi,' Clare says.

Vita finishes her cigarette and throws the stub down on to the road. 'D'you know what I want to do? I want to *dance*.'

'Singing, singing,' Gertie says.

'I love it,' Renee Chatterjee replies. They have never met before, and although they would have a million things in common, neither of them has bothered to find out more about the other. It is too loud, and Gertie is out of sorts. She wants to tell someone: tell them how much May means to her, how wonderful a child she is, how they sat next to each other on the settee and sometimes the child's hand would stroke her own, and the companionship of it means more than anything. The singing stops. Men gather around the piano, their hips thrust forward, elbows gathered to their sides, their hands awaiting the next clap. Nil brings Rita a drink, leaves it on the top of the piano. Kumar leans on to Rita's shoulder, and Mr Basit pulls him back, pushes him out of the inner circle.

'I have to take the child back,' Gertie says to Renee. Renee follows her line of sight. Through the French windows beyond the piano, children can be seen running in and out of the bushes, playing hide and seek. Lolly and May hold hands, and Deirdre chases them. Although it is dark, she can see May's face, wide with joy, suddenly just a normal child.

'Why?' Renee asks.

'Her mother wants her back. She hates her because she is black. But she wants her back.'

'The mother is white?'

'Yes, and the father was black. She expected the child to be like her.' Gertie wants to tell of the scars on the child's back, where the mother bleached her.

'Does the child know?'

'No. I don't know how to tell her . . .' and her voice breaks. Renee takes her hand.

'Then don't tell her. Just take her.'

Gertie stares, wide-eyed. 'That would be a *sin.*'

Mrs Chatterjee pats her hand. 'You enjoy each other for the last few days. She will remember you, you know that.'

'Her mother hates her. And I have to take her back.'

'Never mind, never mind. Life is hard for us all,' Renee says, and as they sit watching the singing, Renee taps Gertie's hand in time, as Gertie dabs at her eyes with her dead husband's white handkerchief.

The ghettoblaster is best in their parents' bedroom, Rohan and Preethi decide. Clare is flirting shamelessly with Rohan, her arm around his neck as he leans down to the deck to put Michael Jackson on. As he presses the play button down, 'Don't stop till you get enough' begins, and he twirls her into the room, first with her arm, then pulling her back into a crotch thrust by the waist. Clare is thrilled, and so is Vita, who has been in love with Rohan since she was born, she thinks. Nil sits on the bed, watching, and Preethi calls to Gehan and his friends. Clare goes back to the 'blaster and turns it up. The children have run in from the garden and are now outside the bedroom, looking in curiously. They all watch as Rohan and Nil, Preethi, Vita, Jenny and Clare all start to dance wildly, their arms in the air, their feet pounding double time to the beat. On the stairs, a late arrival: Mohan has run up the hill from the station in order to be with his family for New Year. It is five to twelve.

Victor stops everything: 'It is nearly midnight! Let's count down! Ten! Nine! Eight!' Before he can continue, the noise from upstairs throbs the counts for him. 'What is that?' he says, but he knows it is his children.

'Another song!' Kumar shouts, but as he shouts, he falls over.

'Three! Two! One!' Wesley says, and then 'Happy New Year!' and everyone shouts 'Happy New Year' to each other, and there are kisses all around Victor, but the music goes on upstairs, so that as the people kiss each other in his sitting room, and their colours mix like a kaleidoscope into smoky patterns, he becomes angry. He remembers home, the New Years when he was a teenager, the faces he kissed there, the night heat and rain, and his mother's orchids, their silhouettes in the moonlight. He remembers the smell of the warmth, of drying coconut and rice. But he remembers also his father's stinging switch, his mother's face turned away. He wants to get to Nandini, because he is all out of it: of the party, of the friends, of his children. Nowhere he can find home, but if he found Nandini, it would be there, in her, and he would be safe again. He looks for pinks, for mauves.

The dancing does not stop. They show off to each other. They dance, brothers and sisters together, they dance because they can. They are exhausted, but they push on, they push each other on, because they are new, they are the ones.

'What to do?' Siro says to Nandini. 'She is determined to marry him, what to do?'

'Good. Let her make a good marriage,' Nandini says. Wesley and Victor sit with them in the dining room. Many people have gone. Gertie and her brother sit on the opposite side of the table.

'Good, good. These children will never go back,' Gertie says. 'Let them make marriages here.'

'But with white fellows?' her brother says.

'Why not?' Gertie asks sharply. 'You think once you give them all this, you can take them back there, take it all away?'

'Why not?' Wesley asks. 'They can get used to anything. They are not English. They are *ours*.'

'What rubbish!' Nandini says, and Siro agrees with a nodding of her quiet head.

'What is their mother tongue, now?' the brother says.

'What does it matter?' Victor says.

'Language – it is important. What is their mother tongue?'

'Ask me what is mine,' Victor says. 'It is the same as theirs. We speak in the language we live in. It is not important.' He sees the yellow fire, as if it were dangerous, this man, dangerous.

'What language do you dream in?' the brother asks.

'Dream?' Wesley answers for Victor. 'We live in our dreams. We do not need to dream.' They all laugh.

The children come downstairs. Vita sits on Wesley's knee. Preethi throws her arm around Victor.

'What is your mother tongue?' the brother says to them both. Clare leans against the doorway. Preethi shrugs. Vita says, 'Oh my God, are you arguing about that stuff again?'

'Do you want to know? I will show you,' Nandini says, and she elbows Siro, and the two of them together poke their tongues out, catching the tips with their fingers. Nandini crosses her eyes. Victor laughs, but he wants to cry.

'We belong *nowhere,*' he says. 'But if we belong anywhere, it is *here*. I have chosen *here*.' He stands. '*We* have chosen *here*. And that is it,' he says, flicking his wrist up as if tossing an imaginary cricket ball into the air. 'We are *here*.'

When everyone is finally gone, and the children are asleep, he and Nandini go to bed. They talk of the brother, of Kumar and stupid Shamini. They gossip and laugh, but when the light is off, he turns on to his side and kisses Nandini on the forehead, on the nose, on the lips. He says, 'I was homesick for you,' and she laughs and says, 'Silly, you were drunk,' as she rolls over and tucks herself into him, pulling his arm around her, her husband, her *husband*.

THE BOTTLE OF WHISKY

'Allsorts!' Basit hears him shout. The young one in the cellar. They call him Allsorts and it makes him angry, but they all have sweetie names. This makes Rita laugh, when he tells her their sweet names, as if they were not the bastard, nasty fellows he knows them to be. She says 'Sweet names, as if they were sweet on each other!' He loves Rita, loves her joy, the way she has taken him on, the way she wipes her hand across his forehead when he's angry. The way she loves his boy, his grown-up son Ali: taking him to work at the hotel, getting him a job so he's safe away from the men *he* works with.

It's not real work, not the way he worked in Sri Lanka. Over there, he pushed along in his father's tailoring business, machine-sewing sarongs with a pedal Singer. He drank and gambled. The black sheep, they sent him to England as soon as he had earned the fare. Off the boat he looked like everybody else, but now, he catches a glimpse of himself in the mirror of the club: grey shiny suit, sharp as broken glass, hair slicked back in a quiff, white shirt, black, thin tie; his jacket buttons done up, a cigarette dangling from his lips; and even though they're inside, the thin sunglasses.

'Allsorts!' the man calls from the cellar.

'Yes, yes,' he says obsequiously, as if startled to it.

'Come here, you wog,' the man says. There is no side to him. It's just what they say. Wily oriental gentleman, the boss said it meant. But to Basit, wogs are the black guys. It is short for Golliwog, and though the black clubs are where he goes when he's world-sore, unhappy, seeking out the friendships of his first days off the boat, he doesn't want them confusing him with blacks. He's not black. He's a Sri Lankan, a Muslim, from Colombo, not the sticks, his parents from a good family . . . he said it at the tables once, and one of the big bosses said, 'You're nothing here, mate. You're what *we* say, all right?' And the other one started laughing, and said, 'Here, your name's Basit, right? What about we call him Allsorts?' And they all laughed, and he laughed with them, because he was grateful for the job.

The man is stuck in the cellar. He's trying to lift a box, looks like a tea chest.

'What you want me to do?' he says. The man looks up; he's no more than a boy really. They call him Bullseye because he has a glass eye, an accident when he was doing his national service.

'We've got to leg it. They'll be coming soon,' Bullseye says, and he looks pale.

'Who?' He doesn't understand why they are here. It's a small club, all locked up, but Bullseye has a key.

'Look, boss said come over, get this box, and leg it, so that's what we're going to do, but you got to give me a hand, all right?'

He can't help himself, he nods his head from left to right, that up and down sideways agreement that was silent acquiescence at home. Bullseye starts to laugh, a little snot shooting from his nose. 'You look like a fucking coolie when you do that,' he says, but he means it kindly. Basit moves in to help him, looks at the situation. The stairs down to the cellar are rickety, riddled with worm and shredding off in places. The chest is too big for two people to negotiate up the steps.

'Let us empty it?' he says.

'No mate, boss says we leave it. Nothing to be disturbed. Secret stuff in there.'

When he got off the boat, he had one suitcase, brown leather, which his father gave him. A khaki shirt, brown trousers and one brown cotton jacket, all of which his father had made on the Singer machine. He headed the way others headed, on the train from Tilbury and then towards the East End. London yielded little. He followed a Muslim once, but lost him in the narrow alleyways. His very first night he spent by the river on a bench. He had never felt so cold. But the sun coming up over the Thames was the shivering sunshine of his future: a paradox, the chilly sun, the whiteness, the clear air of it all; this was his home now, this illogical island. It was *his*, he decided that day, and when he stretched his creaking limbs and stood, he found he had grown, and the world so large, so enormous, new and shiny, was inviting.

Bullseye is jammed on the stairs. He can't move up because his hips are grinding backwards against the rickety stair rail. He can't move down, although his right leg has some traction.

'If you'd helped,' he says to Allsorts.

Basit looks at the boy-man, and tries not to laugh. His son Ali is about the same age, that indefinable age when boys start to become men, the age when they fall in love, are sent off to war. Ali is cleverer than this boy.

'Wait, will you,' he says. He cocks his head, looks down into the cellar. 'We must empty the crate.'

'No. Boss says no,' Bullseye says.

'What is your name?'

'Why?'

Basit shrugs. 'I don't like these names the boss gives us. What did your mother call you?'

'Terence. Me sister calls me Terry.'

He has never known a Terry. It sounds like the name of a woman. The friends he knows are Victors, Harrys, Eddies, Johns. His own name – not even Rita calls him by his own name: he is Basit to Rita, and to his friends.

'Terry,' he says, trying the sound, disliking it. 'Terry, you can move?'

'No,' Bullseye says sullenly.

'Ah.' He looks around for something to lever with. Only round-backed chairs, and now he focuses on the room, they too are old, worn. 'Then,' he says, wringing out the word into many sounds, 'we must empty the crate.'

Bullseye says nothing. It is his fault, but Basit knows it will be blamed on *him* if there is no good outcome. So far, he has only had good outcomes. He has worked for these people for three years, and he covers his back, looks around, triple-guesses every situation. He will not step wrong: the big glittery world he lives in will not break, because he will not let it.

'It is nailed down?'

Bullseye says nothing.

'Terry,' he says sharply, and he hears his father's voice.

'Yes,' Bullseye says. 'I've got pins and needles.'

'What is this?' Pins and needles: he thinks of his grandfather, pins in his mouth, his father, pins cushioning at his womanly chest, maybe entering his skin and he wouldn't have noticed.

Bullseye doesn't reply. Basit walks down the stairs. He tries the box lid and it is tight on. He tries to move it this way and that, to a sudden shout from Bullseye: 'Oi! That hurts!'

Basit takes his knife from his pocket. It is a single flick knife, ebony handle, blade like silver, presses the button. 'Oi,' Bullseye says, and looks straight at him. No trust between any of them.

'It is all right,' Basit says. 'Here, watch,' he says. He puts the knife into the gap and levers gently. A nail creaks against the wood. He can smell tea. He is transported briefly . . . and then back again, to this strange nether place. He can feel Bullseye's breath on his mouth: the warmth disgusts him, he hates this boy-man, so small and useless. He stands still, stuck, like a ship waiting for Tower Bridge to open.

He proposed to Rita by Tower Bridge. Rita was young, vibrant. His first wife died in Sri Lanka the year before he came to England. His teenaged son Ali looked like he was becoming his father: skipping school to go to the cinema, quiffing his hair like Elvis, staying out late and drinking. They put him on a boat to England with an old friend of Basit's. As if the last of him was eradicated from the island, as if they didn't want a trace of him left to remind them. And then Rita came along, little Rita, with her curly hair and her Burger pale skin. She was Sri Lankan, the cousin of the friend who accompanied Ali to England. She cooked at a hotel in Fulham; brought home tasty treats for them both. Rita agreed to marry him the night England won the World Cup. As the city erupted, they held close to each other: it seemed their city celebrated them, shouted for them, beeped their horns and yelled for them.

The last nail comes out of the box. Bullseye has said nothing. Basit levers up the nail and the lid comes off. There is newspaper on the top. He sees the date on *The Times* is 1944. Bullseye holds his breath. Basit pulls the paper off. Inside there are guns. Maybe ten or twelve.

'German,' Bullseye breathes dramatically. Basit stares. He hates the sight of them, their liquorice lustre, their power to mesmerise. He reaches for a wrapped object, and tears at the newspaper: it is a bottle of Johnny Walker, black label, the lead seal intact. It looks old.

'Hurry up,' Bullseye says. And suddenly Basit is all action, leaning into the crate and unpacking each weapon, resting them on the stairs. After each gun is lifted, he tries to un-jam the crate. It is only when he takes out the last gun and then the bottle, that the crate can be shoved back and forth. Eventually he pulls the crate upwards, away from Bullseye, and then up the steps of the cellar.

The boys at the Jamaican club got him this job. He tried to set up a proper gambling den with Jules, his Jamaican friend. But Jules was more interested in music, and Basit won too many times. Jules had a friend who knew the bosses. They asked Basit to come to their club on the Old Kent Road, watched him shuffle, deal. Hired him on the spot. Quick fingers, Freddie the Pony said. They couldn't call him Quick Fingers, because there was a famous croupier up Golders Green way called that, a Jew boy. Basit thought he was in, but he was never really *in*, though if an outsider called him coon or nigger, they'd get it from one or other of the bosses. He was all sorts, yes, but he was theirs too. And they were fair to their own. He had taken Ali with him on one job, lifting job, taking goods from one lock-up to another, and Freddie and some others had given him a bag of chips, told him he was a good-looking boy. One of the bosses looked at him funny, so Basit asked Rita about jobs at the hotel. No funny stuff for Ali.

As the box comes away, Bullseye starts to yell. He's not swearing at Basit, just swearing, shaking his feet, his hands. His voice is loud, so loud that Basit, who is supposed to be the lookout, doesn't hear the key being tried in the lock. He has a habit of shifting the catch down on Yale locks from the inside. The key is being tried, and he only realises when people start swearing on the outside of the door.

'Terry,' he whispers fiercely. He pushes his hand down into the boy's face.

'Oh, fuck, oh fuck,' Bullseye says. 'What about the back door?'

Basit runs, grabbing a chair, fumbles with the bunch of keys to lock the door, and jams the handle with the chair. He runs back to the cellar steps. Bullseye is handling the guns. He looks up at Basit, and Basit sees how young he is, how frail.

'What d'you think?' Bullseye says, pointing a weapon at Basit.

'Put it back. Come on, put it back and come, will you?' It will take the others five minutes to get to the back of the building; they'll have to go round the promenade of shops and down the alleyway at the back. They can make it out the front.

'What, leave it here?'

'Yes. Come on.'

'Nah, mate. We may as well stay and be killed. Bosses will have us.'

Basit and Bullseye wrap the guns in the newspaper. They

look around for something to carry them in, and there is nothing. They were told to move a box, so they came in their suits with a Ford Anglia Estate that belongs to Bullseye's dad. Basit is now sweating, but he is also cold. He suddenly hates the boy, Terry. Hates his whining and his surrender and his wilful waste of his life: why would he do this work in this country when he is white? He could be anything. He is inside the big, wide gleaming world, and all he needs is education, and to work hard. Basit's hands shake. He hates the boy for his wasted opportunities, the way he hates his own banishment from the world where he could have been something if he hadn't squandered it all.

He puts the guns back into the crate, throws them in so they thud and fall like bodies. He takes the whisky and wraps it three, four times in paper, and places it on the top of the pile. He stops to listen: are they there at the back door? What can he hear? He's not sure. He begins to lever the box by himself to the door. Bullseye is inanimate, and when the back door handle is tried, Bullseye wets himself.

Rita, he thinks. Rita.

He is at the front door, turning the latch when they finally burst through the back door. Only two of them, but they're big fellows.

'Well, well,' one of them says. They don't say anything more. One takes the box away from him, gently, politely. The other punches Bullseye, but there is a graciousness about the way he lets him fall back on to a chair. And so begins a long afternoon, when they are beaten, questioned, beaten again. They are both tied to chairs. Neither of them says anything. They have nothing to say: the information wanted is unknown by anyone but the bosses.

He thinks of his other life, his good life.

On a Friday, if he has the night off, he takes Rita out dancing to Jules' club. She's one of those Portuguese black Burgers, the sort his mother would call 'fast'. In Sri Lanka, her family would have had a party every Friday and Saturday, cooking small eats all day, and serving bottle after bottle of arrack. The Baila music would be played by her uncles on guitars and drums and accordions, and they would sing and dance under the stars, in the garden. He could imagine her, the soul of her family: it was strange to them both that they had never known each other there, in Colombo – such a small place compared to London. But here they were each other's, and here, their dancing, to calypso beats, with stronger drinks and wilder friends, this was their own. Though they were both scared, they drove each other on, as if it made them bigger, as if the glass palace they wanted to enter, this great Britain which hated them and found them dirty and disgraceful, would see them dancing through their windows, and want to come out and join a more joyous, raucous party: because they were the new *great*.

Rita, he thinks. That is all he thinks. Bullseye lies wasted and used on the floor of the club, bleeding from his face, which is mushed like a stubbed-out cigarette, his glass eye rolling gently under a chair. As he regains consciousness Basit sees the men are post-coital after their day's activity and are resting at the bar. They have their backs to him. He is worn too, and angry, with Bullseye and the men, but mostly with himself. He gave up too easily. His hands are tied to the sides of his chair. He feels for his knife in his Chelsea boot, and flicks it open. He easily slits the tufted rope from his left hand, and watching the backs of the men, he cuts the rope from his right hand. He has done it all silently. The gentle material fall of the rope is too loud for him, and he puts his hands back into the position they were tied in. He gathers strength, thinks of the prayers of his youth, before he stopped going to the mosque. Recites one in his head, and then, before finishing, he stands, walks swiftly to the men, stabs one, withdrawing the knife from muscle with effort, and then punctures the other before they have time to turn around. One swivels to him as if to ask for the time, and falls. The other says: 'You fucking coon, fucking coon,' but slumps forward. He thinks it should take longer for someone to die. He turns to Bullseye. He seems dead. He kneels by his side.

'Terry! Terry.' He prods his arm, pulls it back and forth. The boy opens his good eye. 'Come on, we've got to go.'

'I can't,' the boy whines, 'it feels like they've broken me legs.'

'Come on, I'll get you to the car, and we'll get you patched up. Come on now.'

But the boy won't try, won't make any effort. Basit looks at him. Stands and looks around him, and catches a glimpse of himself in the mirror again. His shirt is bloody, his suit torn; his face is swollen, bruised. The men lie dying or dead about him, and Bullseye moans. He can suddenly see clearly the life he is living. It isn't shame that makes him plunge his knife into Bullseye's heart. Not anger either. Maybe nothing but the whining pettiness of the boy. Perhaps the line that he has to cross to do it is the line he crossed before: from the place he loved to the other side of the world.

He takes the keys to Bullseye's car, takes the bottle of whisky and leaves.

Two months later, after he thinks it is all over and done

with, Freddie comes into Jules' club, where he works intermittently, in between the hotel jobs.

'No hard feelings, Allsorts,' Freddie says, shaking Basit's hand, squeezing his shoulder. 'But the bosses are wondering what happened to the bottle of whisky.'

'The bottle of whisky?' Basit said. 'Those men drank it. Then Bullseye got free. He untied me, and he ran them through with a knife. But there was a terrible fight, and they killed Bullseye. His last words were "Run, Allsorts, run." So, I didn't know what else to do. I ran,' Basit told Freddie. Freddie took that story back with him to the bosses.

A few days later, Freddie came back. No one found the bottle there. That was 1930s whisky. The bosses were saving it. Expensive, best whisky.

'What are you saying?' Basit asked.

'Where is it?' Freddie said.

'I'm a Muslim. I don't drink. I don't have the whisky,' Basit said. It stood, in a cupboard of their flat in Fulham, next to Rita's London snow globe. The Tower, Big Ben submerged and glittering, as far from Basit now as they had always been.

Rita called from work two days later. Ali had fallen down a lift shaft. A dreadful accident. He was at the hospital, but his neck was broken. Basit went to the hospital, identified the body. Funny thing, among Ali's belongings was a miniature bottle of Johnny Walker black label. The boy had never been a drinker.

The bitterness of seeing Ali's carcass never left Basit. Everything in the world dulled. When he thought of London he thought only of the colour grey. Rita was already pregnant with their daughter Jenny, and he went to work on the buses, and then at the council. Freddie gave up with the clubs a year later and Basit got him a job at the council too. He was Freddie's boss for twenty years, but he realised not even being a boss would let him in. He and Rita would always be on the outside, looking at it all: the beauty, the greatness. He had never had any idea why he kept the bottle. So many years later, when Jenny was a teenager and Rita dying of cancer, he gave the whisky to an acquaintance at a party. After all, he had paid for it. It was easy to give it away.

THE CLANGERS

Her grandmother is the Soup Dragon, and they are the Clangers, she thinks as she wakes. Her mother goes out to work before Archee, the Soup Dragon, wakes Preethi and her brother. They walk about the cold house in housecoats made by Archee, and slippers bought at the market. It is Preethi's first day at nursery school today. Her mother has left written directions, and Archee will walk there with Mrs Cullen from across the road. She has Darren starting today.

Rohan, Preethi's brother, talks loudly and without need of a reaction. The Soup Dragon, picking the cereal spoon up and plunging milky Weetabix into Rohan's open, talking mouth, makes noises in the back of her throat in reply: 'Hmm, hmm.' Preethi watches them both from her chair, solemnly, eyes wide. She likes her Archee, and Archee smiles her a quiet answer. Preethi picks up her oversized spoon and inserts the mash of wheat into her small mouth, feeling it spill to her chin, and leaving it there because Archee has heated the milk and it is warm. Yesterday the Clangers had visitors on their moon, it was Spacemen, Rohan says, but they did not seem like visitors, because everything on that moon is normal and everything is also strange.

They get dressed quickly, because of the cold. They have no central heating, and although it is April, just after the Easter holiday, it feels like it will snow today, and there is icing on the inside of the windows. Preethi scrapes at it, reaching up above the Edwardian sill, taking black sooty dirt under her nail and wiping it on her trousers. Archee has watched her, and again the 'Hmm, hmm, hmm'. She makes Preethi brush her teeth, admonishes Rohan into allowing his hair to be tugged and mauled with a brush. Rohan goes to the toilet, gets his coat. Preethi suddenly wants to go for number twos but is worried because her daddy is not here: he always washes her. Rohan says, 'Preethi wants a jee-ya,' and Preethi starts to cry. Archee leads her to the toilet, and she sits there, looking at the man in the paint who only she can see. When she is finished, she tries to wipe herself, but Archee walks in with a plastic jug of warm water, and washes her just as well as her daddy.

Archee ties Preethi's pink fur hat on her head, does up her coat, buckles her red shoes. Rohan has already gone out of the front door, as if it were not a portal into a large, frightening world, but a simple step into a new day. He is sitting on the front wall. 'Preethi!' he calls. 'Preethi! I've decided, *this* part here is *my* garden, and you can have *that* part.' He is pointing at the clusters of ugly yellow flowers on the opposite side of the front steps. Preethi says nothing. She waits behind the front door for Archee to put her mother's old coat on. It is pale green with large cream plastic buttons. It is familiar, a friendly coat.

Archee looks about for the keys, and Preethi notices the

worn-out quality of her unsmiling face. Archee wraps a scarf about her neck, then takes it off and ties it about her head. Looking at herself in the mirror in the hall, she unties it again and wraps an end around her neck, then she pulls the scarf over her head, and tucks the other end back around her neck. She seems satisfied with this. 'Come,' she says, and offers her hand to Preethi. Preethi stands and takes the hand, and Archee, patting her hand on the coat pocket where the keys are, pulls Preethi out into the day and single-mindedly closes the front door.

Mrs Cullen and Darren wait outside. Rohan has started to walk up the hill with Matthew, Darren's brother. Matthew and Rohan are seven, old enough to lead the way. When they get to the top of the hill, they walk by themselves the rest of the way to school. Even though it was cold in the house, once they are halfway up the hill, Preethi feels the sun. She takes her pink hat off and hands it to Archee. Archee can't take it because she is holding her bag and the skirts of her sari in her other hand. Mrs Cullen does not speak, and Archee does not either. Preethi holds the hat as she walks. She and Darren walk in between Mrs Cullen and Archee. She wants to say 'Isn't it a funny thing that the Spacemen came to the moon,' but she's not sure if it is funny, or if it is normal. Is it normal for *people* to go to the Clangers' moon? They walk slowly, so when Preethi looks to the top of the hill, she sees Rohan hopping and scotching, and Matthew looking at bigger boys walking past.

'That's enough, Darren,' Mrs Cullen says. Preethi looks sideways at Darren, and he is crying. She looks up at Mrs Cullen's face, and then up at Archee's face, and Archee is looking solidly ahead. Preethi looks to where Archee looks, and they walk on, silently. At the top, Rohan says 'I'm going. Bye!'

and just runs down the road, away from her, away . . . Rohan is Preethi's first thought in the morning, her last conversation at night. She presses Archee's hand with her fingers, and a surprise: Archee pulls her closer, clutches her hand tighter. They turn in the opposite direction and walk down towards town where nursery is.

Darren cries and cries. Preethi waits until the teacher finishes talking to him. She waits, holding Archee's hand. The two of them are silent as the other children bustle around them, and the mothers talk to each other, and with loud voices say, 'I've found your peg! Shall we hang your coat here?' Preethi wonders at their loud voices: do all other mummies talk in loud voices? Is it only her Ammi who talks quietly, feeding her and undressing her and reading to her as if they were friends, as if they were exchanging ideas?

The teacher turns to her.

'And this must be Pree-tti?'

Archee moves her head from side to side with a small, puzzled smile.

'This is your peg, dear,' the teacher shouts. Preethi places her hat on the top part of the peg, and Archee removes her coat, and hangs it on the bottom part. The teacher has made a card with Preethi's name on, and under her name she has drawn a picture of an angel with a white dress, white wings and yellow hair. The teacher says slowly to Archee: 'Back at twelve fifteen.' She shows Archee her watch and says 'Twelve fifteen,' even slower.

Archee waits outside the door and watches Preethi walk in

and sit at a small table where glossy blocks of paper have been laid next to plastic pots of crayons, each standing in its own ray of sunshine. After the initial thrill of pure white paper and the huge chunks of unsullied coloured wax, Preethi looks around for Archee, but Archee's face is not behind the glass at the front door.

Mr Cullen is a plumber, always out and about, so when he gets back home for his elevenses and the school calls simultaneously to say that Darren needs to come home because he's distraught, Mr Cullen puts the paper down, sighs leisurely, finishes his fag and tells the mother-in-law to tell Betty that he's gone for Darren and should be back in fifteen minutes, mind, so coffee better be poured and ready, he's got a twelve o'clock. At twelve-fifteen, Archee is outside the glass doors, has to step backward for the doors to open, while the other mothers wait in the yard beyond. Preethi has drawn the Soup Dragon, in purples and oranges, even though the Soup Dragon is green on the television, Rose and Olive told her, but her television is black and white. (They said 'Is your telly black and white?' and she said it was brown, and they laughed, and explained, and she thinks they are now her friends, but they have already told her they are cousins and are each other's friends. But Preethi is good at playing and she knows secretly, she can be a cousin too.)

She has put her coat on carefully, but carries her hat and her picture.

'It's the Soup Dragon,' she tells Archee.

'Good, good,' Archee says. She takes Preethi's hand and

looks about for Mrs Cullen, who is at home dealing out a small helping of shepherd's pie and a smack on the leg to Darren. Preethi and Archee wait in the playground for all the children to come out. When Darren does not appear, Preethi takes Archee's hand, and they walk out of the school gate. The sun is shining, and Preethi looks about her at trees she did not notice when she came to visit nursery with her mother, who held her hand tighter than Archee, and took her to the market stall in town after, and bought her grapes. The town, she thinks, and they are walking away from town.

'Archee, this way,' she says, pointing down the hill. Archee stops and looks at her.

'We came down hill, now up hill,' Archee says.

'Town?' Preethi says. Archee shakes her head. 'I have bought!' she says, and indicates her bag bulging with vegetables and fruit. Preethi glimpses a rare, squinting smile.

They make slow steps up the hill. They are both tired. Preethi looks into each garden gate, into the windows of the houses at their paisley swirled, orangey, yellowey curtains, at brown-tinged nets, at vases on window sills. Ahead of them she sees Rose or Olive talking to her mum, and her mum talking too. Preethi stops and unbuttons her coat. Archee unbuttons hers. They walk on. At the top of the hill, they know which way to go – right. They walk along the road, and although it is unfamiliar, they are both sure. Archee points at bluebells in a garden.

'Snowdrops,' Preethi says confidently. 'Blue snowdrops.' (When Rose called her chocolate drop this morning, she called Rose snowdrop, and she was sure that would make them friends.)

'Hungry?' Archee asks. Preethi nods. Archee stops and

produces a round, greeny-yellow apple. They continue to walk, as she levers small bites of sweet cold flesh into her mouth, dripping juice on to her coat.

They get to the top of her hill. She is convinced of it.

'Here, Archee,' she says. Archee looks about, as if for someone, something. They go down the hill. Each house is familiar, and not familiar. The hill is steeper than she remembers. There is no turn to a white-walled driveway on the corner. There are no rose bushes to fear in the next garden. They are on the wrong hill. Preethi says nothing, but tears start. Her breath is short. Her apple falls and rolls away into the middle of the road where a cat is grooming its kittens. She looks to the opposite side of the road where Darren's garden gate is green, and it is not there. Archee walks on, looking at each house. They walk to the bottom of the hill. Their house is in the middle of the hill, and Archee has walked to the bottom. Preethi looks up at Archee, the tears now joining the apple juice on the lapel of her coat.

A woman is walking towards them. Archee squeezes her hand.

'Ask,' she says.

The woman wears a long blue coat, a white hat and small, white-framed glasses. She is almost past them when Archee raises her hand and touches her arm. The woman jumps back.

'Yes?' she says sternly.

'Sutton?' Archee says.

'What? What are you saying?'

'Sutton Road?' but she says it like the Soup Dragon, her mouth making extra noises, her mouth making words Preethi understands but the woman does not. The woman looks as if she has swallowed medicine.

'Ask,' Archee says, and pushes Preethi forward. 'Tell.'

The woman looks at Preethi. Preethi thinks she looks like a peering spaceman, a stranger in their little world.

Preethi says 'I live at 28 Sutton Road,' and the woman turns around and points to the next hill along, points, turns back, continues on her way. Not a stranger, Preethi thinks. Spacemen *do* go to the Clangers' moon.

❂

When Archee feeds Preethi her lunch, she kneads mackerel curry with lentils and rice and makes little balls on the side of the plate. Each ball is a house in a village, Archee says, and Preethi thinks perhaps a house on their hill, or a Clanger house – or maybe a house in the village in Sri Lanka where Archee is the headmistress. When Archee feeds the mush into her mouth, Preethi closes her eyes and it tastes of Dragon Soup.

THE FLUORESCENT JACKET

'It seems,' he says, 'the rain coming every day.'

He says 'sims'. The girls do not stifle their laughter, but burst with a kind mirth in their corner of the kitchen. Their mother turns her face from him and he knows the stare that silences them: the same grimace her own mother would have given to her. He remembers his aunt's fierceness, her vicious tongue. 'They're doing no harm,' he says in Sinhala, but his cousin shakes his excuses off, her ponytail-tremor the only movement in the dark Edwardian kitchen, the rain the only distant sound. He cannot even hear the girls breathing.

'It *seems* like it rains every day,' Shamini corrects him, now. He glances quickly at the girls, and they are waiting for him to repeat the words. They are taller and fatter than girls he is used to in Sri Lanka. The older one has ribbons in her hair, the younger, a fringe, which covers one eye. The skin of their cheeks is taut, as if it is stretched over gourds. He chooses the smaller one, her one eye, and he repeats to her, 'It *seems* like it rains every day.' She smiles encouragingly. She must be eight?

Her hand comes up and she pushes the hair from her eyes. She looks at him and he winks at her. Both girls laugh again. Their mother makes a swipe at the air in front of them and they stumble up and clear plates and the Pyrex butter dish, the pots of jam and the golden syrup tin. They are like puppies, he thinks, watching their bottoms wobble. They are like week-old dogs.

Soon, he limps out into the grim, London day. He goes to the train station, and following the instructions Shamini has written, he buys a ticket from the machine. He presses the button for New Cross Gate, then waits on the wrong side of the station, boards the wrong train and goes most of the way to Croydon. He shows his directions to an African on the train. The African shakes his head. There are no other people he can ask, only white fellows. The African points to the door and to the other train. The door is about to close. He jumps off. He gets on to the other train as its doors slide to, and he stands by them, looking out to the train he just left. The African is at the doors. He smiles, lifts his hand. The African turns away as their double doors smoothly glide in opposite directions.

He watches the rain on his window. He watches the incessant water beyond the window: the steadiness of the droplets on the glass calms him, and he dares himself to reach forward, to follow the route of one of the threads of water. But his hand is scared. His body is frightened of being out alone in this huge, fast world. He sees his reflection when they go into a tunnel, and finds it remarkable. It is his face, but his body is in too large a coat, and water is percolating through him, as if he were simply not seen. As if he were a filter for rain.

At New Cross he walks back and forth along the streets, following Shamini's map. He cannot find the street she has spelt out. He shuffles: his shoes are too big. He sees more Africans, leaning against a car. One of them shouts to him, but he puts his head down and walks more quickly. He looks behind him, sees they are laughing. He is worried he will lose the station and will not find his way back to Shamini's. He steps into a road, and a car sounds its horn, but not like in Colombo where everyone uses the horn. The car is like a bull, shouting an anger. He steps back, looks about, and people are watching him, and people are everywhere.

He does not find the building, but he finds someone who wants him. A man is beckoning him, and asks him if he wants work. He nods.

'Name?'

'Kumar,' he whispers.

'What?'

'Kumar.'

The man writes it down.

'Your trousers're too long. Roll them up. You're gonna get covered in shit,' the man says. He points at Kumar's legs, and when he realises he does not understand, he mimes rolling, as if he were winding a clock, or wringing a towel. Kumar rolls his trousers up.

'Here,' and the man hands Kumar a fluorescent jacket. It is yellowy-green, the colour of too-ripe limes. Around the bottom edge is sewn an orange strip, its colour as loud as the yellow. Kumar takes off his coat, the one that belonged to Shamini's ex-husband. He puts on the fluorescent jacket.

'Get in the van,' the man says.

Shamini asks 'Lunches made?' The girls nod. 'Go, then, go – brush your teeth' she calls after them. She turns to Kumar.

'How long more with these people?'

'Five days.'

'They are paying you nothing.'

He grunts authoritatively. He knows she will start to nag and to whine if he does not shut her up.

'When will they give you the money?'

They give him the money at the end of each day, but he has told her it will be at the end of the week. He has already bought a present for the younger girl, Lolly – a plastic doll with blonde hair and enormous breasts. He has bought ribbons for the older girl. Also a bottle of whisky. The rest of the money he has put into a biscuit box in the bottom of his suitcase. At the end of the week he will give Shamini twenty pounds. That is what they have agreed. He clears the breakfast now. He washes up before he goes out. He waits to hear Shamini's car door slam and then he uses the bathroom. Before he leaves the house, he makes Lolly's bed. He shakes her duvet, breathing in her sleepy odours, picking up her pillow and smoothing the sheet below, holding the pillow against his chest. The bulk of it against him, mixed with the headiness of her aura, makes him hard.

It is not raining, and he notices that the park on the way to the station gleams in the sunshine, the way that paddy fields are luminescent after rain in Sri Lanka. He is wearing his work jacket, and he sees there are others with the same jacket working in the park. He will miss the first train, but he goes in. He wanders towards where the gardeners are digging. An African with long, braided hair looks at him and points at the tools leaning against a railing.

'You're late,' he says.

Kumar takes a fork, and climbing over the knee-high fencing, he joins the African, watching him to make sure he knows what he is doing.

'Take it all out, man,' the African says.

Kumar begins to dig.

He drinks whisky in the morning, after they have left. He drinks then dons the jacket. He does not eat, because he has stopped paying Shamini. He drinks more if it is raining. He slurs when he speaks, he has noticed. So he does not speak. At the park, they point at tools, sometimes give him a cup of tea, but he is not earning money. He has walked into their team, employed by the council, with structures of paperwork converting their callouses into the notes and coins in their pockets, and he does not speak or hear enough to understand this magic trick. He earns a small amount cleaning and restocking the twenty-four-hour shop, but they are Tamils and they don't like him. They pay him enough to buy a bottle of whisky and a loaf of bread every day. The blurred pictures he sees in this huge world make him feel inured to it. He is used to it, yes, but he is still afraid. His English has not improved. He does not practise, because no one speaks to him, at the park or at Shamini's house. And the Tamils speak Tamil to each other.

He tried speaking Sinhala once, to the boss, and the man looked the other way, frowned.

Lolly's sister, Deirdre, is causing trouble. A few days ago, he heard her use the word 'stinky'. He had watched enough American soap operas to know that this word meant his smell. Shamini ignores him though. She asked for money at the end of the first week, and then stopped. He knows she owes his father money, and that is why she continues to have him under her roof. He wonders if she needs a man in the house now her husband has left. He does not question his status in their house any more than he questions the wet air around him.

When he arrives home this evening, the door opens to wailing. He hears Deirdre and Lolly crying in their rooms. Shamini looks glass-eyed.

'What has happened?' he asks her and is surprised at his own words, because they are English words, not Sinhala.

'Some girls from Lolly's school have disappeared,' Shamini says. He takes the news into him the way he takes in water or whisky or breath. His head tilts this way and then the other, the lines of his mouth pushing down into his chin, his lips pursed in a non-committal acknowledgement.

'What to do?' Shamini says.

Children go missing all the time in Sri Lanka, he thinks. In Sri Lanka I went missing for a time. No one cried for me. He removes his jacket and takes it out to the porch to shake it into the dark early evening. He looks down the street at the cars driving fast, and the traffic lights at the bottom of the hill. Everything so orderly and smooth, like it is all on the inside, the roads conveyor belts like at the airport, the cars suitcases, the houses people, their eyes staring at him, their mouths pursed in disapproval. He closes the door and comes inside.

He goes to the bathroom and washes his upper body under his arms, splashing the water up into his armpits. He looks briefly into the mirror. His eyes are bloodshot and his hair is long. He has grown a moustache and beard that looks like coconut husk. Kumar goes to his room and gets his wash-bag. Lolly looks out at him as he goes back to the bathroom. He winks solemnly at her. She looks steadily back.

Shamini talks on the telephone after the dinner he has been invited to join. He hears her hushed voice as he washes up, and he knows she is talking to their family in Sri Lanka. The girls have been sent to bed, and now he sits on the edge of his own single bed, in the boxroom, in silence. He takes his whisky bottle from his suitcase under his bed and glugs back the remains. The room is blue, and he feels its coldness. The bed is surrounded by tea chests, which have failed to be carried into the attic. The ladder is at the foot of his bed, but he has not been up there, it is not his business, it does not interest him.

He remains on the edge of the bed, waiting for Shamini's voice to stop, for sleep to come, or morning. When he is at the park, digging earth, he feels happy. Earth is earth, whatever its colour. In Sri Lanka, the earth is red and dusty, as if the setting sun has crumbled like cake, but here the earth feels heavy and is black, wrought from ore. It feels good in his hands, it feels like he holds people in his hands, people from pasts he has no knowledge of. When he dies, he does not want to be swallowed up by this country, to become part of the heavy blackness. He will go back to Sri Lanka, he thinks, to die. To disappear into dust there, that is his ambition.

Lolly comes into the boxroom. He has dozed off in his clothes, lying sideways on his bed, his feet still in his shoes, still touching the ground. She puts her ear to her shoulder and smiles into his eyes.

'Ammi said she's going to get rid of you. She told someone on the phone,' she whispers.

He does not move. She hypnotises, a demon in a plump child, the spit on her lips enticing.

They stare at one another, then in a sudden movement he sits up straight, and she flinches back. He pats the bed.

'Come, sit.'

She looks at him, pulls her robe around her nightie. Her hair is dishevelled, the curly strands sticking up in places.

'How old you are?'

'Height,' she says, and he does not understand why she talks of height. She says it again, then holds up eight fingers. He says 'eight' in Sinhala. They sit gingerly apart. His fingers judder across the worn candlewick bedspread. He can see her giggle, her hand coming up to her face. Her eyes are hidden from him, so that when he pinches her arm, he cannot see if she is pleased or scared. He does not want her to be scared.

'You very pretty.'

'No, I'm not,' she says straight back. 'Deirdre is the pretty one. I'm the clever one. Ammi says.'

'Hmm,' he says. He pinches her arm again.

'Ow, don't do that.' She presses her fingers where he hurt her. He looks at her fingers, so small and sweet, their nails broken and bitten.

'Come closer.'

'No.'

'Come, will you?' She edges towards his part of the bed.

He smells her, her creaminess, her warmth. 'Closer. I will tell secret.'

'What?' she asks, open-mouthed. He sees the little tongue at the back of her throat; it is an obscene, dangling sign of welcome. He leans toward her.

'I have present,' he says, and winks.

'What? What is it?'

He holds her gaze, then moves suddenly again, enjoying her shudder. He pulls the suitcase from below the bed. His body bends and stretches the way it does when he digs plants into the earth. He takes the plastic doll from the suitcase and places it in her lap.

'Oh,' she says.

'Why? You don't like?'

'I've got one.' She places it between them. He pushes the case back with his feet. 'I have to go back to bed. Ammi will be cross.' When she gets up to go, he reaches and holds her hand, tugging her back. She looks scared, and he enjoys her fear, smiling into her face, squeezing her hand until it hurts her, until it hurts his own fingers. She says nothing, but looks into him and understands. He remembers feeling how she feels. He lets go of her hand.

'Go to bed.'

She opens his door and putting her head down, she darts back to her room. He can hear the television, laughter carrying up the stairs from the living room, and it makes him feel even colder. He draws the bedspread up and around his shoulders and lies back down, tries to sleep.

The next day in the park, he is sent with a young white fellow, Cal, to the brambles behind the toilets. They tell them to clear it all. When the supervisor walks away, Cal sits on the ground, his back against the wall, and takes out cigarettes. He offers them to Kumar. Kumar takes one, surprised at this kindness.

'This is fucked,' the boy says. He nods towards the scrubland, where ash saplings and brambles are their painful day ahead. Kumar shakes his head loosely in an indifferent agreement. He smokes the cigarette down to the filter, throwing it into the bushes. He walks to the edge, sees the width of the sharp-thorned creepers, and looks back at Cal, still seated.

'I'll watch you, mate,' Cal laughs.

Kumar brings the wheelbarrow round and finds gloves and long-handled cutters. He begins to hack into the wilderness, pulling at the weeds with his left hand, grasping loosely so that the thorns do not pierce him through the gloves. He looks back at the white fellow, and realises that he will not help. His head is against the wall, his eyes shut. He wears a fluorescent jacket, but it seems for nothing. He wears it for no reason.

Kumar works swiftly, cutting down woody limbs to the left, to the right, straight ahead, until he has a sizeable patch cleared. He stops, fetches the wheelbarrow, and fills it with the remains he has cut. He pushes this to Cal, and pressing the wheel against his foot, indicates with his head where it should be taken. The young man sucks his teeth, but stands and picks up the wheelbarrow and wheels it off. Kumar takes a fork and starts to dig at the roots of the plants he has just cut down. It is heavy, hard work, but the sun is beginning to warm through the clouds, and he becomes sweaty and happy. He removes his fluorescent jacket, takes off his jumper and puts the jacket on again.

To the left of the toilets there is a different patch, which seems to have been better cared for. The brambles have been cut back, and there is a sort of tunnel through the saplings, a pathway perhaps, made by wild animals. When Cal comes back, Kumar points to the other long-handled cutters and says 'You, this place.'

'Nah, mate. *You* fucking do it. I'm fucking ill.' He sits back down. Kumar is not angry. It is not his business. He continues with his work, cutting back, cutting down. He wishes he had a sickle or a machete and a mammety, the beautifully shaped spade, folded sideways, that cuts and digs the earth as if it were food on a plate. He feels the sun hotter on the back of his neck, and the sound of the breeze closes his eyes, so that he is home, in the hills, and if he opens his eyes, he will see the startling green of a paddy field.

'Hey! Oh my fucking Christ!' Cal shouts, and when Kumar opens his eyes, he sees his jacket first, and it is a paddy field swimming up, but beyond the paddy field is a child's face, in the black dirt. He stands quite still. The white man is screaming. Below Kumar's feet, a curly-haired child stares at him, lying in that tunnel of scrub, dead. He steps back.

Cal has run away, shouting. He looks at the girl. She is brown, her hair black. She is a pretty child. He stands and stares at her. He looks at her hands. Her fingers are long. She has no clothes. He looks away from her body, looks beyond her, and he sees another face, another pair of eyes. That little face is white, and the eyes are blue. There is a white child, lying in the earth. This is what scares Kumar, the blue eyes. He steps back, steps away. He walks backwards, still staring, and when the African with the long hair reaches him, he is shaking.

'Aw, man,' the African says.

Kumar turns and walks away. No one notices him go. They are all crying because they found the little lost girls. As he walks out of the park, he hears the police sirens. So many, coming in every direction. He stops and watches them descend on the park, halting their cars at angles to the front gates so that cars driving past have to give way to each other. Leaving their doors open and their blue lights circling in the air, the policemen race in, like toy men, their arms and legs making clockwork motions. Two men open the main gate wide and a police van and an ambulance drive in. He turns away and walks up the hill.

⭘

He is arrested four months later. It takes four months because there are no records for him. No one could understand why he would work for free: and then the penny drops. They swoop on Shamini's house in the middle of the night. It is two or three weeks after he has started touching Lolly.

When the police interview him, they ask Shamini to be there to translate. She refuses. She hates him. They call in a Sinhala speaker from the local community, a member of the church one of the detectives attends. He whispers the Sinhala words to Kumar, then speaks the English reply loudly, clearly, as if the interviewer is deaf. Kumar thinks his arrest is because of the wrong he knows he has done to Lolly. When he is asked about the lost girls, he says readily that he found them. He says he walked away because he was scared.

When he is asked why he worked in the park for no money, he replies that he liked working with earth. The translator says: 'He is a farmer in Sri Lanka. In Sri Lanka, he planted rice.'

This becomes part of his lore, the story the headline writers use. And in prison, they call him Farmer Boy, and Paedo Paddy, and he learns this is a funny joke because only the Irish are called Paddy. They also call him nonce, and they beat him. Once he is left for dead.

*

No one fights for him, because he never claims his innocence. His English improves and he learns to read books. He takes courses so he may reduce his sentence and be put in a better place in prison. He learns the rules, he learns who to trust and who to work for. He buys cigarettes and chocolate and puts on some weight. He showers daily and shaves. In prison, he becomes somebody.

But he does not forget the moments in the cold boxroom with Lolly. He lies awake at night and thinks of them, and when he thinks of them, Lolly has blue eyes. He is more scared of this power she and the lost girls have over him than he is of the world outside his door. Prison, in its churning routines, its boredoms and unpredictable violence, becomes – safety. In here, even the rain is safe, even the rain.

*

'In Sri Lanka, the rain falls hard,' Kumar tells his English tutor.

'Write a paragraph about rain,' the man, Jim, says.

Kumar writes about rain filling streets up, like taps filling bowls. He writes about rain that batters coconut matting roofs, until the roofs tumble and people inside the huts look up into the deep sky, as if they could dive into the sky and swim.

'This is good,' Jim says. 'Now write about when you were a child. Try and write about how things felt, Kumar, how it felt to be in a monsoon, what you heard, how your skin felt.'

He thinks about how his skin felt. The fingers of water piercing him through, the rattle on the corrugated roofing of the shack.

'I cannot write about *that*,' he says.

'But why?' Jim asks, and Kumar nods his head to and fro, like a nodding dog in the back of a car, Jim thinks. They smile at each other.

Kumar remembers the day he was carried away, through the flooding streets, and a schoolboy, clutching his shoes, looked at him as he floated past, and suddenly lunged at him, dragged him into his arms, pulled him up on to a wall, and then into a Temple flower tree. They sat like monkeys, watching the water flow away. Kumar remembers the boy woke him, and carried him down, carried him in his arms until he found people who knew Kumar's parents. He remembers the boy's face, straining, and his white uniform murky and wet. He remembers his mother's cry and his father wresting him out of the schoolboy's arms. And how his mother knelt at the boy's bare feet, touching them with her forehead.

Jim says, 'You nearly drowned? In a monsoon? Can that really happen?'

Kumar nods up and down: he has learned to nod yes properly.

❂

It is fifteen years until they find the man who really killed the girls, when he does it again. The DNA is matched, and as easy as a flip of a coin, Kumar is released, through a sliding, rackety gate, into the fast-moving world he cannot comprehend. He has rejected the clothes he came into prison with: they remind him of Shamini and Lolly. Lolly frightens him. She will be twenty-three now, and he worries that he may figure in her nightmares as she figures in his. He wears other people's hand-me-downs, the clothes of those who never left the prison. And he wears his fluorescent jacket, for that, he thinks, truly belongs to him. He goes to the lodgings he has been directed to, using the change they have given him for the bus fare.

When he has worked on the roads for a few months, his social worker asks him if he would like to meet some Sri Lankans. He is asked to dinner by the local preacher who translated for him, and that way gets a job in a garage, and then on the trains. Up and down to Hastings, seeing the sea every day, and he is happy.

One day, Shamini is on the train. He nods to her, and she turns her back to him. He is glad not to speak to her, but it is he who paid for her life in England, he wants to say. When I was twelve, they sold me to a German man for the summer.

She turns back as if she has heard his thoughts, fumbles in her bag, bringing out her purse.

'No, no. *Eppa*,' he says – no thanks, in Sinhala, the first Sinhala he has spoken in years.

But she takes his hand and palms twenty pounds into it, and then she is gone. He looks at the closing door into the wet October evening. He only sees his eyes reflected back at him. He can actually see himself clearly.

LOVE ME TENDER

Preethi ran down the hill. And once there, she stopped. Across the road were flats: red balconied blocks, compact and sound. They stood in their own land, laid mostly to grass, with squat elm trees lined up like defending soldiers, their branches cut square and short. She crossed the road and looked closer at the trees: their leaves were new and fleshy, the colour luminescently yellow. Preethi looked in to the grounds, wondered if the one girl she knew who lived there might be playing outside. Her name was Sofia, and she was younger than Preethi, but had followed her home last year, shouting names at her, because Preethi had not been with her normal friends. The grounds were empty: she thought of returning home, to the hall with the black and white tiles, the sun shining through the stained glass of the front door, the clock they had inherited from the previous owners ticking its admonishments from the darkly wooded dining room. And then:

'Oi,' from one of the trees. She leapt back from the metal railings. 'Up here.' She turned to leave. 'No. In the tree!'

She swung herself under the railing, smelling the dog wee and the grass, the sourness of the smooth metal on her hands. She wiped them down her orange dress, and looking over her shoulder and to the opposite houses, walked slowly towards the tree. Her eyes adjusted, as she looked up. She recognised the boy: Danny, the mong.

They called him a mong in school because of his arm. She had never looked closely at it, feeling it to be private, like looking at a man naked. She glanced now, saw its two prongs and looked away again: a nausea rose in her throat when she thought it could touch her. Above his head birds flitted, sparrows old and young, as if the leaves and branches restricted them like a cage. He concentrated on the birds, recognising, it seemed, or counting, like a miser with coins.

'Are they yours?' she asked lamely. What was there to say? No one talked to Danny in school. He was talked *about*: how he could draw animals as if he were tracing them from a book, how he dug up worms in the beds around the playground and carried them in his pocket. How his arm was made by a witch from a chicken wing. How he ran from one corner of the field to the other on the morning in October when the dew-covered spiders' webs appeared, calling to others to look, as the sun came up and steamed them invisible. Stopped a little one breaking a web with a stick with his nasty arm. And the little one cried in case he touched him.

'Nah. Birds don't belong to no one. I just . . .' He shrugged.

'Oh.'

Preethi waited. He had called her, and she did not want to go home.

'Wait there, I'm coming down.'

She moved back to give him room and watched him use

both arms deftly, his body just like her own: muscular and dependable. As he jumped, she noticed a nest that his head had camouflaged with his hair.

'They let you get so near,' she said.

'Yeah, they're stupid really. I could be a predator or anything.'

'Do you feed them? Is that how you do it?' He was standing very near her: it scared her, the arm, and his bulk – he was taller than she had imagined. She tipped backwards, pretending to lose her balance, and then recovering it three steps away.

'What you doing down here?'

'I dunno,' she said.

'Wanna come and play?'

'Play what?'

'I've got a den.'

He led her around the trees and to the back of the flats, across the grounds to the box hedge on the far side. There, he had leant branches against the straight-cut shrub, and under the branches were rugs, books, a sketchpad, pencils. Two apples and half a sandwich. He lowered himself under the branches and sat down in the impression his body had left. He crossed his legs and indicated with the arm for her to sit opposite. She sat. He picked up an apple with the two fingers and leant forward to her. She shook her head, but he thrust it still. She reached her hand forward, not looking at the apple, but at his face.

'Go on,' he said.

She took the apple as they stared at each other still, and when her fingers touched his, they were warm. She put the apple to her lips, and bit. He smiled. Then he did something extraordinary: he leant forward to her feet and tied her shoelaces, the two fingers on the arm weaving the thick white laces into an extra loop in a complicated route so that the bows on her shoes sat tight and hard, as if her feet were packaged up like two matching gifts.

Slap, on the arm, so not *so* cross, she thought. Just one. Stay quiet.

'Did you polish Rohan's shoes?' her mother said.

'Yes, Ammi,' and pulling herself in, her tummy, her arms, into herself, she walked towards the door.

'Where are you going?' She recognised the quiet threat in her mother's voice. 'Preethi?'

'I'm just going to get my books, Ammi,' she said. She ran upstairs to her room, rubbing at her arm, saying the same prayer on the dark stairs. She switched the lights on, threw her sheets and blankets back up on to the pillows, smoothed over the coverlet, rubbing her hands along its worn lines.

'Preethi!' she heard Gehan call. He was younger than her, but he knew all his times tables, understood algebra, had started to learn the periodic table in his spare time, to taunt her, she thought. To hurt her. 'Ammi says come,' he shouted up the stairs.

She looked at the exercise book of sums her mother had left her that morning. Long multiplications: she had attempted them, then stopped. What was she to do? She took them downstairs. Slap, across the face.

'What did you *do* today?'

'Nothing, Ammi,' she said through the sting of tears.

'Nothing? Nothing! I see "nothing". Why? Why?' She

wanted to reach towards Ammi, say, 'Don't, Ammi, it will be all right,' but she stood still.

Gehan said, 'I saw her walking down the hill today.'

'What? I *told* you to stay here,' and slap again. Slap, and Gehan smiling. That was all she saw. Tomorrow she would go out again. Ammi put the book in her hands.

'Upstairs until you're finished. Finish quickly. Papa is back in half an hour and we will eat then.'

Rohan came in to her room, sat on her bed and looked over her shoulder.

'What's two times six?'

'Twelve.'

'Carry the one. What's four times eight?'

She shrugged. 'Thirty-two. Add one. No, add the one.'

He waited.

'You really can't do this, can you?'

She shrugged again. He dictated the rest of the answers, telling her where to put the carried tens and cross them out. 'You must have been taught this . . .'

'Yes, of course I have,' she said.

'Then why can't you do it?'

'I just can't.'

'What *do* you like?'

'Reading. And poems.'

'Yeah, I'd noticed. But apart from that stuff?' She shrugged.

When she went downstairs, Preethi heard Papa in the study. Shyly, she went and stood by the door. Watched him hang his coat and hat, take the bottle from the shelf and pour a glass of the amber liquid, and as if administering medicine, throw it bitterly against his throat and swallow. He put the bottle and glass back, then turned to the door.

'Hmm, hmm, what are you doing? Why did you leave your sums?' But he asked kindly. She smiled, reached her hand to him. He took his hand from his pocket, and instead of holding hers, slipped a pink, cellophane-wrapped boiled sweet into her fingers. He gently turned her from the shoulders, and walked her into the kitchen, where Rohan had set the table, and mackerel curry and rice were already waiting.

'This one, Neville, called me at office: someone has daubed paint on their front door,' Papa said.

'Everywhere,' Ammi said. 'Everywhere, these letters.'

'Hmm,' Papa poured himself another shot of arrack. His eyes were murky already, Preethi could see. Ammi looked at the glass, then turned away, towards Preethi.

'Tomorrow, you will write out all of the times tables. Write them out every day for the rest of the week.'

Papa nodded at Preethi. 'Clear now, clear,' he waved his hand at the plates. Preethi jumped up, but the boys remained where they were. Gehan never helped. She and Papa normally cleared, and did the washing-up together.

'I talked to her teacher last week,' Ammi said. It was old ground, a well-rehearsed speech. 'It is not that she is not bright enough.'

'Hmm, hmm,' Papa interrupted. Preethi heard the harsh punishment of the drink, the way he gulped it into him.

'Have you thought she might be dyslexic?' Rohan said. Preethi looked at him: it was very brave, this sudden thought. Unexpected, and brave, particularly when Papa was like this. Papa laughed, and Ammi, looking first at Papa, laughed too.

'What is this "dyslexic", child? You think you're at medical school already?' Papa said.

'Ammi said her teacher said she had a "blockage". I have read about dyslexia . . .'

'What nonsense,' Ammi said feebly. 'Nonsense.' She jutted her chin towards Preethi, to the sink and the pans. 'She is a bright girl. No more nonsense,' she said. Rohan took the rest of the plates to the sink, and together they washed and dried, as Papa unsteadily walked to the sitting room. Soon he and Gehan were laughing with the audience on the television.

Sometimes Danny said hello in the playground. Now and then, she sat on the cement kerb at the back of the steps up to the classroom, and he would sit on the opposite kerb, and they would look at the others playing. Gehan wandered alone in the playground too, but he never played with Preethi. She had friends, but if they played Charlie's Angels, she had to be the baddie, or if it was a fairy tale, she was the witch. Princesses were always blonde, forlornly pallid.

Princes had two straight arms. Kiss chase happened between boys called Philip or Stephen and girls called Jackie or Donna. Danny said there was something dirty about kiss chase. Preethi agreed. A boy holding a girl by her shoulders and rubbing his body against her looked like animals in the park. Danny and she talked about birds, of course, and animals: her cat; his desperate longing for a dog.

'But me dad's going,' he said one day.

'Going where?'

'Nah, *going*. He's got cancer.'

'Oh. Does that mean . . . ?'

'Yeah.'

'So you can't have a dog because he's got cancer?'

'No. I mean, if he goes, then we'll move out of the flat. We can't have a dog at the flats.'

'Where will you move?'

'To my grandma's in Hampstead. She's got this posh house, but me mum says it's just 'cos she's married well.'

She knew he had told her because he felt the small loss she felt. What had started so recently would soon be over, this sideways talking, these quiet moments in their school day.

She began to walk home with him. Normally she walked by herself, behind Gehan on the main road. Now, she walked down the first side hill, and along the adjacent main road, stopping at the sweet shop so they could buy Bazooka Joes and pop bubbles until they got to the trees at his flats. She would come with him to see the nest, then say goodbye and walk up her hill home. Once Sofia called out a name, but it was so rude, so disgusting, Preethi could not even understand it fully and she smiled at her because she did not know what else to do. She always reached home first, despite leaving after Gehan so he wouldn't see her walking with the mong.

The summer holidays came and where she would go to school in the autumn term was still undecided.

'What's cancer, really?' she asked Rohan one day. They were eating breakfast together silently. Gehan had gone out early on his chopper, soon after Ammi and Papa had gone to work.

'It's a disease,' he said, not looking up from his book. 'Sometimes people can survive it, if the doctors catch it early enough. But most people die. Why?'

'Oh, nothing.' Preethi watched him reading. 'What's that about?'

'This? Science and stuff. I *am* starting my O levels in a couple of months.'

'I know. But don't you want to read stories? I mean, if I knew I had to go and study, you know, all that stuff, I'd spend the holidays reading *proper* books.' He laughed.

'Proper books? What – like *Charlie and the Chocolate Factory* or something?'

'Yeah.'

He picked up his book and leafed through: 'Says here that Hippocrates named the disease cancer because the conglomeration of cells looked like nesting crabs.'

The thought of it made her feel squeamish. The layers of crustaceans in rows, round like overlapping warts on dirty skin. 'Don't read to me from that book. I don't want to know about bodies. I'm not like you,' she said angrily.

But he was sunk in, ignoring her, and despite the maths her mother had left her, she walked out of the house, into the sunshine, and sat on the wall. She heard Rohan pad into the sitting room, saw him throw himself down next to the record player. Soon, she heard Elvis sing.

She walked down the road, to the den. Sometimes, Danny wasn't even there, but she still stayed, hoping, watching the birds fly back and forth from the trees.

She fought with both her brothers that summer, Gehan especially.

'It's your fault we're not in Sri Lanka,' he said suddenly on a Saturday: Ammi and Papa were marketing in Peckham.

'What do you mean?' Preethi had never considered that they might have gone that year. It wasn't their year to go, was it?

'Yes, stupid,' he said, watching her lips move as she counted her fingers behind her back. 'It's the third year. We always go every third year. I heard Ammi say that we have to save money, so you can go to the private school.'

'I don't want to go to private school. What private school?' Preethi panicked. She had assumed she would go to the local school, the one all the other girls walked to first thing in the morning. She had watched them for years, thinking she would wear their navy skirts, their blue polyester shirts: she would clip her hair back like the teenaged Greek girls across the road.

'It's *your fault*,' he said again, and she remembered their cousins in Vavuniya, the two boys the same age as she and Gehan: how they would all be shy on the first day, and then . . . and then! The joy of barefooted cricket, climbing to the roof of their house and spying on their father and his brothers on the veranda, watching their mother sitting at the kitchen table with her sisters-in-law. She thought of food cooked on the open fire in her grandparents' kitchen, she sniffed the air, her eyes closed, as if coconut shells were burning in the sunshine outside the back door. Gehan punched her. She cried out, jumped forwards to him, bit his ear, scratched his face. 'I *hate* you,' he said, pinching at her body, twisting the flesh on her lower arm.

'I hate you too,' she shouted, and pulled at his hair. But

then, she ran into the back garden, and round to the patio doors into the sitting room. Rohan lay on the sofa, face down, his head dangling near the record player. 'Gehan punched me,' she said over Elvis.

'Did you hit him back?' She nodded. 'Well then. It's hot, isn't it?' The song finished, and he pulled himself up slowly and selected another record from the box set. Each sleeve had a picture of Elvis on it: on the one he chose now Elvis grinned sideways, his hair long, around his ears, white shoulders studded with rhinestones. Rohan tipped it, and the record slid in its paper cover into his hands.

'Why do you love Elvis so much?'

'Because he's . . . what is he?' he asked sternly.

'The king of rock and roll,' she recited.

'Good girl. Why were you fighting?' He put the record on to the record player. The rhythmic plucking of a guitar, then harmonic backing singers: '*King Creole . . .*'

'Because he said,' but Rohan wasn't listening. 'Ro – he said that if it wasn't for me, we would be in Sri Lanka.' Rohan beat his hand against the black PVC sofa. 'Is it true?'

'Maybe,' Rohan said. He glanced up at her. 'Ammi wants you to go to a different school. She's worried you won't do so well down the road.'

✪

As she walked down the hill, she wondered why they knew, but she didn't. When she got to the den, Danny wasn't there. She didn't want to wait, was anxious suddenly, needed to run, and be safe too. She wanted Danny, though, and for the first time, she heard it in her mind that she liked him, that she wanted to see him. She saw some small boys around the back of the flats.

'All right? Which one's Danny's flat?'

'Who's Danny?'

'You know, Danny,' she said, 'with the arm.'

'The Flid? The mong?' they asked. She nodded. 'Up the top. Number thirty-two.'

She walked up the steps, into the cool cement corridors. As she reached the top of the third flight, she emerged on to the balconied landings, and paused to look down to the den. From there, the den couldn't be seen at all, nor the trees. She walked to the last door, and waited a moment before rattling the knocker on the letterbox. Once, then twice. There was no movement. They were out, she thought, so rattled it harder, twice more, then turned to walk back down. The door was opened suddenly by an old woman, her grey hair short, pulled about. She wore a dark dress, sensible sandals. She had been crying.

'What do you want? Oi, what you banging on the door for?'

Preethi backed away. 'Danny,' she said. She moved back more, and stopped against the balcony.

'Get away. We don't want your sort round here. Go on,' she said. She extracted a tissue from her sleeve and blew her nose. Preethi looked past her down the dim hallway of the flat, and saw Danny standing in the kitchen. He looked at her the way his grandmother looked at her. The arm tucked against his side like a rifle, he stared. Preethi lifted her hand to wave, but he turned, and before the grandmother closed the door, she saw him bring his good hand to his eyes, and wipe sideways viciously, as if to swab her away.

When she walked up the hill, she could see their car parked outside the house, hear the music coming from the sitting room windows thrown open. She walked into the house, looked in the kitchen, in the sitting room. She saw them in the back garden. Elvis sang his way through the trees, to the houses beyond their fence. She watched the four of them: Papa digging a bed over, Gehan swinging from the low branch on the pear tree, Rohan lying on the grass, Ammi hanging washing out. As she walked up the steps, Papa saw her, and at the top of his voice he sang 'Love me tender . . . !'

Ammi called '*Victor*!' and his eyes widened, as Ammi's arm slipped around Preethi's shoulders, and he directed his singing at them both, his hand splayed towards them. Ammi threw her head back and laughed joyously. Her arm hugged tighter, and she kissed Preethi's cheek, a deep hard kiss, as if she really loved her.

⚬

They went to Lewisham that afternoon. In a sports shop buying rugger boots for Rohan, they heard the noise of people shouting rhythmically. Rohan heard it first, one foot tied in a studded shoe, the other in a sock.

'What's that?' he asked the young guy unpacking the boxes. They all stood very still, looking towards the glass door. The manager, a small curly-haired woman, walked out into the sunshine, and they watched her flex her shoulders back, cross her arms, assess, then return. She locked the glass doors, top and bottom.

'Right,' she said to the family, 'in the changing rooms.' Preethi ran towards the door with Gehan: they wanted to see. The noise was louder, and she could see policemen. Across the road, the sign outside the church said 'All One in Christ's

Love' in giant, red capitals. A middle-aged woman in an incongruous church-wear blue hat screamed along to the chants, and a policeman fell over. 'In the back!' the manager yelled at them. Preethi and Gehan retreated, and the manager took their place. One of the crowd threw a rock towards where Preethi and Gehan had stood.

'Yaaaaah haaaaaaaaaa!' the manager shouted, putting two fingers up on both hands.

They waited in the booth at the back, Ammi held tight by Papa, Gehan sitting on the floor, Rohan on the bench and Preethi on his lap. The march went by quickly. It was nothing, her parents said. It was nothing. And when other families gathered to eat with them that evening, Preethi heard them only talk of this nothing: and ask each other if *they* were nothing, in this country, if that hatred actually made them nothing.

A few days later, Elvis died. Rohan cried all day, and in the evening, Papa and he sat in the back garden with the record player, drinking passion fruit cordial and eating Bombay mix and patties. Preethi crept out and sat with them, watching her father top up his glass with arrack, and as the evening cooled, he told them of the Lyons House in fifties Sri Lanka, he and his friends with their Brylcreemed quiffs and pastel shirts, drinking bottled sodas and listening to Presley's latest hit. He mopped a tear or two at times, and when it started to rain, they sat for a while still, until Ammi shouted that they were all idiots and should bring the damn machine in before it was ruined.

Preethi still went down there, to the flats: someone had to feed the birds. She took a crust from her breakfast, and when she climbed up where Danny usually sat, the birds would fly about her, eating from her hand, no different in their expectations, and she realised how Danny felt. The birds were a freedom, that was all.

And then, the day after Elvis died, when she had left the times tables and the periodic tables behind her, Danny came. He looked up at her, startled. His hair had been cut. He wore dark trousers and a proper shirt. And a black armband. They shrugged at each other.

'D'you want to feed them?'

'Nah,' he said. He leant against the tree. 'I can see your knickers.'

'Shut up.' She hitched her skirt up from behind, then pushed herself off the branch and landed next to him. 'What d'you want to do?'

'Let's go to the den.'

They sat and said nothing.

'I know what cancer is,' she said. 'Shall I tell you?' He shrugged. 'It's clusters of cells. Like crabs.' He didn't look up.

'Well, it doesn't matter. He's dead anyway.'

'Are you going to get a dog now?' He shrugged again.

They sat still for a while. And then the arm, covered in its nice shirt, reached to her, and the fingers that she had become used to, the two fingers with the bent nails, touched her belly.

'Show me your cunt,' he said gruffly. She looked at his face.

'What?'

'Show me your cunt.'

'No.' She sat still, wondering if he would change back to Danny, the boy with the unkempt hair and brown, dirty legs.

'Go on,' he said, and his fingers moved lower, to where her wee came out. 'Let me touch it,' he said.

'No. Get off,' and she hit at the hand, as if it was animated by an outside power.

'Go on. I want to see,' he wheedled.

'No.' He pushed towards her, both hands on her shoulders, trying to pin her down. She kicked at him, kicked about as his weight stretched on to her, kicked one of the bowed branch legs of the den, crashing it down. 'Get off,' she wailed, and his weight rolled away. He was crying.

'Paki cunt,' he said. 'Fuck off, Paki cunt.'

She crawled out from under the fallen branches. He was sobbing: she wanted to go back. But instead, she walked away, and up the hill, hearing that chant, hearing that nothing, saying, 'it's nothing, it's nothing,' to herself.

At home, the house was quiet. She let herself in with the key that hung from the inside of the letterbox, and climbed the stairs with her eyes shut against the ghosts. She went to her room, and sat at her desk with the periodic table in front of her. She stayed there even when Gehan came crashing in at the front door, pushing his bike into the hall and calling for her to come and make him hot Ribena. He came up to her room.

'I'm thirsty,' he complained.

'So, make it cold.' He watched her from the door.

'Have you learnt any yet?'

'Yes.'

'Have you been there all day?'

'Yes.'

'Liar. I saw you with Danny the mong.'

She turned angrily in her chair. 'Don't call him that! His dad just died. Don't call him *that*.'

'Make me Ribena,' he whined.

'No, I have to do my work.'

When she heard Papa come home, she left her room, stood at the top of the stairs until he had put the bottle back on the shelf in his office. He came out, switched the lights on in the hall and on the stairs, and saw her.

'Ah, you are ready? Gehan says you have learnt,' Papa smiled. She knew Gehan would have made trouble.

'I'm not ready yet, Papa.'

'Why? Hmm, hmm, come, come,' he said, pulling at the air in front of him. She came down the stairs. Professor of Tamil literature he had been, he told her once. No good to anyone – sciences, that's where the power is. She saw his eyes were bloodshot.

'Why not ready? Gehan said, all day at your books, good girl,' and he patted her head, pushed his hands into his pockets to find a sweet. There were none.

He took her into his study. When she was tested usually, it was Ammi who asked the questions, Ammi who slapped and shouted. 'Victor!' she heard her mother call.

'I am testing Preethi,' he called. Preethi heard her mother come to the hall, heard Gehan behind her. Heard Rohan come out of the sitting room, stand opposite her: she could see his face over Papa's shoulder.

'Go on,' he said.

'Al Aluminium.'

'Good, good.'

'Cr Chromium.'

'Yes?' Papa looked back towards Rohan. Rohan nodded.

'Cb Cobalt,' she said. 'Co Copper.'

'Yes?' again, and Rohan nodded again.

'No,' she heard Gehan: 'Co *Cobalt*. Cu *Copper*.' She could hear Ammi's short breathing. She looked at Rohan. Papa frowned.

'This . . . *this* is all you have learnt today?' She realised suddenly – *I am Papa's favourite*. She thought of the elements on the page, winged and flighty, interchangeable, magical letters, numbers, pecking down, caged in Gehan's head as if of their own accord, but flying free, far from her own brain: she was lost again. Gehan stood next to Rohan now, and Preethi smiled, defeated, as he watched her with fear. *I am Papa's favourite* she thought again: Gehan had been in the study before, with the door shut. She had seen his crying face, Rohan's too. Papa pushed the door to.

'Again,' he said. She shook her head. 'Again,' he said louder. She looked towards the window and waited. The door opened, and Papa turned. Ammi stared, and Gehan smiled a sad, small smile, and something passed between them, a hate: for their parents, for who they were, for this tingling moment of heat and fear.

'Well?' Papa said. He stumbled against a chair as he went back to the door to push them out.

'I'm sorry, Papa,' she said.

'Sorry?' he screamed, and in a precise movement, bent her almost double and with all his strength, beat her on the calves, the backside, the back, until he overbalanced, and Preethi fell to the floor crying. He landed heavily against the chair, juddering his knee. He looked down at her, bringing the back of his bruised hand up to wipe spittle from his mouth. The door opened, and Rohan came and picked her up, tried to pull her with him to the hall. But Ammi blocked them.

'You *have* to work hard,' she said. Preethi watched her mother's mouth, the way it curled bitterly about the words. 'You have to become something. Stop! Stop this crying. When you work hard, you are above everything. *Everything*. You are *free*,' and she stepped aside, letting Rohan take Preethi out. Ammi stayed in the study, watched her husband take the bottle down, and Rohan, Preethi, Gehan stood behind them, in the darkening hall, waiting to be told what came next.

Ammi took time off from work the next day and took over the supervision of Preethi's studies. It was a hot but wet day, full of frustrated tears and longing for a time before: when the den was safe, when the study meant sweeties.

'You're getting fat, that's another thing,' her mother said. 'You do nothing all day, that is why. Seven times eight?'

'Fifty-four.'

'Fif-ty-six,' with each syllable a hurt – pinch, pinch, pinch. Preethi picked up a pencil, wrote it down again. At the kitchen table, the table with the furrows full of toast crumbs, darkly stained oak, hard and unforgiving.

The doorbell rang and Ammi answered it.

'Preethi! Someone for you!' She met Preethi in the corridor: 'Get rid of him. He is not our sort.'

Danny stood on the top step. He had his shorts on again, his old T-shirt. Still the same brown legs, but it was not him any more, his short hair disguising him, his eyes different.

'What?' she said.

'I brung you something.' His good hand clutched into a ball, his two fingers resting on top, over the gaps.

'What is it?' she asked, holding back from him. She stood inside her home, he on the second step down from the door.

'Look.' He offered her his hands. She shook her head. 'Come on. Look.' She walked towards him, couldn't believe that he would come here, up to her house, just to trick her.

She leant down, not touching him and he lifted his fingers. Inside, a fledgling, it looked like, or maybe a fully grown sparrow, weak, scared, dying perhaps.

'Did you catch it?'

'No. Found it under the tree. Thought you'd like to look after it.'

'Why?'

'Well? Don't you want it?'

She told him to follow her to the side of the house and up the alley to the shed by the back gate. She found an old box and some dried grass. They sat in the shade on the back steps, watching it try to fly.

'Looks like its wing's broken,' she said.

He said nothing, then: 'I'm sorry,' very quietly. She ignored him, but it was done, and she was glad.

'Are you going away?'

'Yeah.'

'When?'

'Dunno. Soon. Before school starts.'

'Oh.'

She heard Ammi call from inside.

'Better go then,' he said.

'Yeah. Bye,' she said, but before he stood, she put her hand to his arm.

'See – not so different,' he said with a smile. He left by the back gate, down the alley and home.

When she went in with the bird, Ammi told her she should keep it in the shed. And later that week, after her father beat her again, she went out there and crushed it in her hands. When she opened them, she saw its breast still moved, so she pressed hard with two fingers against its throat until it stopped.

⚬

Preethi asked around, and found out that Danny and his mum had moved out of the flats, and a West Indian family, the Russells, had moved in. The daughter was called Glenys, and she and Preethi became best friends at the local comprehensive Papa had arranged for her to attend.

THE TURTLE

In the dark they are back to the people they always were, Jenny and Mike with their son Lucas. They are three stumbling human beings, walking in black air, with multitudinous stars above them, and Jenny and Mike, with Lucas in between, can just be people on holiday.

With her pashmina wrapped about her, and Mike holding Lucas's other hand, she feels safer in their family, stronger in her belief in it. The guide with the torch is far ahead, and a group of worthy Germans and Italians walk his invisible footsteps in the sand one step behind. Mike and Jenny and Lucas take their time because Lucas is only four and Lucas does not like the feel of the sand as it enters the holes of his Crocs. 'I like wet sand,' he says to Jenny, 'but not *this* sand.'

'That's funny, because I would have thought it would be the other way round,' Mike says.

'No, no, Daddy. It is *this* way round,' Lucas says. 'I think this sand is yucky,' he says to Jenny, conspiratorially. She nods in the dark. 'I SAID . . .' Lucas shouts –

'Yes, sorry, I heard you,' Jenny whispers. 'Remember the deal, Lucas? We whisper, and then the turtles will come out. Do you remember?' she asks urgently. Up ahead, she has seen a few of the Germans' heads turning towards them.

'Would you like a carry, littley?' Mike says.

'No, Daddy,' Lucas says. He has developed a habit of calling Mike 'Daddy' in a formal manner, as if addressing a newly bought dog that needs to learn his name. It is done kindly, but Jenny hears it every time as an admonishment to them both.

'Let me carry you,' Mike continues. 'We could catch up, and see the turtles sooner.' Jenny feels the change in the air as he stoops to pick his son up. She stiffens as she feels the child's hand become rigid in her own.

'No, Mike, don't . . .' she says sharply, and it is nearly too late, but he has learnt, from her emails and her sobbing phone calls in the middle of the night, to stop as soon as she says no, to do as she says, at least where Lucas is concerned. They walk on, but she feels she is dragging Lucas, and she realises he has let go of Mike's hand.

There are dips in the sand, great hollows where her foot thinks there will be ground and instead there is air, and she unbalances two or three times, giggling embarrassedly, without humour. She pulls Lucas down with her once, and he shouts again. Mike lags behind, then comes up unexpectedly at her shoulder, holding her arm with his hand. She wants to shake him off, but she contains the anger.

They reach the group, and the group acknowledge them, Jenny is sure, with stares and disapprobation, but she can't see – it is so dark she cannot see her own hand. She looks down at Lucas: his face reflects the guide's red light and is an ecstasy of expectation. She only notices now that the guide is still waiting for a group of Japanese who straggle up behind them.

'Where is the turtle?' Lucas asks, quite reasonably, she thinks. It is a rational request in this circumstance. It is fine for him to ask that, at that pitch of voice. The guide does not reply, simply looks ahead towards the older Japanese couple still struggling towards them. Lucas steps forward and tugs at the guide's *dish dasha*. 'I said,' he says louder, 'where is the turtle?' The guide flicks Lucas's hand away. Jenny hushes him, takes Lucas's hand, leads him off into the dark. Mike follows.

'Can I have attention, *please*?' the guide says. 'My assistant is now looking for turtle. There is turtle nearby, but we have to wait, so please to sit. Sit . . .' He gestures expansively. He has wide eyes, a broad smile, satanic in the red-bulbed torch he uses to search out the laying turtles. Mike and Jenny take Lucas up a dune, behind the rest of the group, and kneel gingerly. Lucas does not want to sit.

'The sand is yucky,' he repeats.

'Look,' Mike says, 'look at the stars,' and slowly he coaxes Lucas into sitting between his knees, with stories about Hercules and Orion. Stars shoot across the wide sky, as Mike's story takes hold. Jenny imagines this as ordinary, imagines they could live here, as Mike wants them to, and she could take for granted stars that transverse the sky.

Twenty minutes later, when they are starting to cramp and Lucas is beginning to shiver, there is sudden movement, an exchange of texts and the guide says 'Please! Please! Quiet! There is a turtle very near here! She is in process of laying eggs, please!'

'Did you hear that, Lucas? We're going to see a turtle now,' Mike says. Lucas is still with the stars.

'Lukey, did you hear?' Jenny whispers. 'A real turtle!' He is dreamy, tired perhaps. They get up, Mike lifting Lucas to his feet, and Jenny notices he is careful not to do more. She is grateful. The group all stand and murmur. Suddenly Lucas shouts, 'We're going to see a turtle!' and Mike and Jenny gasp, shush him, tell him no. Some of the group laugh. The guide says 'Quiet! Quiet . . .' He tells them facts and figures about the turtle, how she will not lay until she is between thirty-six and forty-two years old. She is two metres long. She swims back to the same beach every year, and the turtles that are born on this beach will return to lay their eggs. He says the turtle lays, then she covers them in a large mound and goes back to the water. Jenny takes the information and speaks it into Lucas's ear. Lucas interrupts her sometimes, to ask her to repeat the words; she knows he is encapsulating the knowledge. She knows these words will stay now, that each kick of a turtle's flipper is a neural pathway opened and connected to another in her son's brain. She is an enabler, that is all, helpless in this assimilation of facts, lacking courage to deny it and make him play as any other child. She fills him up, day after day, and it seems to make him stronger, seems to make him more.

'Come now,' the guide says. 'Let us go. But when we approach, be calm and quiet please. The mother lays eggs *now*! Now!' They follow his torchlight down on to the main beach, falling in and out of holes which Jenny now realises must be old nests. The assistant is squatting next to a hole containing a dark green, hexagonally patterned rock. The rock has a head, which moves from side to side like a toy. Lucas has started to tremble.

'See, it's a turtle, Lukey, can you see it?' Mike and Jenny and Lucas stand back, away from the rest of the group, letting Lucas understand.

'I need to see,' he whispers. He allows Mike to pick him up. Jenny watches him crane forward, his arm carelessly about Mike's neck. She does not look at the turtle, only at that arm, the skin in full contact with Mike's skin. It is simply there, and she is nearly faint with not breathing.

'Come!' the guide whispers to them. 'Come and see the eggs!' As they approach, the guide asks others to stand and move away. He kneels again, shows them where they should sit. He takes Lucas's chin in his hand and points it, just so, like a midwife. 'Look!' he says, and Lucas does not object to his touch, simply looks and there are large pearls dropping from the turtle's tail, precise and round, a pile of luminescent blobs of matter, perfect in their potential.

'Oohhhh!' Lucas says wildly. The guide nods, pats Lucas's head. He does not move them away.

It was the hottest night of the year, the night Lucas was born. He was stuck in her birth canal, his English head too wide for her. 'You are made for round-headed Sri Lankan babies,' the Chinese midwife said. 'We need to unhook him. Episiotomy . . . forceps.' Words mentioned, not understood: she was feral with fear and pain and anxiety for the child. Mike stood between her and the doctor, stood with his eyes to hers, cradling her head as cuts were made, holding her hands as tight as she clung to his, while cold metal plunged high into her abdomen to retrieve the tiny man stuck inside.

'It hurts, Mike!' she screamed, and he held her, telling her she was the bravest, telling her the baby was nearly there. 'Ohhhh!' she screamed.

And it was this noise she heard, when Lucas cried out. It was this red-hot anguish she thought of, the white light, the blackness inside her skull.

Jenny looks down at the turtle: there are tears rolling from the creature's eyes. 'She's crying,' she says to the guide.

'Yes, tears. But she is secreting excess salt, nothing more. It is not pain. It is not sadness!' He laughs, as if it were a joke. His phone beeps, and he reads the message. 'Oh! My goodness! You are lucky group! There is baby here! Baby!' He turns to Lucas. 'Come! You see baby?' Mike and Lucas stand and follow the others. But Jenny stays there, in the dark with the turtle, in fellowship.

Much later, in bed finally, Lucas's limbs are still, and he settles into her. She holds him close, as if he were a normal child. 'My egg,' he says. His T-shirt is damp with sweat in the closeness of the night room.

'You're a little egg, all tucked up and safe in our bed,' she coos.

'No. *My* egg,' he struggles awake. 'Be careful with it. It's in my pocket.'

When he's asleep, she looks in his trouser pockets. There is an egg there, dented, worn by the world it seems, still pale but its skin dull, dead. Mike is making tea in the kitchen of their suite. She shows him, and he reverently washes out a yoghurt pot, places tissues inside, and puts the egg in, tucking more tissues around it. Its value to Lucas somehow brings them together. Yet, when they go to bed, they say goodnight, nothing more, and stare at the ceiling, listening to the waves outside their window, knowing the sky above them is still full of stars.

✿

The egg focuses Lucas, Mike thinks. There are fewer scenes than in England. Perhaps Lucas is growing out of it, he thinks, but he knows it is a foolish thought. He has always chosen to ignore the worst of Lucas's foibles: the way he crawled back and forth on top of the patch that was burnt by a falling iron in the carpet in their sitting room, running his hand along its texture, then crawling, then backing up and doing the whole procedure over and over, as they both watched helplessly. His mouth dribbling from a sticking-out tongue. Jenny's anxiety made Mike ashamed – of himself, of his family.

'You were the same,' his mother said, when he broached the subject. Had he been? He asked his eldest sister, who was ten when he was born. Had he been madly obsessive, too bright, easily upset? She was part of the problem – she had the same symptoms, so could not provide the solution. 'But we did OK, didn't we?' she emailed back. Did we, he wonders? Did we? Jenny and he on this cusp – and his brothers and sisters all divorced or near enough. Lucas is going to be happy, he decides. This holiday, this childhood, this life.

They wake up early every morning, and Lucas is awake before them, singing in his bed, as if in answer to the call to prayer at five.

His egg sits by his bed: it is the first thing he sees when he wakes. He has replaced the tissue with sand from the beach at Ras Al Jinz: he brought it back in his jacket pocket. Lucas had taken in everything. The guide said, 'The sand of this beach is the mother of these turtles, and it is to their mother they return when they too become mothers!' Lucas's egg is at the bottom of the yoghurt cup, weighed down by sand. Sometimes he tops the sand up from other beaches, but he is careful not to allow the cup to tip so that the 'Mummy sand', as he calls it, stays integral to the egg.

'How can you tell the difference?' Mike asks.

'Oh, I can,' Lucas says, showing the fineness of the Ras Al Jinz sand compared to the rice-like desiccated shells of the Ras Al Haad sand. He is now an expert on turtles and an expert on sand.

As they have travelled about, Lucas has held the egg in its carton, with its clingfilm (with holes) lid, on his lap in the back of the car. He has refused air conditioning, preferring the temperature of the car to be the temperature of the warm dry air of Oman. As they drive past mountain after mountain of pinky orange rock and plains of sandy earth, Lucas looks steadily and calmly about him, understanding little, 'not engaging' as Jenny puts it, but holding his yoghurt pot. Mike is fine with this. It *is* fine, he thinks. It is perfectly ordinary for a four-year-old child to behave in this way.

The driving makes Jenny talk to him, and Mike is grateful and quick to reply, so that the friendship that began their relationship is rekindled soon enough. They do not laugh yet, as they used to, but the interest shown and given is enough for Mike to be encouraged.

'I used to love stick insects when I was his age, you know.'

'Really?' she smiles. She is the most beautiful of women, pale brown, with her long black hair making her seem paler in this deeply coloured, heavily sunned country. He cannot see her eyes under her over-large sunglasses, but he has noticed that she has steadily lost weight since Lucas was born, and her wrists are tiny, her cheekbones too prominent. He dares not look at her breasts, her waist. He looks at the empty road as he drives and they speak. He does not dare imagine making love to her.

When he was offered the job in Oman, he expected her to be negative. The vehemence, though, her downright refusal to contemplate a move, disquieted them both. But the break away from the family, from the pity, from the routine visits to various caring professions: all would be banished, he argued, and we could do it ourselves. It would be just *us*, he said, bringing up *our* child. She had not considered it. Had not thought it through, he realised. He took the job. He knew it was the right moment, the right opportunity, and she would follow, or she would not. And with the extra money Oman offered, he would be able to pay for Lucas and Jenny to have the life they needed, in Oman or England. There were no other choices. He came to Oman.

'I had a snail farm,' she says. 'I collected snails for a whole week or so – you know, those ugly, grey-brown things that eat everything, and I let them crawl up my arm, and Mum took pictures and thought I was some sort of science genius, but I wasn't.' He notices a line of sweat-dots glistening on her upper lip. He would like to lick them off. She looks out of the open window.

'Camel!' she cries. 'Did you see, Lucas? Oh, slow down, Mike!' and she puts her hand out and touches his forearm. It tingles; the warmth of her fingers he feels down in the base of his penis. He cannot help his erection, and he slows the car down, stops on the hard shoulder of the highway, so she can hang out of the window with a camera, and he adjusts himself, and shifts in his seat. Lucas is asleep behind him, and the pot is sideways in his lap. Mike leans over and takes the yoghurt pot, puts it into the drinks holder at the front. He starts the car again.

'You don't have to be a tourist, Jen,' he says.

'Let's not talk about it,' she says.

'Why? Why not?' She does not say anything. He drives up

the last hill, in a culvert cut through orange cliffs. He knows at the top there will be the first sight of the ocean, navy and straight, the dash of a child's loaded brush across this white day. They are on their way back to Sur. They will soon be passing the Sur lagoon where young men play football at dusk. Sometimes, he plays football with the office crowd in a park in Muttrah, a rowdy, good-humoured game where often he finds himself floored by a handsome Omani who picks him up and slaps his back. Football is the language here – even in the desert, a Bedouin served them coffee in a Beckham shirt. He could teach Lucas, he thinks, and then smiles at his optimism. 'Shall we stop for a drink?' he asks, pointing to the hotel on the lagoon. Its door stands open invitingly. The tide is receding, and here the water is yellow with silt and glinting around the already stranded dhows lying on their sides.

'Lucas is still asleep,' she says.

'We can leave him in the car. It's safe here. We can sit over there, look,' he says, pulling in through the gates. In England he is never so decisive. In England Jenny tells him where to park.

'OK,' she says.

They sit at the table, and he drinks a mango lassi, and she drinks lime juice through a delicate, opaque straw. Everything about her looks taut, as if about to break. They are Mike and Jenny, Jenny and Mike, who hold hands and drink in pubs by the river.

'Please, Jenny?' he says. And just this question brings it all pouring out, the misgivings, the resentment, the torture of being left by herself in England, the 'I will *never* . . .' that she has stored up for this occasion, the quiet reflection after the tears, the talk of divorce. And he hears it all, but it is as if it is something that can be dealt with in the morning, on a fresh day, like a bad Excel spreadsheet that has come in at 5.30. Tomorrow it will seem easier, and when she has finished her drink, and takes off her sunglasses to really look at him (a technique he is wise to), he only says, 'Oh, my, you are lovely,' and she smiles, she – smiles. At least, she smiles.

Just down the road, he can see the men pulling up in their cars, in shorts and vests and mirrored shades. They don't wear shoes, but slip swiftly over the rocks on to the lagoon bed. Lucas's scream, 'My egg!' he greets calmly, and Mike walks steadily to the car, takes his son from his seat and the yoghurt pot from the front, and they stay for another drink and watch the sunset game.

Jenny wakes up abruptly on the beach. She watches a bird fly out across the waves. It has come to her, the sudden idea. It does not make her lift her head from the towel. She lies there, still, and thinks – if he is to drown Lucas, he must do it soon. Now. I will give him *this moment.*

Just as suddenly as the idea has come, it becomes anathema, and she sits up, curling her legs beneath her. She feels the breath judder into her, her head twitching to the side. In the distance, Mike and Lucas walk along the sea edge, hand in hand, looking down at the water. They stop to silently watch an Omani family in the sea. A father struggles with a ball against the tide and two boys run in and out of the water. She hears the boys' laughter, and she turns away.

On their last day, they stop in Muttrah. He has taken them to the Grand Mosque, and round the Sultan Qaboos University Campus, should she be tempted to take up the provisional teaching post he has begged for. He drove past the International School. He did not need to point it out. She saw it: he saw her head turn.

They sit at a juice bar, opposite the bay, fanning themselves with menus, the heat swabbing them, getting between them. Will she launch into another tirade? Not yet. She sips. He hears the sigh.

'You see, what I'm afraid of . . .' she says. Here it comes. 'You see me as some kind of catalogue bride. Bring me out here and I'll facilitate for you. I'll look after your fucked-up son . . .' His fucked-up son is playing with an ugly black street cat under the next table.

'. . . and be waiting at home with my sexed-up clothes under my hijab . . .' And so she goes on. He waits silently for her to finish. She can see his jaw twitch in patient frustration. 'I don't want to talk about it any more,' she finishes.

'Have you thought,' he says suddenly, 'that Lucas may benefit – ' But she does not let him carry on. Off again, the het-up, angry words, female and hot. He talks over them: 'Maybe a new country . . . maybe it is not stepping backwards. Maybe a new culture . . . Maybe you'll be free to be *you* . . .' But Jenny does not see the new culture, the new life. She sees a turtle, in a hole, flapping its back flippers to bury its eggs, its head nodding this way and that in exhaustion. She sees the lady on the next table, her hijab-ed head nodding this way and that.

'No, Mike. I *can't*. I can't be *trapped* . . .' but as she says it, she thinks of the turtle climbing out of her hole, walking down to the foam, swimming out to sea.

'Oh, Jen. I hate to say it, but you have got to – *shut up*!' He sees she is shocked. He has spoilt her, being so polite, so gentle. 'I'm sorry, but you have to *listen*.'

She will not, and she stumbles up, he knows in tears, and takes Lucas's hand roughly, so that as he stands, he glances his head against the corner of the table. He shouts, and begins to cry, but a painful, ordinary child's cry.

'Be quiet, Lucas,' she says, in anger, and Lucas is quiet. She starts to march away, pulling at his wrist. Lucas drags back, and they tug at each other. Lucas says: 'I want Daddy. I want to stay with Daddy.' Mike takes three Omani Real from his wallet and tucks them under the ashtray. He picks up Lucas's rucksack and takes Lucas's hand. Lucas shakes Jenny away.

They walk back into the soukh, Jenny ahead of them. Around them, men offer pashminas, perfume. The smoke of frankincense carries them through.

'You know you're going on the aeroplane tonight, don't you?' Mike says.

'Yes. Can you check my egg?' It is a ritual now. Where is the egg? It is in the main pocket on the right side. It is in the dark, under your muslin. Mike opens the bag, makes a pantomime one-eyed probe, and Lucas giggles. Jenny has disappeared around a corner into the gold soukh. He saw which way she went, but he is in no hurry to find her.

'Lucas. So you know you're going home, don't you?' He wants to appeal to the logic in the child, make it easier, the way things were made easier when he was a child, by teachers at boarding school.

'Yes,' Lucas says. But unexpectedly, he says, 'And when will you come for us?'

'Come for you?'

'Yes,' Lucas says. 'When?' And he has learnt that use of a deep, direct look into Mike's eyes.

'I don't want you to go,' Mike says, and he looks away, towards Jenny.

At the airport, they are dreadfully alone. Mike has kissed Lucas again and again, and Lucas has kissed Mike tenderly and carefully. Jenny allows him to kiss her cheek. It is night, almost ten. Lucas is tired as Mike picks him up, holds his full length against him as if to memorise it. Lucas walks backwards through the security doors. Jenny looks back once, sees Mike brush a tear away. She and Lucas have to become a team again. She pushes the trolley, and he carries his rucksack. She tries to check in, but they have not opened the desk yet, so she sits Lucas on the trolley and they wait, watching the men and women in their flowing robes. She is grateful for the air conditioning, the vacuum of the airport. An Omani manager is kind and beckons them to a different desk. The bags are on the conveyor belt when Lucas says, 'My turtle.' It is a low-pitched gurgle of a noise.

'Did you pack these bags yourself?'

'Yes.'

'Mummy,' he whispers. 'My turtle.'

'Lucas,' she says sharply. '*Wait!*' She has learnt that his feelings are not always precious, and that he will not break.

'Did anyone ask you to carry any packages for them?'

'No,' she says, talking to both of them. Lucas looks as if he needs the toilet. 'Do you need to go?'

'Yes,' he says urgently. 'Mummy, my turtle. It's hatching. It is.'

The man at the desk smiles at Lucas.

'It isn't, Lucas,' she says, chattily. She wants to get through this, get back to England, and the cold and dark, which make her safe. The taxi is booked to meet their flight. The old shuffling George who takes them to Lucas's appointments will be there, white bristles on his cheeks, hair unkempt and the black anorak pervading smoke and Fisherman's Friends. Lucas jumps from one foot to the other. He is going red.

'He needs toilet?' the man says.

'I think so.' She is embarrassed, the way she always is, in a matter of fact, my-child-is-special-needs way.

'Go – go,' he says with a smile, and points towards the lavatories across the hall. She takes Lucas's hand roughly and they go through the double doors.

'See?' Lucas says, unzipping his rucksack. Inside, clambering over his muslin, his colouring pencils and his shells is a small black creature. It is comical, its head bobbing about, and it tries to climb up the black nylon interior. Its eyes look up at her, and Jenny yelps. Someone is coming in. Jenny pulls Lucas into the toilet and locks it.

'Oh, God, what are we going to do?'

'I want to take him home,' Lucas says stoutly. He slides to the floor with the bag on his lap. Jenny looks at him and sees Mike. She thinks of Mike carrying the yoghurt pot through Oman, and it makes her cry, the suddenness of the turtle's appearance. Oh, Mike, she thinks.

'We have to take him home,' Lucas whines. He is looking at Jenny, the way he looks at her when she is to say no, no, Lucas, we can't.

'Take him home? Where to?' she asks him. She will not say no.

'To the beach, of course,' he says. She was sure he meant his little room, with its dinosaur mural and plastic animals on the floor.

'Lucas! We're just about to get on a plane! We're going home!'

'No! Jenny.' He calls her Jenny in moments of crisis, like an old man, like a friend. 'We need to take him to his beach.'

'Lucas . . .' As Lucas begins to shout, she realises she had never imagined a time when Mike was not part of her, when she was simply Jenny again.

She calls Mike from the desk, but he is not home. She cannot remember his mobile number in her fluster. She takes the bags off the conveyor belt, tells the man they are not going. They fight their way out of security, and all the while Lucas laughs, and is manic, allowing his rucksack to be held safely by his mother, while running up and down the concourse, skidding on his knees, getting in the way of busy men and tourists. It is nearly midnight. She should take a cab, but instead she goes to a desk and hires a car.

She asks the man for a map, pays by credit card, loads the bags in with no help from anyone, straps the rucksack into the seat next to Lucas. 'You do *not* touch him, understand? You allow him air to breathe, but you do *not* touch him, OK?'

'I won't hurt him . . .'

'Lucas. I'm warning you . . . what did the man do when you saw the baby turtle?'

'He guided him down the beach with his torch.'

'Exactly. We will do the same.'

'At Ras Al Jinz?' Lucas's eyes are wide, excited.

'No. I don't know,' she says. 'We'll ask Daddy.'

They stand at Ras Al Haad, watching the sea. Lucas's shoulders still heave from the crying, and the singing of the muezzin is unexpected and disturbs them. The sun will come up soon. Lucas holds Mike's hand, and Jenny stands apart from them. It will take time, she thinks. And later, months and years later, when Lucas and her daughters are willowy and stand tall next to her, she thinks of this moment, on this beach, as the moment of knowledge. The moment she covered what was exposed. The moment she opened what was shut away.

SOPHOCLES' CHORUS

At Cassie's party, Preethi stood and watched Ollie, the beautiful boy-man, golden, crisp from their day in the sun – all of them ringed with blurred lines of sweaty light as day transformed to evening and then to night. His hair was short, but out of shape, in need of a cut, its thick fronds jutting out from behind his ears. She had talked to him once before today, at the cast party for *Midsummer*, when Freddie and Preethi had been the glorious two, the ones to watch, comedic and loud-mouthed on stage, gangly and shy in a corner of the party where others kissed and drank and sang around them. Ollie had joined them, sat quietly with them, told Freddie how great he was, adding, 'You too,' to Preethi, with a simple twinkle.

Today they were aware of each other, as Freddie's friends. They were aware of each other's sexuality too. It is the way it happens at their teenaged parties: eyes meet, few words, but mouths fall on each other after a preparatory glass of wine, and if the bean bag fondling goes well, and you're a softy and he's a softy, you'll be walking through Dulwich Village holding hands soon enough. If it goes even better, and a condom is found or you are one of those miraculous girls who has put herself on the pill for such an occasion, and penetration has been achieved on the bundle of coats in a bedroom, then you may be walking through the Village clutching books to your chest as he walks with you, smoking behind sunglasses. Definitely not soft; serious, to the point of a small death, serious. Preethi was aiming for the second status with Ollie. His beautiful face, his knowing eyes, his wiry arms too tight for his school uniform shirt, the way he smoked a fag that remained pinned to his lips as they played football in the field, his right eye strained closed at once to deflect the smoke and aim the ball to score yet another goal. He played barefoot. When they had a grass fight later, they both played dirty, rugby-tackling, holding one another down, intimate, knowing; knowing nothing of each other.

They had played on the redundant rugby field, opposite the boarding houses just below the tollgate. Then Cassie said her parents were expecting them all at their house in the Village. There had been some argument among the girls, and some of the Hong Kong boarders, because Judi's parents were also expecting them, and the large group divided into scientists and artists, the soon to be medics and engineers walking off towards Alleyn Road with Judi and the rest of them sauntering slowly, pushing their bikes with their sweaters slung over shoulders. One or two of the girls walked barefoot in the dusk, Ollie and Freddie and Preethi lagging behind, enjoying the peace of the huge buildings of the college. The first group up ahead went in through the gates of Blew House: J.D. needed to pick his camera up from his bedroom. They took the detour through into the courtyard at the back of Blew and walked into the car park and then across to the playing fields in front of the college.

'Will you miss it?' Preethi asked Freddie. He stared up at the red and black bricks, the shining windows, the whole building, burnished and pompous.

'No,' he said, and turned away, shrugging. There was an element of Freddie that no one could really know, Preethi thought.

Cassie had spent the last two years studying, and having done seventh term, was off to Magdalen to read PPE. She was *that sort.* Preethi and her friends thought her rich, spoilt even, but felt sorry for her, for she was on a trajectory that would never give her the self-knowledge and peace that they knew already. The peace that came from failing a little, failing enough for highly strung parents and teachers not to have too high expectations. Cassie had never had a party in her house (neither had Preethi, but for different reasons). When they had arrived at the front gate, Cassie had looked about her at them all, worried, Preethi could see, and unable, because she lacked experience, to say the self-deprecating joke, the easy 'don't break anything' or 'it's all inherited' that others in the same position would have. Cassie's father was a banker from up north, and sometimes her cut-glass was muddied with a Yorkshire smudge: everything in front of them was self-made, not effortless, paid for with resentment and sweat and pride.

The white house was three storeys tall. One of Cassie's friends, Suzie, had once told a hushed sixth-form common room that she had delivered maths homework to Cassie (lying in bed with shingles), in a flat of her own at the top of the house: 'She has a little red sofa, and a kitchenette with a toaster and a kettle and a mini fridge!' Preethi and the other girls looked at one another, standing outside the white house, and wondered which one of them would ask to see the flat. When they went up the stairs into the hall, Cassie nervously volunteered a walkabout tour of the house, but refrained from showing them her quarters.

When they walked into the basement kitchen, their supper had been laid out on gold-rimmed white plates: slivers of ham and tomato salad and crusty baguettes and pâté and cheese. And a case of wine. They all gasped, and Cassie looked embarrassed. The tour upstairs had already made her falter: glass-fronted bookcases in the library, the wood-panelled sitting room, each shrinking her more. Preethi, in the spirit of the day, linked her arm into Cassie's.

'It's all right, posh girl. We'll still talk to you on Monday,' she whispered, and Cassie squeezed her arm closer.

Ollie sauntered into the kitchen, picked up bread and cheese and ate it as if it were a normal moment in his day.

He stood now, in the dark, with a bottle of beer on the veranda, and lit another cigarette. Freddie and Preethi were in the kitchen with the others. Freddie with his back to the French doors, Preethi stood facing him, joining in the conversation, allowing Freddie to stare at her. Occasionally she would look at him, then blur her gaze beyond him, as if to stare into the distance, understanding his need to drink her in, as she watched Ollie.

When they were full, they all erupted into the June night and lay on the lawn, making a criss-cross of limbs, a few girls laying their heads on each other's bellies. The music, 'American Pie' and 'If you leave me now' and 'I'm not in love' gently pervaded, and someone said, 'So where are you guys planning to travel to this summer?'

Freddie said, 'We fly to Delhi, stay at Shiv's parents' house in Kashmir, then take the train down, and somehow get to Sri Lanka. And then we're taking a plane from Sri Lanka to Australia.'

'Is Daddy paying, Ollie?' Ollie punched a bloke in the dark. It was Simon, who was jealous of the boarders and came from Forest Hill, like Preethi. Simon said, 'You're from Sri Lanka, aren't you, Preethi?'

'No, south London,' and people tittered. She said it to be cool, but it sounded defensive. She never knew where she was with these spoilt brats.

'*No*,' he said, because he was that well-meaning, prosaic sort of boy. 'I mean you were born there, weren't you?'

'*No*,' she mimicked. 'Paddington.'

Freddie and Preethi had had a conversation about Sri Lanka the day before, about where he and Ollie should go, about how much things cost, and how ideal it all was. She talked as if she knew, when really she had only been to Sri Lanka three times, the last time almost four years ago, during a period of danger and curfew. She and her family were taxied about by uncles and cousins, spending their evenings looking out from a veranda into the darkest nights, envying the freedom of the dogs who gathered on street corners, sharing their scavenged meals and howling. Freddie asked for names, people he could call: as if Preethi's family were the same as his, as if her uncles worked in government ministries or the arms business, and could facilitate a quick ride out on a private plane. Preethi's dad's brother was a retired bank manager, her mum's sister still taught at the village school where her grandmother had been the headmistress.

Now, in the dark, Ollie said into the air: 'But Freddie says you've given him some ideas . . . is it really as lovely as it looks?' Others murmured, asked similar questions, and Preethi allowed herself to be dragged back into this illusory evening, where these people were her friends. She talked of the aroma, as soon as you land, the smell of dried rice, the humidity, the soil: its colours rose up in front of her, the reds of the earth, the greens of the trees, the whites of women's teeth as they bathed in the rivers. She did not mention the shanty towns her father never failed to point out as they drove from the airport, the mounds of rubbish and their stink. She edited, so that chaotic driving became eccentric and delightful for her audience, the Kades, where her father insisted they eat, became an opportunity to try the working-man's meal. She was selling dreams, and she was on the edge of them, as if an insect, buzzing back and forth from teacup to wineglass to coffee cup, and in each receptacle was a liquid of each world that surrounded her: home, Sri Lanka, school, church. When she read a book, it was familiar immediately, because she could play parts: she could be everyone. And here, in this champagne flute of an evening, she could be immersed in sparkling intoxication, and roll on to her side and look at all of these blonde, auburn, brunette heads in their jeans and shirt sleeves, their Laura Ashley dresses, with the daisy chains still in their hair, and she could imagine she was as beautiful as they were.

Ollie stood and lit another cigarette. Preethi stood too.

'Can I have one?' she asked. Freddie was quickly at her side.

'Do you want another drink?' he asked. She craned her neck up to look at him. He was infeasibly tall, and she realised that in any light, he was very ugly. She saw him smile down at her, avuncular and eager.

'Yes, all right,' she said, and dismissed him. He went inside with a group of girls, and she and Ollie watched as Freddie gesticulated wildly, making jokes, so that the girls about him put their hands out to tap him lightly on the arm as they laughed.

'I didn't know you smoked? Do you smoke?'

'No. But I'd like to try.' She had tried before, and actually, it had made her sick. She liked the idea of holding a cigarette, though; she liked the way she looked. He put two Rothmans in his mouth, lighting both with a match and took one and flipped it around to offer it to her. The smell made her dizzy – Ollie made her dizzy. She took the cigarette and walked past him towards a swing seat in the corner of the garden. Ollie followed her, as she thought he must, as she had envisioned he would when she moved. The dark was complete here, under a wisteria which climbed the white wall of the large Dulwich mansion.

Everything here was like Shakespeare updated, a Bohemia that had no outside contacts to loud striking miners in Trafalgar Square, or the church fundraiser her parents were helping at. In the dark, on the swing seat, she could see Ollie's profile, the cigarette glow, his hair pushed back so that it stood craggy on the top of his silhouetted head. He sat down. She leant forward, turned his face to her, and kissed him. He responded, and the kiss, extraordinary as it was that two people who knew each other so little could kiss, was a very good one. The initial plain-lipped kiss opening up slowly and becoming satisfyingly erotic, the lunge of the tongue just right: not overtly wet or overpowering. Then the drawing back, one peck, then two, and a pulling away so he could kiss her face and her neck, and then the turning of her head, expertly done, she thought, so that their kiss became more powerful, as if they both really meant it, as if they could both, actually, maybe, fall in love.

Freddie saw. Freddie came out with Preethi's drink, and saw the end of the kiss, and she saw him. She drew back from Ollie, squeezing his hand to warn him, and the squeeze of his fingers felt more intimate than their kiss. To see Freddie stand there, as she held Ollie's fingers: she felt as though they were older, grown up, in their twenties, and she lipsticked and high-heeled and he suited, and they were at a dinner party, and here came a man who was notoriously badly behaved and wore his heart on his sleeve, and he would say . . . Freddie spoke. 'Oh. God. Oh, God,' and still she held Ollie's fingers, until he shook them off, threw his burning cigarette to the ground and rubbed at it with the toe of his shoe. She still held her cigarette in her other hand, and she looked at it as a proposition. She put it to her lips, puffed at it, coughed a little, threw it down to the ground and watched it smoke there, until it rolled away into the undergrowth.

Freddie brought the drink and stood in front of them both. And then he said to Ollie: 'But you knew how I felt about her,' and Ollie said, 'Yes, but I got carried away,' and Freddie said, 'You always get carried away. But she's not like the other girls,' and Ollie said '. . . well, that's why, I suppose.' And Preethi watched the smoke, wondering if a plant could be set alight, thinking that she wished she was at the church, or with Rohan, on the march. They discussed her back and forth a little longer, as she watched the smoke and somehow felt dirty. Ollie coaxed Freddie to sit with them on the swing seat. Freddie took a swig of the wine he had brought out, and handed Preethi the rest of the glass. It was that nasty white wine all the girls drank, semi-sweet and syrupy. It made her feel sick usually, but she swallowed it down in one gulp, aware that she had placed her lips where Freddie's had been, deliberately, so he would see. So her sensuality would taunt him, as it had through these dozen weeks they had known one another.

'You should go out with her,' Ollie said into the dark silence. He stopped the swing of the seat, holding it with tensed thighs. She could see him clench his jaw and hold them there on the cusp of the decision. She watched him turn to Freddie, smile deeply, as if they had agreed a plan.

'But,' Freddie started, and they both looked at her.

'But, *what*?' Preethi asked. But – what? She stood, walked away. Went inside where everyone seemed diminished in the electric light and the sterile-white kitchen. She took her glass to the sink and started to wash it. There was a shower attachment above the taps, and she pulled at it, and a hose came out.

'Cassie? You're *that* posh that even your kitchen has a shower?' she said idly. She meant nothing, felt dismayed about everything: her behaviour, their behaviour. These were the boys – the men – she had wanted to know for ever. Freddie and she were reading Dostoyevsky *together*. She had already finished *Crime and Punishment*, but he was savouring it, going slowly because he loved it so. She was reading Forster, while he caught up. What was she to do now? Cassie, drunk and lying on a sofa by the French doors said, 'Preethi, don't touch that . . .' but it was too late, and Preethi had soaked them all. Cassie and Maria, Katie and Paul – all were drenched, and laughing and running into the garden to shake themselves dry like so many spaniels, running in a pack. Preethi looked about for a drying-up cloth, soaked up the splashes from the floor, and when she was sure it was clear, she found her cardigan and left, letting herself out of the side door by the back stairs because she could hear Cassie's parents coming through the front door, loud and cheery and full of questions that she couldn't bear to answer.

o

It was the kiss that stayed with her. It was a kiss of sweetness and longing. In it she tasted the eroticism of becoming a woman, the eroticism of making a choice to kiss Ollie, not being chosen from the pack of girls at a party, like a boy taking a Top Trump card. She had chosen him with ambition: he was the most wanted boy of the year, and with him came status, an ease into the best parties, the bettering of herself. The kiss was something, it was certainly something – perhaps a potential, or a future. Perhaps she and Ollie would be the ones, the ones who lasted.

She could taste his kiss on her lips as she turned the key in her front door. The wine and the cigarette smoke lingered there, although she had chewed chewing gum on the night bus so that any waiting parent would not know she had been smoking. The black girls at the back of the bus, coming home from Brixton, had lit up their cigarettes, and her hair and clothes smelt so much that she climbed off the bus at the bottom of the hill, to walk the rest of the way home in the dark. It was funny, their smoking was a good excuse, but she didn't want an excuse for this evening – she didn't want anything of it to be wrong.

In the hallway, she was greeted by a short, white man. Above his lip grew the startings of a moustache; his eyes were small and staring, and his mouth smiled palely. He wore a white T-shirt and very grubby working trousers, which could have been navy once. Rohan and her father stood with him.

'Where've you been?' Rohan said.

'Party. I told Mum,' she replied. The man smiled and nodded. He looked as if he were welcoming her to her own house. He looked as if he were the only one at ease.

'This is Bill,' her father said.

'Hiya,' Bill said, quite loudly. She winced slightly – her head had begun to hurt. 'Good party, was it?' Bill smiled.

He was a miner, had no money, had come down on the coach, didn't know where his mates were and Rohan had brought him home. Ammi had fed him chicken curry and rice, and now they were trying to decide where he should sleep. Their sofa was small and would not hold him. He had a sleeping bag. Preethi noticed her father's face. Gehan, her other brother, slept in the bedroom next to her parents' room. He was studying for his O-levels, and was already asleep. She and Rohan slept on the floor above, in attic bedrooms. Her father's worries were merely sexual. He thinks that we might meet in the middle of the night on the way back from the bathroom, and I might spontaneously be laden with child, she thought.

She followed him to his study, where he had gone to look for something, saying, 'I'll lock my door,' and kissed him on the forehead. She went up to bed, not bothering to brush her teeth, but digging under her duvet in her knickers and T-shirt. She lay looking out of the uncurtained window, staring at the moon. She wondered if Ollie was thinking of her too? Was Ollie thinking of the potential of that kiss? Had her impression on his lips, on his fingers, become a solid place, like a mould of her around him, like he had around her? As she lay there, just as she allowed her eyes to close, she could feel his mouth on hers, its weight, its beauty, its heat.

She woke suddenly, thinking it must be late, and Papa must be calling her to church. She had heard a gruffness in her dream. The window was still lit by moonlight, though, and she looked towards her alarm clock and saw she had only been asleep for half an hour. She could hear voices. Not another argument, she thought. Rohan and Papa were constantly trying to instil their own sense of what a man should be into each other, and it was tiresome for the rest of them. She sat up to listen again, thinking that perhaps she could stop it. But it was not her father's voice. Then she remembered Bill. Oh, God, Rohan, she thought. She stood up, and went to her door, standing behind it. She could hear Bill's voice, and Rohan's. They were talking at the same time, louder, then softer, then louder. It was almost like singing. She turned the door handle gently. The house was Edwardian, and the fixtures had not changed since they were first put there eighty years before. The door rattled, and the voices quietened immediately. She had forgotten to lock the door, so it eased itself open, sliding gently across the anaesthetic carpet.

She stepped out into the hallway, listening still. Below her, she could hear her parents snoring in unison. She was comforted by their noises, which she often relied upon when she came in late, or wanted to steal downstairs to drink a nip of gin from one of the bottles in the kitchen. She heard the sing-song of Bill's voice again: he said 'Yes, yes, faster, no faster – Oh God, you're gorgeous,' and she moved closer to Rohan's door, spied through a gap and saw them fucking. Her brother stood behind Bill, his arse naked and shadowed, and Bill's back lay forward in front of him, a glance of moon lighting him as he writhed. Rohan's head fell back, his face creased in what looked like tears, and she wondered: should I stop them? Should I go to him, because he looks like he is in pain? But she knew he was all right, and she stepped back into her room, shaking.

In the morning, when she came down to breakfast, Bill and Rohan sat silent on the opposite sides of the table, and Ammi put fried eggs, bacon and fried bread in front of them both.

'Ah! What time did you get home, Madam?' Ammi asked.

'She was home by midnight, Ammi,' Rohan said, quietly.

'Bike didn't turn into a pumpkin then?' Nandini said. Bill laughed. She could not look at them. 'You want tea, darling?' Nandini asked, putting her arm around Preethi's shoulders.

'Where's Gehan?'

'Gone already. He had cricket practice,' Nandini said.

'Where's Papa?'

'He went to the early service. Are you coming to church? Where is your bike by the way?'

They agreed that Ammi would give her a lift to Dulwich to pick up the bike, and she would miss church just this time, and take a slow ride home to clear her head. Rohan was going to accompany Bill to Euston, where he would put him on a train to Leeds. Preethi did not say goodbye to them. Bill caught her mother around the waist and told her he would never forget her, then kissed her. Where Preethi had been sitting, he put a page of NUM stickers. When she returned home to an empty house later, she found them, and instead of throwing them away as she wanted to, she stuck them into her diary, and on her bike and on to her school bag, as if their topicality and reactionary quality were in some way a payment for his presence. And when her friends asked where the stickers came from on Monday, she said casually 'Oh, my brother brought a miner home from the march on Saturday', knowing that this statement alone would deem her worthy, extreme, likeable.

⚬

She saw what Ammi thought of Cassie's house.

'Is she a nice girl?' she asked.

'Nice? Yes I suppose so.' She jumped out of the car and waved goodbye before her mother could ask more. She decided it would be better to ring on the doorbell and let them know she was taking the bike. It was, after all, sitting against a bush on their front lawn. But when she rang, nobody came. She thought of walking around the side, to look through the kitchen window, but as she started down the side path, she caught a glimpse of their garden, an expanse of lawn and the wisteria in full bloom, climbing high up the white walls. In the daylight, it looked shiny, like the park of a museum, and she felt as if she were preying on it all, as if the museum were closed, and she was breaking in. She could see the swing bench in the corner of the garden, and she stood for a moment, looking at Ollie and herself kissing.

'Hello!' a voice said from above.

'Hello?' she said, craning her neck back and squinting into the sun. Ollie. He stood on the steps by the front door.

'How odd. I was just thinking about you.'

This made her hot, made her lose her words.

'I was just thinking . . . well, never mind. What are you doing here? I left my jumper here, I think. It's my last one, and I'm leaving soon: I doubt my mother will buy another and . . .' He stopped. She looked at him hopelessly as he stopped at the bottom step. Extraordinarily, he leant towards her and kissed her gently on the mouth. 'You look lost,' he said quietly. At the kiss, her heart leapt, not for the kiss itself, but for its intimations: its acknowledgement of the potential she had been thinking about. And yet, as he kissed her, she thought of Rohan and Bill, washed with moonlight. She hated herself, but it disgusted her, the passion her brother and his lover had felt.

She had still to say something, anything. She smiled at him, then touched her lips.

'I'm sorry,' he said, looking grim.

'No. Don't be. It's fine. I mean, it's fine.' She tried to be jolly, but could not. She pointed towards her bike and walked unsteadily across the lawn, not sure if she were allowed to walk on its pristine surface.

'I was wondering what you were doing back here. I knew you hadn't stayed the night, and anyway, all the girls that did are in the park having a picnic breakfast.' He raised his eyebrows.

'Oh.'

'Do you want to join them? I'm walking up that way . . .'

'D'you mind if we don't? I had a horrible night, and I'd just like to calm down a little,' she said, and without it meaning to, the secret came tumbling out. What made it worse was Ollie whistling a little and shaking his head.

'Rohan was a prefect when I was in the lower sixth,' he said, and she saw he was adding things up, remembering her brother differently.

'No, look, no. He's *not* like that,' she said, but he gave her a knowing smile. 'Look, can you just forget about it? Can we talk about something else?' she asked desperately.

'Of course. Where are you going now?'

'I don't know. Where are you going?' She felt that she was wrong, for telling, and for telling Ollie, someone she hardly knew; but now she had, she felt a relief, she felt a change in herself. And here was Ollie, standing with her, kissing her, talking to her. 'Shall we go up to the woods?'

They walked up past the college, past the playing fields and the boarding houses. She left her bike chained to the gate to the woods, and they walked in, and when she slipped, he reached out and rather matter of factly held her hand. It was dreamlike and steady, this walking upwards, this heartbeat pace. And once into the wood, they stopped talking and he kissed her again. They sat against a fallen tree and kissed and kissed, and when he broke off and pulled a cigarette packet out, he did not ask, but lit two. She lay down in front of him, her hair splayed about her head, and he leant down and kissed her again, and even later when she was married with children, she remembered this moment, when she was seventeen, smoking the second cigarette of her life. She remembered his hand, a square-fingered, heavy hand, reach across her body, stroke down from her neck to her shoulders, across her breasts, rest gently on her stomach, and to her pubic bone, where it seemed it dare not go further. His eyes did not leave her face, and when she raised her eyes to his, he looked at her, not through to her, simply at her.

When they finished their cigarettes, she sat up, sat next to him again.

'So, what are we going to do?' she asked. Her bustle and efficiency broke the mood. He lit another cigarette for himself only.

'Nothing. We'll do nothing.'

'Why?' She was horrified: she was sure it was the story about Rohan. She would say she made it up, as a silly joke. She would say – look, how ridiculous it is, the idea of a *miner* coming to stay. 'Freddie. I can't take the girl he idolises from under his nose.'

'Freddie?' she laughed, incredulous. Freddie, the ugly idiot savant, who told the best jokes and looked at her across rooms as if she were a saint. Freddie who in his last letter compared her bitterness about the unfairnesses of the world to Antony – to him she was not Cleopatra, but Antony! She had forgotten Freddie, she had forgotten his straight-backed, righteous love for her, which she had never implied she would return.

They parted at the gates to the wood. This time, she leant to Ollie and kissed him, not tenderly, but with a hard, grazing intensity, so that for the rest of his days he would miss her. But as he walked away, she saw his step was not sad or slow. His head was jaunty in the midday sunshine, and around him the day haloed.

It turned out there was another reason for Ollie to turn away. He had asked Cassie out on Saturday, and the sixth-form common room was awash with hormonal screams and mutterings. Preethi kept her meeting with Ollie to herself. It belonged to her, she decided, and one day they were destined to be together. Besides which, he was going travelling with Freddie soon.

She had life to get on with, friends whose groups she needed to become part of again, essays to labour over, an A4 diary to catch up with, in detail, to describe the kiss, the hand stretched over her body. Soon, on Monday, she was absorbed in *Howards End* and Forster's abyss, and as she read of Leonard Bast's walk which the Schlegel girls found so enlightening, it suddenly came to her: the overwhelming guilt and loss, a feeling that hollowed her out like a pain of three-day hunger, and it was Freddie she thought of, Freddie whose ugly face ricocheted around her head until she laid her face on her arms in the library and cried.

She wrote him a letter, about selfishness and the guilt she felt, and at lunch went to post it. On the way back, she saw him in the distance, and Ollie was next to him, walking through the Village. She thought to cross the road, or hide behind a tree. He had seen her, though. She smiled, he waved, but when they came close, she saw Ollie's face, his eyes, and how beautiful he was, and how his lips were still hers. Freddie said, 'I was just thinking of you,' and she smiled up at him. Ollie walked away, and they went into the park.

'I just sent you a letter.'

'I'll look forward to it.' Freddie's face was bitter.

'I wanted to say I'm . . . sorry,' she started, knowing how useless it sounded.

'Yes. What have you been doing?'

'Exam practice: an essay on *Howards End*.'

He groaned. 'I hate Leonard Bast. I hate the Schlegel women. So affected . . . stupid.'

'Oh, stop,' she said, relieved that they were reverting to who they had been before. 'I see them all around me: the Schlegels and the Wilcoxes. Dulwich is full of them: my year is full of them! Girls who think they are original and exciting, and *understand life*: as if you *can* understand life.'

'And Bast? Bast – who is he in your picture of the world?'

She smiled and shrugged, but he knew already, she had cast him as that outsider, and cast herself as Margaret, who understood *love* at least, where he only stumbled about trying to save himself from the abyss. He stood suddenly, and started to walk away.

'What are you doing?' she shouted after him lamely.

'Going home,' he said over his shoulder.

'I'm sorry!' she shouted. And she went back to school and wrote an essay that garnered an A.

'Preethi!' she heard her father call. 'Phone for you!' She shot from her room. Perhaps it was Freddie, perhaps he was phoning from far away and the seconds ticking between her getting from her room to the telephone in the cold hallway would cost too much and he would be cut off.

'Who is it?' she shouted as she slid and ran down the three flights of stairs. Her father had already disappeared to the kitchen.

'Hello?' she said, panting, almost scared. What would she say to him? But he must be missing her as much as she missed him.

'Well, there's no need to get excited, it's only *me*.' Her heart fell. Clare, boring, stupid, Classical Civilisation Clare.

'Oh, hi,' she said breezily. Her father came out of the kitchen and pointed at a mug. He was making tea. She shook her head.

'Look, it's your turn to go through *Antigone*, and I wondered if you'd done the notes yet?' Preethi closed her eyes in frustration. She had been so busy writing notes on Forster.

'No, I haven't. But I'll do them tonight.'

'Well. OK. I was going to offer,' Clare said.

'No, Clare. I said I'd do them.' She had been tricked like this before: Kate called it passive-aggressive, whatever *that* meant. Something to do with Clare always doing the work, then telling everyone – including the teachers – about it. 'Was that it? Thanks for reminding me.' Clare was quiet at the end of the line. 'OK. See you tomorrow,' Preethi added.

'Look, someone has to tell you, Preethi. I heard some major bitching in the common room.'

'Oh.'

'Cassie knows about you and Ollie at the party.'

'Oh.' Her mouth was dry. 'But . . . technically, that was before they were going out, wasn't it?'

'Well, the thing is, she and Ollie have been on and off for months, and she's just been waiting for the exams to be over. I don't really care, myself, but you're both my friends, and well, I hate to hear people calling each other names.'

'What did she call me?'

'Well, a whore, for starters.' Preethi sat down on the leather pouffe by the telephone table.

'Right. I see. Well, thanks for telling me, Clare. See you tomorrow.' She couldn't talk about it any more. Freddie and Ollie were gone, and she was left to face the pack of wolves in the common room. And still a week until the end of term.

'Wait! Preethi? Are you still there?'

'Yes.'

'There's something else she said, and that's why I phoned.'

'What?' She was annoyed now. She rifled through the letters on the table, and saw a small, white, handwritten envelope, postmarked North Yorks. Bill.

'Cassie said something about your brother. It wasn't nice.'

She did not go to school the next day, a Thursday, or on Friday. She pretended to, getting on her bike with her school bag in her wicker basket and blowing everyone a kiss as they got into the car. Then she rode down to the shops, bought cigarettes, a newspaper and chocolate, and went to Hornimans Park. She sat by the petting zoo, feeding chocolate to the goats, reading about Princess Diana and Prince Charles and the baby due in September, and smoking a cigarette to the middle, until she needed to throw up. She walked unsteadily to the toilets, vomited her breakfast and the chocolate and went home to bed.

Later, she went out again, as far as Lordship Lane, and when she saw the first school coaches making their way up the hill, she turned her bike around and cycled home. In her room she read *Antigone* and tried to make notes, but fell asleep twice. She need not have bothered to go through the charade of returning: no one was in when she arrived back. It made her feel better. When her mother returned, Preethi made her tea, started chopping onions for supper, then went back to her room.

Rohan came into her room on Friday evening.

'Ammi's worried. What's the matter with you?'

'Nothing.'

'She says, you're always out at friends till six. You always have people calling. Nothing over the last few days. What's the matter?'

'Nothing.' She looked at his face, beautiful and shining, his vigorous confidence, his joking manner.

'Come on,' he said more tenderly. 'You can tell me.'

'I haven't been to school. I can't go back.'

Rohan looked shocked. 'What is it? What happened? They want you to do fourth term! Have your grades gone down? I can help you – there's no need to skip school.'

'No, no,' she said miserably. 'Someone told a secret, something I told them, and now the whole school knows. I can't go in,' she said suddenly. 'I can't face it.'

'It's only a week, *putha*,' he said, stroking her hair.

'You sound like Ammi when you talk Sinhala.'

'Do I?'

She lay down on her bed, and he sat at the end, and neither said anything more. She could hear the silence, could hear dinner being made, and Papa and Gehan coming in and birds, and children shouting in gardens on the opposite side of the road. He stayed with her for a little longer, and then he went into his room and she heard him put Bowie on, and sing along to 'Let's Dance'.

On Saturday, there was a postcard from Freddie. It chatted about nothing, and about Ollie, and she tore it up, because even seeing his name made her feel revolted, made her feel anger so that if he stood in front of her, she would kill him. On Sunday, Clare phoned again, told her it was time to stop hiding. Told her to bring the *Antigone* notes in, the Oxbridge meeting had been postponed because of Preethi's sickness, that she would stick by her, it would be OK.

That Monday morning was beautiful. Her remorse, her anger, her misery floated above her for the moment when she rode past the chapel, across the roundabout. She wore sunglasses and a white dress, white plimsolls, and slung around her shoulders a purple cardigan. She threw her head back to look at the trees above her, and a window cleaner across the road shouted, 'All right, darlin'?'

When she got to the traffic lights at the foot of the hill and saw everyone walking, running, shouting into school, she thought she would die. For them to know this of her. For them to understand her brother so completely, in one, filthy idea. For them to think she was somehow part of his profligacy too, simply because she wanted Ollie. Clare stood on the other side of the road, and waved and beckoned, and somehow it was too late to turn back, and she went in.

Everything had changed. Her life and the way she was perceived had changed in two days. As she approached school, girls in the lower forms made way and as she passed, giggled and whispered. Clare turned sharply to them and hushed them, but Preethi could hear it all about her. She put her head down, and they walked silently to the bike sheds. She saw Cassie and her friends across the field, and looked in panic about her. A few of her other friends came smiling towards her. It would be all right, it would be all right. But then, as she walked towards the sixth-form building, Debbie, a small, fat fifth-former said to her back: 'Your brother been fucked in the arse by a miner: pretty much like the rest of the country, eh?' And all around her laughed out loud. She used her advantage: 'All *you people* are degenerate, aren't you?'

Preethi continued to walk, stride now towards the block, and then she turned to Clare and shrugged. It would be the easiest way out. She turned back, almost ran at Debbie and struck her hard, across the face with the back of her hand. As the girl reeled, Preethi looked around at the other girls, who were gasping and shocked. Then she took another step towards

Debbie, who put her hand up to deflect the next blow. Preethi saw her fear, saw her own face in the fear, and still she hit her again, and then again, on top of the head once, until the girl fell to the ground, crying. There were shouts from a teacher, and thundering steps of someone running to her, tangling her arms up in their tight grip, and she was led to the headmistress's office, where the teacher, a flaky PE-sort, sat with her, jigging her knee impatiently and smiling at anyone but Preethi.

Mrs Divorcee they called her, their headmistress, so full of bouncing, tall energy, certain that the young women at her school would *all achieve*. They would all *be something*. But perhaps not me, Preethi thought.

'Well? Can you explain this behaviour? You realise I have already asked my secretary to inform your parents. You will be immediately suspended for a week, which takes us to the end of term.' She saw Preethi's face lift with relief. 'It will be questionable whether you can come back,' she continued, and to her satisfaction she now saw shock. Preethi did not speak. 'Oxbridge! You would give up a chance at Oxbridge for a petty fight! Surely you would have known this before you let a silly little girl like Debbie get to you?'

'No.'

'Ah. You *can* speak.'

'Yes.'

'Well? What is it about? You *hit* a child – *what is your explanation*?'.

'I . . .' she shrugged.

'Oxbridge!' the headmistress said again. 'Look, sit down, sit down.' She bustled to a salmon pink chair. She offered a blue sofa to Preethi. Preethi looked about at the duck-egg blue walls, the glass-fronted walnut bookcases, the antique desk and the wide, long windows. Edwardian, she supposed, a place the Schlegels might live in, or Forster himself. She did not think of the violence of her act, or her swollen little finger. She thought of Ollie, and Freddie. Where were they now? Where was she, that girl they had argued over?

'Now, we cannot have this. You must tell me why.'

'My brother,' she started. But she stopped. She had already told one too many people.

'What does it have to do with your brother? Look, can't you see what you have done? Preethi, look at me. We work *so hard* here. You do . . .' She bent a dramatic, pale hand to Preethi, as if a ballet dancer, or a good witch, and then brought the hand up and placed it gracefully on her chest '. . . and *I* do. We work so that women can break through the glass ceilings in all walks of life. Don't you see? You could be a remarkable scholar! Your English essays, I am told, are extraordinary, *exemplary*. Your behaviour, until now, has been such that, within the one year you have been here, you have made many friends and gained much admiration from the staff. Your dyslexia has never to my knowledge got in your way. All of this adds up to a model student, someone I could not recommend more highly to any university in the land. Come now, please explain.' She waited in silence, her head turned towards the window, watching the late girls sneaking through the gate and raising her eyebrows. Preethi sat in silence. A clock ticked loudly in the lobby outside the office. She scratched at the texture of the sofa. The headmistress sighed.

'Preethi, our school is like a city, a golden, glorious city. We work for each other, and we work for ourselves. What we give to you is self-worth, your importance in the world. What we want for you is *everything*.'

'Yes.' Preethi had nothing more to say. There was a knock on the door, and Nandini was ushered in. Preethi saw her eyes, fearful and furious. And to her shame, she began to cry.

Clare brought her bike back later. She met Rohan at the door, and refused to come in. Preethi would not have wanted to see her. Her mother had hit her, and she had spent the day crying in her room. Papa and Ammi went out to see some friends, and now that the exams were over, Gehan went with them. Rohan went up to London to see a play.

Preethi ran a bath, and while it ran made a large gin and Rose's lime and drank it down, without ice as there was none. She smoked a cigarette in the garden, wondering where Freddie was, wondering how he was, how Ollie was. She thought of the kiss, thought of it a million times, the kiss that somehow made her dirtier than her brother. She smoked another cigarette, and then went up to the still too hot bath. She stepped in, one foot then the other, and allowing the heat of the water to encapsulate her skin gradually, she sank into it. She remembered Ollie's hand, as she lay back into the water, looked at her body, which he had stroked through her clothes as if he had owned her, as if he could love her. She left the bathroom door unlocked, and using one of Papa's new razor blades, she opened her wrists.

She was dreaming, and characters, famous people were all there, and talking about her, about fate, about the abyss. There was Mrs Godfrey, dear Mrs Godfrey her English teacher, talking to them all, walking from person to person, facilitating the party. Edwardian dress, with coal-scuttle woven hats, men in tails. There were Ollie and Cassie, holding hands, walking across the grass under a tall oak, and Freddie stood in a corner, waving, beckoning to her to join him. And Margaret Schlegel, on the arm of Mr Wilcox, stopped to talk to Freddie, and Freddie was rude. And then, suddenly, Freddie was no longer Freddie, but Prince Myshkin, the Idiot, and it made sense, and she thought, but of course, of course, I should have known. Mrs Godfrey was saying something, saying something to all the guests, and they were throwing their heads back and laughing, and each time she said it, it was funnier than the last. Preethi tried to get closer, to share the joke, and when she finally stood by Mrs Godfrey's elbow, she heard Mrs Godfrey say: 'But you see, the joke is, he was not "taking it up the arse"! He was "giving him one", as they say!' And people laughed around her. 'He's one of us! He's one of us!' And everyone laughed.

Preethi started to scream. Her eyes tried to open, but they could not. Her mouth moved, and her father and her mother and her brothers stood traumatised and scared of the screams, and of their own part in her suicide attempt, Victor clutching her bandaged hands, Rohan pressing a button to summon a nurse, Nandini leaning heavily against Gehan.

In her dream, she was dressed in a white cotton shift, belted with rope. Her hair was braided around her head, and her feet were bare. Wound around her arms were golden cloths. In her dream she walked around the party looking for Rohan, and when she saw him, beyond the fence of the garden, she knew he was dead, and no one would bury him. She looked back at the party, where people still laughed, and climbed over the fence and ran across a field to where the body lay. She took the bandages from her arms and laid them, bloodied and disintegrating, on to his already decomposing body. She dug at the ground, trying to cover the body with crumbling earth. The whole party turned to her at once, she could see they were all chanting, and finally it was a sympathetic chant, but grudgingly so. Some pointed, some shook their heads. She lay down next to him, her lovely brother. Lay down, and then, as if this part of the dream had been the only reality, she woke up.

NIL'S WEDDING

On the morning of her wedding, Nil lay in bed and listened to the noise of the family, the harmonies they sang, the melodies which struck each other awry, until she could hear shouts and laughter. She heard Mohan calling for Vita, Vita answering 'What?' She heard her mother Siro in the kitchen, her father, Wesley, in the garden. She listened to his voice. She could see him in her mind's eye with his two brothers. They would be sitting in the shade of the pear tree, Wesley's arm carelessly around the back of a grey-tinged plastic chair, telling a quiet story, sipping tea from his old brown mug. She thought of them all as she stretched, thought of her family walking down the aisle with her, a gang of De Silvas laughing and playing as they strutted towards Ian's more dignified family, waistcoated and be-hatted, like a set of Etonesque sixth-formers. She lay still and listened again, and heard her two aunts in the kitchen singing in their high voices, and Vita laughing. She heard her mother's voice on the stairs, talking quietly to Mohan, and Mo saying 'Don't stress, Ma, it's fine.'

She could hear Mo's feet coming up the stairs. Nil closed her eyes, holding herself still. He walked into her room, opened the curtains, looked down at the garden, knocked at the open sash window. She lay quiet. She knew he had turned to watch her. He laughed.

'I know when you're awake, we shared a room for long enough,' and he pulled the covers from her. She yelped, pulling them back.

'Go away, Mo.'

'Dum dum de dum,' he sang loudly, 'Dum dum de dum. Ian's getting lucky tooo-night . . .'

'Ah, shut up, would yer?'

She heard her father shout, 'Mohan! Leave the child alone!'

Mohan started to leave. Then he came back and sat on the bed. He tousled Nil's hair.

'Are you nervous?' he asked.

'No. Why?'

'I would be. Marriage. New house, new life. No Mum to come home to. I don't know. You're very young.'

'I'm twenty-three. Mum was married a year by my age.'

'Yeah. Well. Aren't you worried about all the other ones?'

'I've had enough of other ones. Ian's good enough for me,' she said.

They sat in a steady silence, and then Mohan lay back, his hands tucked under his head, next to her on the pillow. They had shared a bed until she was six. He listened with her to the voices, the singing in the garden, laughter from the kitchen.

'Mum's stressing,' he said, as commentary. They could hear their mother shouting into the garden: 'Wesley! The flowers!'

Nil turned on her side and looked at Mohan in profile.

'I'll miss you guys,' she said.

'Will you?' he asked, but he didn't seem to be interested, a little smile on his face as he stared at the ceiling.

After Mo left, Nil lay in her bed for another half an hour and tried to answer his question. She wondered why on earth marriage was so important at this stage, when men were practically falling into her lap from every angle. She heard another wave of laughter from downstairs. She realised that she took comfort from the knowledge that that other life – of dark crawls across hotel bedroom floors at two in the morning to find her clothes, before she made her way drunkenly back down the corridor to her own room – was over. Ian was a good bet. Ian was a freedom, and a shutting off. He was the groundwork for everything else. But was he love, she wondered? Was he the love that creates laughter, and home, and the tenderness of all of this? And she knelt up in her bed, and looked down into the garden, where she saw her father reach out for her mother's hand as she hurriedly walked past him, clutching Nil's bouquet.

Nil went for a walk. The front door was open, and the hallway lined with flowers, small oasis-filled plastic plates, poked through with froths of gypsophila, prongs of creamy freesias, plump mauve roses, pinewood-smelling greenery. She stopped short when she glanced into the shady, green dining room, where she saw her own large bouquet on the table, leaning up on its handle, the ivy and stephanotis trails artfully falling off the edge. Why is it all so necessary, she thought?

Nil could hear Siro in the kitchen.

'No, Wesley,' she was saying forcefully. 'We must have

someone in the house at all times. Who will pour the champagne, take the clingfilm off the platters?'

Wesley, replying, 'This one, this woman, what is her name?'

'Margaret?'

'Yes, the cleaning woman. She said she would come.'

'But she is a *cleaning woman*, Wesley! What if one of the guests doesn't know where the church is and comes to the house?'

'So Margaret will tell them.'

'A *cleaning woman* cannot direct guests to my daughter's wedding, *nayther*?' she asked, and Nil knew her mother was looking around at her husband's sisters, who for the past week had sat at her elbow from morning till evening, giving credence to Siro's interpretation of the ancient laws of Sri Lankan wedding etiquette.

Nil walked down the hill she had lived on since she was five. She strolled past Molly-the-widow's house, stopping to peek through the perfect round hole in the fence she had discovered as a teenager, which gave her a small view of the magnificent garden of hollyhocks and delphiniums, fuchsias and honeysuckle. This was beauty, she thought. A glorious England, a place of history. She walked past Debbie's house, her friend and constant companion when she was a teenager.

She walked on down and stopped outside Rosemary-the-dinner-lady's house, the last one on the road. Its front path was terraced up through a rockery, which Nil knew and loved. Rosemary had always allowed them to go in and search for snails, ladybirds, butterflies. If I find a ladybird, I will count its dots, and times them by my age and then by Ian's age, and then I'll find the mean of our ages and divide the answer by that, and that will be how long we'll be married. She found a ladybird with one spot. This had never happened before, and she took it as an omen. A good omen or a bad omen, she wondered?

Nil walked into town, went into Boots and bought hairpins. She looked at the front cover of the *Guardian* in Smith's. Thought seriously about buying it. The first 'civilian' in space, a teacher, Christa McAuliffe, had been announced. Nil thought about the first moon landing, when she and Mohan watched the little black and white TV in the dining room. They took Mamma's Hoover apart so they could attach the hose to the tea chests, which had just been unpacked after they had moved into the house. Christa and me launching into new territory, she thought.

Walking back up the hill, she saw the dogs with their people, children on bikes, a normal July day. The oppression she had felt before had lifted, but when she looked into the park, she felt it again, this weight, as if the wedding were a story and the real world, going on its way in and out of the park, were an admonition to her family and its fantasies of equality, acceptance, normality.

The doorbell rang and rang. Nil showered, then had to wet her hair again, so the hairdresser could tease it into a French knot, and then they realised they had done everything in the wrong order, because how was the hairdresser to pin the veil into her hair while she still sat in her knickers? So Siro had to be called up to dress her, because Nil had never put a sari on by herself. She'd only ever worn one – with her mother's help – for a fashion show in the sixth form, and even that she had resented because she didn't want people thinking that she was, well, *ethnic*.

Nil stood in her parents' bedroom in front of the only full-length mirror in the house. The bedroom was a dark room, large but full of furniture – a simple double bed with no head-board, dressing table, wardrobes, cupboards, a chair. Nil looked at it all through her nearly married eyes, and thought about the house she would move to at the end of this week. She saw its large windows all opened, the whiteness of the walls swallowing her up in their space, taking her into their blankness, shaping her into something different.

Aunty Marjie and Aunty Ivy watched from the bed. Aunty Dorothy stood by Siro's elbow holding the pins. Marjie's straight back and thin arms did not disguise her tenseness – Siro often told Wesley that Marjie would *die*, of a *heart attack*, if she did not learn to relax. Ivy, her opposite, sat slouched into the amalgamation of her chest and tummy, and Nil giggled and looked away. Both aunts fiddled with their hair, and sometimes with each other's. They had lived together for most of their lives; Marjie had once made a foray into married life, which had been short-lived and was never talked of. Siro's sister, Prema Aunty, the younger, light-skinned double of her elder sibling, remained quiet and undisturbed, not allowing any infringement on her sister. She was Nil's favourite aunt by far. She laughed easily, fitted in to plans and escapades, made no judgements but only small sounds of approval at times when they were needed. She pressed the white sari as Siro lifted it gently from the ironing board, fold by precious fold on to the floor. Then tucking, pinning, creasing, she carefully manoeuvred it about Nil's body. Siro walked the material around Nil, and Nil stood still, watching herself, watching her aunts and her mother in their savouring of their duty. Vita had slipped into the room, and stood by the door, her small, dark face showing its sixteen-year-old innocence. Her almond-shaped eyes hooded over with apprehension and what seemed to Nil like distaste.

'What's the matter, darling,' Aunty Ivy said, stretching her hand out and stroking back Vita's hair.

Siro stopped what she was doing and appraised her other daughter, with her head to one side.

'Have you showered?'

'No.'

'Well?'

'I wanted to watch.'

'Hmm . . .' and she continued to walk the sari about Nil. Nil looked at Vita in the mirror and winked. She waited to see that Vita smiled back, but the small face was intense, following their mother's movements. She seems afraid, Nil thought. Siro pleated the sari and tucked it into the front of Nil's underskirt. Nil looked at her mother's hands, and somehow a prick of anger came to her: the rough fingers that overwrought the simplest of tasks – even this putting on of her sari was an act of Sri Lankan drama. It was as if she, Nil, were unimportant within it all, simply a vessel to carry the rectitude of the Sri Lankan methodology.

'It is a very fine silk, *nayther*?' Prema asked.

'It was a bargain,' Siro said.

'Rea-ea-lly?' the aunts chorused. Vita took a step back towards the door. Nil said nothing.

Siro took the final part of the sari, walked it about Nil once more then pulled it up on to her shoulder. The *pallu*, the embroidered panel at the end, lay splendidly down her back.

Her mother looked appraisingly at it, then undid it, pulled one of the pleats from Nil's middle, and re-draped it. She squinted at her daughter's back. Nil balanced her head with its large hairpiece curled into a French knot and stuck tight to her scalp. She tried not to laugh.

'Longer?' Siro asked Dorothy. Dorothy and Prema both walked to Nil's back and looked. Dorothy reached her hand forward, but Siro gave it a stinging look, and the hand was quickly withdrawn.

'Are you pleating it, or leaving it?' Prema asked.

'What do you think?' Siro asked Nil in the mirror.

'How am I supposed to know, Ma?'

Wesley was called for an opinion. She heard her father's voice on the stairs, wondered if Ian would ever care about the way their own daughter should be dressed on her wedding day. Would they even get so far as having a daughter?

'Pleat the *pallu*,' Wesley said, straight away.

'Hmm,' Siro said.

'No?' he asked.

'All right,' she snapped.

Wesley looked at his wife in amusement. He put his hand on her arm, then, reaching to her head, stroked back her hair. 'Why, darling?'

Nil watched her mother adjusting, pinning and unpinning, her father watching her mother, in love.

Nil wore her mother's wedding diamonds. It was the first time she had seen them out of the box. But when Siro put them around her neck, they realised the catch was broken.

They pinned the two ends of the necklace under her blouse at the back.

'*Cummak na, nayther?*' Siro said uncertainly to the aunts. She patted the blouse down over the bump.

'*Ekka nena*,' her aunts muttered, smiling at Nil, but looking at each other uneasily. Nil knew her mother had said it doesn't matter, does it? And her aunts had answered, of course not, but she looked at them and wondered why it would matter at all? It's just a necklace, just a wedding.

Vita was the bridesmaid in a mauve sari, her shorter hair dressed with lilac freesias. Mohan wore a suit that matched his father's. They had both bought expensive black suits that were more fashionable than anything Ian's side would wear, Nil knew straight away. She wondered if they would be seen as what they were – two men with flair – or as jumped-up immigrants, wider than wide boys. She thought of Ian's father, his mother. They wouldn't understand this pageant, her family. They would parade like a tribe in full costume, her parents, Mohan, Vita, her aunts and uncles and cousins in their brightly coloured silks, their shining jewellery, their polished shoes and silver and gold slippers, and it would be their best day. The day their family shone, she thought, and she looked at them all warily, sizing them up with one eye, the eye that looked through Ian's eyes, then balanced the image with the other eye, full of pride. She wondered – why am I marrying him, when I hate so much about him?

It was an inevitable rush to the church. Who was going with whom, not enough cars, and too many ladies in saris; and then Vita, who would she go with? Nil walked down the stairs in all her finery, and the crowd in the hall turned as one to stare and smile. Prema in a pale pink sari, Dorothy in beige silk, their hair tied in knots on the top of their heads. Marjie's hair had a stolen sprig of freesias decorating the side of her head, and Nil saw that Siro had noticed and scowled. Nil and her father and mother paused for photographs, and then she entered into the rituals, eating a morsel of milk rice, drinking fragrant beflowered water, being blessed by her parents, aunts dabbing their eyes, uncles, cousins, tiny children kissing her through her veil. The routines she had seen at weddings in Sri Lanka, uprooted and replanted in London. They seemed odd, out of step with the day-to-day living of an hour before. I am an astronaut, saying my goodbyes, eating and drinking my strange last meal.

Nil and Wesley drove to the church in the hired Mercedes in silence. Nil tried to erupt from the car because she was already fifteen minutes late. Wesley held her back.

'It's all right. He'll wait a little longer. Let us catch our breath.'

She sat back and looked at him, as he bowed his head and said a silent prayer. He looked up and saw her, and offered her his prayer, as if offering a refreshment. She refused quickly, smiling encouragement as if he were a little boy.

They walked slowly along the South Circular to the church. It had been their church for the whole of their lives, a place of familiar, stained-glass windows and thirties architecture that all three children knew intimately, from playing there after service, from Guides, Scouts, Junior Church, Youth Services, until when Nil and Mohan turned eighteen they refused to go back. Nil had not wanted to marry here. If she had really had a choice, she would have married in the chapel of New College in Oxford. 'But how on earth will all the Sri Lankans get to Oxford?' her mother had asked. Wesley held the huge train from her veil in his hands, and she lifted the skirts of the sari.

Nil began to shake, a small tremor, but detectable by her father. She had only now realised that she was about to get married. She looked at Wesley and smiled wanly.

'What is it, darling?' Wesley asked.

She stopped short of the door, feeling her legs begin to shudder. Now he had asked, she realised: 'Dad, can we go back?'

'Where do you want to go?' He had her elbow and was pushing her gently forward towards the church door. They could hear the organ playing. A couple tiptoed past them, a lady in a fuschia pink sari, the man in a dark suit and pink tie. They smiled, waved. Nil did not recognise them. Wesley nodded at them.

'Who was that?' Nil asked.

'You know, that travel agent chap, Milton.'

'Why the hell is he at my wedding?' Her teeth chattered as if she were really cold.

'Now, Nil. Come, you're just a little nervous.'

She glanced towards the newsagent on the next block. When they were small, after church, she and Mohan would run down and choose sweets. She always had Jellytots. What she wouldn't give for a packet of Jellytots right now. Or a double vodka.

'Come, darling,' her father coaxed. 'You were so worried about being late.'

She thought logically and reasonably about how easy it would be to run in the sari. Her mother had convinced her to wear a sari about six weeks ago and had again told her the story about the midwives in Sri Lanka who all wore saris and cycled into the far-off villages, sometimes carrying their bags and an umbrella. She would have to ask her father to unpin the veil from the top of her coiled hair.

'Thing is, Dad, I'm not entirely convinced that I actually, you know, *love* Ian. I mean, he's a good bloke and everything, but it isn't like you and Mum or anything.' She was floundering. No one ever spoke these sorts of truths out loud, not in their family.

Wesley laughed. 'I am *sure* your mother felt the same way about me on *our* wedding day, darling. What you see when you talk about our "love" is years and years of practice. How can you achieve love if you do not practise it on a daily basis first?'

'Yes, yes!' Nil was animated by this idea. Wesley edged her towards the church door, but was pushed back by Mohan, poking his head through questioningly. Wesley shook his head at him, and he pulled back in, then pushed out again to wolf-whistle his sister. Nil ignored him.

'I mean, why do I have to get married to do that, Dad? I mean, you're absolutely right. Come on, we'll go back to the car, and Mo can get Ian, and I'll tell him that you think it's fine that we live together.'

She started to walk away, but in the direction of the newsagent's. She was thinking about Jellytots, and white chocolate buttons, which she and Mo always bought for Vita. But what would Mo have, she wondered? Wesley pulled on the veil accidentally. Nil shrieked as the comb in her hair tugged at her scalp. Her whole body now felt taken over by the veil, the sari, the materials of this day. There was an ache in her chest, she thought, an ache from near her lungs – could it be her heart? Her heart was beating so fast it hurt.

'I'm sorry, darling. Come now, come. Let us go in, and we can talk about it inside.'

'No, Dad. If I go in there, someone'll convince me to get married to Ian and I'm really not sure I want to.'

'Come now.' Wesley was suddenly firm. He had clicked his fingers. She followed. She didn't know why.

They went into the lobby of the church where Mohan and Ian's brother Michael stood with Orders of Service. Vita smiled nervously from the doorway leading into the main body of the church.

'What's up?' Mo said cheerfully. Wesley made a small gesture with his hand towards Michael. Michael turned solemnly away. Mo felt in his pocket.

'Here,' he said, and he undid and thrust a small hip flask under the veil over Nil's face. She took the bottle and sniffed. 'It's arrack,' Mo said. 'S'all I could find at home.'

'Oo, can I have some?' Vita asked.

Nil swigged a small nip. It buzzed into her, flowing down into her belly, and then she swigged a larger amount, handing it on to her father.

'Not in *church*! I'm a Methodist, for goodness' sake!'

'Go on, Dad,' Mo said. 'Just once in your life. Jesus would forgive yer.'

Nil passed the bottle back to Mohan, who drank a little and passed it to Vita. 'Only a *little*,' he commanded.

'All right, Grandad.'

Michael turned, and Mohan offered him the bottle. He smiled and refused gently. Nil thought how alike he and Ian were. With the arrack inside her empty belly, she felt stronger, she felt ready to marry. She thought, I could marry anyone now: Milton the travel agent, Michael, Reverend Joseph who christened me waiting there at the end of the aisle, any man carrying a packet of Jellytots. I now feel in the marrying mood. I mean, what's the use of wasting all this, she thought, and she looked round at it all, this grand design of her mother's. Swathes of white lilies and mauve roses stood in every corner of the church. The women on her side of the church all sat in searingly bright saris, greens, blues, pinks, reds, and on the other side, more muted women in their pale blues and yellows and creams, suits, dresses, and hats! Nil thought, Christ, they're all wearing hats!

'Do you remember Mum singing last night?' Mohan asked.

'Yes,' Vita said.

'D'you remember the chorus, Nil?' Mo said.

'You tell me,' she said.

'Love is all you need,' her father said. She took a deep breath. Wesley and Vita dispersed her veil around her, and Mohan squeezed her arm and as an afterthought, gave her a quick slap on the bottom. Her father smiled, kissed her.

'Come on,' he said, and the 'Arrival of the Queen of Sheba' began to play, as Michael and Mohan opened the doors fully.

It was when she was kneeling, she and Ian looking at each other, that she became aware of the photographer. She had specifically said to her parents that there should be no photographs during the wedding. It was the thing, the one thing she had asked. And there he was, this little man in a grey dress coat and a lopsided toupee tiptoeing down the aisle, taking a shot of Ian leaning in to tell her he was about to faint.

'I didn't know I would be this nervous.'

'Oh, shit,' Nil said. 'And everyone can see how much my shoes cost.'

'Have you been drinking?' Ian asked, and his eyebrows arched in that way she hated.

She smiled sweetly. 'Did you think I could marry you sober?'

Ian threw his head back and laughed. He reached for her hand and squeezed it. He's doing it for show, surely? It was this photograph – the one she had specifically asked her parents not to be taken, the one where Ian's synthetic laughter screwed up his features and combined with her simple yet meaningful smile – it was this photograph which was to become everyone's favourite. It would be the photograph which filled an antique silver frame in Longacre, Ian's family home; it would be hung in a dark mahogany frame in Siro and Wesley's sitting room; and indeed in their own Clapham castle, it would sit on a mantelpiece, dutifully dusted for the eighteen years they were married. Nil walked past it most mornings of her married life and did not register it, because if she did, out of the corner of her eye she would see the tiny patch of red at the bottom corner of the picture, the sale sticker on the bottom of her right shoe, and she would remember the things she had left undone in her life, the things she had simply, carelessly forgotten.

As they were blessed, as they turned to walk up the aisle, as they waited for the organ to start Purcell's 'Trumpet

Voluntary', Nil felt the weight fall upon her again, but now as a foreboding, an awe. She glanced at Ian, and he smiled back. I do love him, she thought. I love him as much as I think is necessary. He was not the reason for this feeling. He was not even part of the feeling. He seemed to be a distant, smiling force, representative of the future. She glanced behind her and there was her father, and on his arm, Ian's mother. Behind them, her mother, escorted by Ian's father. She felt a lack of breath, a panic rising as she looked at her mother, who unsmilingly looked back. She hadn't noticed this morning because Mum had been a wedding automaton, she hadn't noticed that Mum looked – what? Disappointed? Afraid? Siro nodded her head forwards. Her hand holding a silver clutch-bag pointed ahead of Nil, and yet Nil stayed, poised at the head of the church, shrinking back behind the altar. Following her mother were Vita and Mohan, arm in arm, giggling. Siro turned and hushed them, and they looked up and forwards towards Nil. Mohan's eyes sparkled. He was never afraid, never worried, Nil thought. And then she looked at Vita, and it was Vita who surmised her. Vita's stare of incredulousness made Nil afraid. She had married on a feeling, a tenuous emotion. She had needed to move forward. But here, back here, behind her, there was an old country, an old world, that she had not finished inhabiting yet. Why could she not have stayed and been a grown-up with these people she loved, instead of jumping into freefall, into the air she felt all about her now?

'SMILE, darling,' Ian said, and he clutched her arm too tight, held it clamped between his elbow and his ribs, a rugby ball that needed to be touched down at the other end of the aisle.

Nil smiled. She looked back, and Wesley nodded a small sideways nod, jutting his chin forwards for her to walk. She had had enough of walking. She wanted to sit, kneel if need be, but not take this walk in this way.

When they reached the church doors, the photographer took another photo, and this one Nil destroyed. No one saw it, not even Ian, and he deserved to see it. Her eyes were cloudy, but his shone, and behind them both were Siro, Wesley, Mohan and Vita, all in focus, and all grave, saddened, feeling her fear, feeling her loss.

MUMTAZ CHAPLIN

My name means excellent, right, and if I said 'I'm excellent' in front of the class or whatever, my teacher couldn't say anything, because that's who I am, and that's it.

But I say nothing a lot instead. I say nothing all the time, and it gets to people, if they don't know me. It makes them small, angry, like you put them in a chair shorter than yours, and you sit at your desk, and they sit in that chair and look up to you. And you laughing, yeah? I say nothing all day. No one, including me, knows why. I laugh at the jokes, and when the boys fall out their chair, it makes me laugh, so I laugh, but no sound come out. It's like farts, when they silent but deadly. But the opposite effect. When I laugh, this big smile is on my face, and my friends say it's like the sun shining.

I watch Charlie DVDs. When I want peace, when I'm on my own. I watch Charlie. And when I walk, I look around first, and then I walk down the road, and I do Charlie's walk, like my hair curly and my clothes holey and especially I like *The Kid* when he has the little boy, and I walk down the road holding the kid's hand. Sometimes I borrow my uncle's shoes, and I walk in them, around the living room, my feet sideways and shhooo, it hurt your hips, sitting back on them so your legs go bandy bandy, like a monkey. My uncle says if I talked I would talk like a black kid 'cos I grew up in Peckham, and I would suck my lips and knife people, he says to his friends, all sitting there looking at me in the living room. But I don't speak, so he don't know, do he? I hear my friends, the ones I left behind, and they never suck they lips. They never talk like what black kids are supposed to. They talk quiet, about different things, and they talk quiet to me, because I don't talk.

When I come up here, my uncle beat me once. I came to the morning prayers, and washed and all that, even though I didn't know how because no one taught me. I just watched him, and I did what he did, and then when we went in the mosque, he prayed, and I stood up and knelt and stood and bowed, like he did, but because no words come out, he hit me. It weren't hard, but he hit me with his hand on my head. And anything on your head hurts, but I thought it wasn't hard like he meant it.

He don't beat me no more, because teachers told him it was in the reports that I don't speak but I hear, and I can write and I understand and I cle-e-ver! They say it to him face. I can do everything because I am clever.

In Peckham there was this English teacher, we called him Fnar Fnar, because when he speaks that what come out. He says stuff like a man on *News at Ten* who talk about people in other countries like they a bad thing. Even white people are a bad thing to the English, if they don't talk English.

'Ah, the English language!' the Fnar Fnar would say. He walk around the classroom, his smile on, and my mate Jared would force one out, and the girls would run to the window and scream and me smile, and the boys in the back row laugh and five each other and punch Jared like it a good thing. But Fnar Fnar would read from he books. And then, you know, then people are quiet, and people are laughing, but I always listened, because he read the English the way the English was written. He could hold you still, like he holding your beating heart. He could still all the hearts in the room, and he say –

'. . . I'll love you till the ocean / Is folded and hung up to dry / And the seven stars go squawking / Like geese about the sky'

– and I know he showing off. He was sad, like a shambling clown, like a man who live in a cardboard box, his clothes spattered with food and his teeth caked with slime. His face had red veins, like the blood congeal in his head and the rest of him dead. Charlie better off than him. Sometimes, Fnar Fnar try to trap me with his voice, he would ask a question, suddenly, 'Mumtaz!' and the class, all loud, would quieten to a whisper, like they in a wider world, and trees waving above they heads, like nature all around and they want to hear the voice of a mouse, they want to hear, creeping by their feet. And Fnar Fnar would look at me, his sadness eyes on my face, and he say, 'I have lost my voice most irrecoverably . . .' and laugh, and the class would talk again. My friends in the back row, my boys, would breathe again. They look after me, they grip the table and knock it over if I look sad. With them, I almost *want* to speak. But if I tried, only grunt grunt, shameful voice would come, like I am an animal, like I am a dog growling.

I tried it once, before the social moved me up here, I tried to say goodbye, in the park. But only strangle noise come. I wrote 'I going away' on a piece of paper. We all on the roundabout, going round and round, and little kids kicking the ground watching us, and their mums watching from further back, not saying nothing, and we enjoying our ride. I stopped the roundabout, got off, and the boys joined me, and I went to lift a kid on to the roundabout and a mother came running forward, and I wondered if my mum tried to save me. I did my Charlie walk for the kid, and Isaac laughing, laughing, says, 'Mumtaz, do it again, do it again,' all the way home, through the park and I walked away from them while they still laughing, my hand in my pocket, my shoulders shrug shrug, twirling my imaginary cane.

How I got to Leeds was one of my teachers told someone else that I was living on my own. My aunt went away, I don't know where, and I just stayed at the flat because I know how to do stuff. She left the keys, and the child benefit book and I just got the eleven quid out and I ate stuff like tortilla wraps and chicken. I can cook a chicken, like it's really easy man, just take it out the wrapping and put it in the oven and that's it. That's it, when the oven works, but it started not to work after two weeks, and I never told no one, and all my mates ask me to theirs, so I ate sometimes, and the rest of the time, cereal and bread. But I think Jared told our tutor, and I could say I never talk to him no more, but that would be a lie, right? I talk to Jared in my head. I talk to him with my eyes, and I smile at him, even though I knew him telling the teacher meant I was on my way. Away. When I see them, my boys, in my head, I don't see them faces. I see an empty roundabout, going round and round.

Teacher says, 'You on your own, Mumtaz?' I nod yes, what I'm going to say – No? And she says 'You hungry?' and I nod yes, and you know, she was nice, she asked if I want a kebab and she took me out at lunchtime, and buy me a kebab with everything on – I mean *everything* – chilli sauce, salad, them yellow peppers the English call chilli and eat to look hard, and she give me a can of Red Bull and watch me eat. I eat it big, man. Then she buy me ice cream. She says, 'You going in a home, you understand?' She black like my friends, so she talk like them when she talk to us. I like her voice and her smile. I like the way she don't try and touch me or hug me like she want to be my mum. I like her just standing there, saying 'It'll be hard in there, you get me?' I nod. And I remembered my uncle, my aunt says when this situation come up, tell them about Uncle Mazoor. I didn't say nothing because I would rather take my chances with a home and stay in Peckham, where Mum used to take me to the library and where the roundabout and the park and the trees I know is. But they know where my uncle is anyway.

I got some photos of my mum, that's all. One of them, is Mum when she's about nine, and she's sitting on somebody lap, but the picture was way old, and it got ripped somewhere down the line, so it only Mum now. I like it, because there another photo, of me on Mum's lap, and I looking at the camera the same as she did when she little. We both smile like we not sure what going to happen. On Mum's picture, she written her name: 'MAY' along the back, like she need to stamp on it that it her. I wrote my name on mine too, but my handwriting better. Mum laughed when I told her. When I went up to my uncle's all I took was my uniform, a couple of Mum's books and my photos.

My uncle never hit me again after that first time. I think he wanted a miracle to happen. I think he thought that if he took me to the mosque, I would remember how to pray, I would say them words, them words that stick there, at the back of my throat, about God, about God. Woah, about God. But nothing come out, nothing ever does, I want to say to him nothing comes out my mouth. I just swallow it all down, the things that happen, the smiles, the kindness, the bad things, down they go, down my throat, away into the inside, where they can't be seen no more. He's young, and the men in the street come to his house and tell him to get married, but he says 'Me and Mumtaz, we're bachelors together!' and he pats my shoulder gently and straightens the stupid hat he makes me wear. He says I should grow a beard, but man – I'm only fourteen, and Jared would say – me tink you look like a tramp more and more, boy!

At the new school, they all white or all Muslim. No place for me in between, so I sit on my own. They talk foreign English, the white ones. They say – owt – when someone says – where you been? Or – what you got? Owt. The first day, Tania come and said, 'Don't you talk?' and I laughed my smile, and shake my head, and she laughed too, and I gave her my straight in the eye – 'why you laughing?' look and she says, 'Well, that was a silly question, weren't it?' and I laughed my smile again.

She said 'Wanna have your lunch wit' me?' and she really talks like all of them up here, and I wonder whether I will too, when I start to talk?

I sit next to Tania and her mates all the time now, and I don't know if that makes me a girl, like a sissy, or whether it's because she thinks I'm cute. I know girls think anyone that does things different is cute. Like I'm a bird with a broken wing that they find on their moors and they bring me home and put me in a cage and every time they see me they smile and say, 'Oh look, he's trying to fly!' I wonder if Tania says to her mates, 'Mumtaz tries to talk to me,' but thing is, I don't. She looks like Paulette Goddard. I don't show her any Charlie moves in case she think that I'm cute – for real. In case she *fall* for me, because Mumtaz mean excellent in *all directions.* I look in the mirror, and you know, what stares back is GOOD (and I mean, for *real*). I don't want to break no hearts. I'm like Charlie – I have a lot of love in my heart, but nah – girls are girls, innit? I loved my mum. That's enough. I could love a kid, though. Like Charlie did. If someone give me a baby in a big old pram, and on his nappy there was a note and it says, 'Please love and care for this orphan child,' I would take that pram home to Uncle's and we would feed him and clothe him and I'd teach him Charlie tricks. I'd have a lot of love for a baby. But not a girl.

⚬

I hear the speaking before I get there. I hear Uncle's voice and a woman. They murmuring like they in love or they have a secret. A secret. It makes me stop in the corridor. Tania is with me. 'I'll show him, Miss,' she said to the teacher when the teacher said there was a woman to see me. I know my way around now, I want to say to Tania. She getting on my wick. I want to say, 'You think I'm dumb?' That my joke, and I say it all the time to people in my head. I love that joke. When I get to the door, I see my fat uncle sitting in one of our school chairs, and that make me smile. I turn to Tania, tell her to go with a nod of my head.

'I'll wait for yer out here,' she says. She sounds like she from Germany or something, talking her funny English. I shake my head, point away. She shakes her head, points at the ground and slumps back against the wall. I don't want her to hear. I don't go in the room, just stand there and wait. See, don't need words, just need to be alive. She sees my eyes. She go.

Woman says, 'Hello Mumtaz,' and she say my name like my mum used to say it. It hits me like a punch in the stomach. It hurt, I tell you. She talk to me about the whys and the hows, and she a this and a that. I nod, look over at my uncle and he look so funny, I start to smile.

'What's funny, Mumtaz?' she asks, smiling. I point at my uncle in his school chair. His big old beige trousers and his beige dress and his waistcoat and his hat, they look like his arse swallowed the chair. I smile and smile. He sniffs at me, a full, swallowing your snot sniff.

'I used to go to this school, you know,' he says to me. That make me really laugh. The woman says, 'Do you not speak because of what happened to your mum?' She says it just like that, and do you know what happens? Because I'm not thinking and I still laughing at my uncle, I just go, 'No.' The sound comes out normal, like one of them coughs, the little ones you do when you nervous.

Uncle and the woman both look at me. Uncle sits straight

in the chair, and the chair creaks a bit. The woman just smile. I shocked. I know I look shocked, I can see my face in my head. If I had taken down my trousers and shown her my dickie, I wouldn't have been so shocked.

'Why then?' she asks. But because I heard myself, because that noise of my voice sounds so strange and so familiar, I can't say anything else. That voice is my father's voice. I can hear it, and when I think that, when I hear it again and again in my head, I feel sick.

I crumple into myself, on the chair, and my uncle stands up and he comes over and he holds my head against his big belly, and he kisses my hair and he says 'You know, Mumtaz . . .' but he hasn't other words. The woman says, 'I'll be seeing you next week, all right Mumtaz?' and her voice sweet, like blackberry juice, her voice strong, like liquorice. I like her voice: I start to stir, to uncurl and I think – I wonder what my voice sound like next to her voice. I wonder if it would stop sounding – wrong.

In his shop, Uncle has Arabic books and leaflets. I walk past them all the time. I think of all the stuff on the news and I wonder what my boys would say about where I ended up: Mumtaz, you a terrorist now? You a suicide bomber? I can hear them. I want to see them, Jared and Isaac, I want to tell them I said a word. I could text because they give me numbers, but me crap at that. Me think they think I dead. I point at Uncle's phone, and he give it me. I try to think of something to say. Nothing comes. I just write *How r u? Mumtaz* because I know that enough. Nothing come in return, and I give the phone back to my uncle. He sitting on a plastic red chair at the counter, his feet bare, and I think his toenails so long, they ugliest thing I ever seen. He sees me looking:

'Get the clippers! You cut them . . .' he says, and I laugh and tap the side of my head. He laughs too. He not serious. He a good man, not a terrorist, even though he ugly. He just pray every day, and run he shop and make food for us both and sleep. That's all he do. He ain't nothing scary. Jared and Isaac would see. In London, everyone the same after a while. After a while, when you live in the same neighbourhood, you take on each other's stuff, you take on each other, whether you can speak or not. The world: everyone the same eventually. That's what I think. That's the Mumtaz lecture for today.

The woman called Sara, nice name. I like her smile and her face, gentle, like a breezy day, like a moment come and almost gone. I like the way when she walk in, she talk to me like we having a conversation. 'How are you? Yeah? Yeah, I'm fine. Rushing around, you know?' and all I have to do is nod. Sometimes when I walk down the corridor, and she walking the other way, I break into a Charlie walk, I twitch my mouth like my moustache itching, and she coming the other way laughing. When I see her laugh, it feels warm inside me. When she talk to me, I say one word, two words. The words I say are yes, no, maybe, day. I love the word day. I love the word love, but I never say it. No one to say it to. Today she says: 'Mumtaz, do you keep in touch with your friends in London?'

'Yes. No,' I say, because she looking serious. Jared never texted me back. Uncle walks in out of nowhere. I look at him annoyed. Don't want him hearing my voice, because where it end? I talk here, he say at home, why you don't talk to me, Mumtaz? He never been back here until today, and I been seeing her half a year or more.

'All right?' Uncle says to Sara and me. He look sad, so does she. I know something happen. Like when I come out from the duvet, like when the police standing there, in our bedroom, and I come out, and no one's faces I know.

'Mumtaz, I'm going to tell you something, and I want you . . .' She doesn't know what to say. I can see her face saying, 'don't stop talking, not now we've come this far,' her face like a little bird, flapping in and out of my face, visiting me with the breeze of her breath, like the wings of the little bird so near, so near, like her breath kisses. 'Mumtaz,' she says gently, 'Jared was seriously hurt in a fight yesterday. We heard this morning that he didn't live. I'm sorry Mumtaz,' and she comes and kneels next to me, her face right there, next to my elbow. I feel the duvet over my head and my mum holding me down, and her screaming and Dad hitting, and her saying '. . . the baby, the baby,' over and over. And then she stop. And then she heavy on me. Enough. Enough, I can't talk about it no more. I can't think about it, I can't breathe, I can't breathe, I can't breathe about it. I can't . . . And then I start to cry, really cry, and I'm crying out loud and Uncle come and hold me, and Sara hold me too, and I hear my voice, all them bad things coming up through my sobbing, like water gushing out a river mouth, like all the bad things washing away to the wide world, to the sea in the sky, like Jared and Mum up there, waiting for the waves come from me, and they wash away, away from me, away.

Jared killed with a knife. I think about that a lot. I think about the knife going in his flesh, the colour of his blood, the colour of the white bone under the muscle, the blue-grey of the sinews and tendons. I think about his heart all the time, a single wound to the heart that killed him, but he bleeding from multiple stab wounds. Wrong place at the wrong time. He on the way back from a wedding with his brother. They go past a fight, and wham, they in the fight, trying to get out from all them arms and legs and weapons. All the wounds I seen and not seen, and all the dead people I know, and all those wounds hurting me every day, like they fresh every morning, the minute after I wake up.

Sara comes twice a week, but I still only say few words. Can't take any more out, can't give them air and sunshine they need, to breathe out of me. Nothing worth talking about. Sara bring me books, about dying, and poetry books and once she brought chocolates for us to share. She a nice person. She tell my uncle to take me to the funeral, but he say it no good for me, I only fourteen. But all my mates will be there, I think. I don't say nothing, and I know she phone him twice, but he say no. I think about going by myself, just take some money from the till and go, but I don't. Sometimes I catch myself in a shop window as I walk down the street, and I don't know who it is: I am a Muslim boy now. The clothes just a costume. I grow a moustache and my uncle think this great, but it so I can be Charlie. I walk down the road like Charlie, but a sad Charlie, after the kid taken away. And sometimes, I sit down on the doorstep and hope I fall asleep, and that everyone come to me as angels, my mum, my mum's baby, Jared, all the people I know in London who all seem dead now. And then they'll dance, like they do in the film, and we'll laugh and sing.

Sara bring me *The Great Dictator*. She says, 'Let's watch it together?' So we do, and Charlie speaking in it all the way through. He playing two parts. He a barber who lost his memory, and he the Dictator, supposed to be Hitler from the war. It is a really funny movie. I think about it after, and Sara say, 'What do you think?' and I say, very quietly, 'I like it,' and that my first sentence.

Be nice, innit, if I say Uncle got married to Sara and everyone happy in old England Muslim land up here in this cold place full of people who talk funny? And it be nice if I say – listen friends, I become an imam when I grow up, singing out the prayers and in the evening I a stand-up comedian, peddling my words for money, letting them shoot out of me like pounds from a slot machine. But see, life ain't like that. Charlie takes this balloon shaped as the world in *The Great Dictator*, right, and he the baddie, and he trying to say in a funny way that he want to rule the world, and maybe he think he do rule the world, and he bounce it in the air and do ballet with this big ball world. But I think that that what we all trying to do, balance the world in the air, in the plain air, like Charlie. And when he walk down the road, a little tramp with a little boy, when it make us laugh, it make us forget the balancing the world in the air. And forgetting is all we can do. Forgetting and remembering. So ends the final lesson. Mumtaz has spoken.

THE COMFORT, THE JOY

So, we're at a work thing, and I'm not really *there* per se, because this is four years after *everyone died* – I say it like that because it gives it its own import, its own *purpose* – and why wouldn't it? Everyone died, didn't they? And we're at this thing, with the drinks, and the people talking animatedly though their eyes are dimmed, like they're happy to be there but behind the eyes there's that knowledge that the person they're talking to told them to do something during office hours that was the equivalent of wiping dog shit off their shoe, and they're all thinking 'I'll talk to you like I want to fuck you, but I really don't want to fuck you, I just want a pay rise', – and we're at this thing, me and Bunny, I call him Bunny because he has a cute behind, sort of perky and womanly, and lovely to run your hand over (even though everyone *died*) – and Bunny says, 'That guy over there keeps staring at you.' Which guy, I think, which *guy*, because hell, that would be nice, wouldn't it? A guy staring, a stranger staring and making the first move, and I look over where Bunny has tilted his head, and sure enough, there's a guy, this guy – grey-haired and thin, not too tall, his hair sort of quiffed but short, like a throwback, like a teddy boy – does anyone say teddy boy any more? He looks at me and I smile and he smiles.

The hotel is the same as last year and the year before. I've come to three of these, one *before* everyone died, and two since. I like these things: I like to watch. I especially like it if people get pissed and behave badly. I like to watch the bosses smiling and scheming. This is the first time I brought someone, and I like to look at people being encouraging, and their faces, their faces – because I'm nearly forty-three, and Bunny is young – he says twenty-six, but he's probably twenty-three – and he's black, which is neither here nor there, because everyone's black deep down inside – everyone's got something about them that other people notice first. Black is just skin, but if you're Irish, someone'll say to your face, 'So you're Irish,' like it's a discovery. Like people say, 'So, you're married?' and I say, 'No, a widow,' and they say, 'Do you have children?' And I say – often with a curt little laugh, a winning smile sometimes – 'No, they're dead too,' and it's fine because sometimes, when I'm feeling charitable, I explain, and sometimes when I'm not, I slug back a vodka and reel about on my heels feeling the waft of moral high-ground about my ankles. When I totter, when I fall, when I'm drunk again (in mitigation, it happens less frequently now Bunny's on the scene), I still feel that punchy, frozen air about me, as I fall through it, as I fall.

The grey hair keeps staring. I slug back the champagne. Gareth from sales, charming guy, stands squarely, suddenly, in my face.

'All right, Claire,' he says.

'Ooh, yes, Gareth,' I say, because I like a flirt with Gareth. He has that sort of stocky body that seems to be made of gun metal. The sort of musculature suited to silk.

'Pacing yourself, are you, darling?' he says.

'Darling?' I say, startled. Grey hair has turned away. I see he is a little hunched. 'Why darling?' I drawl.

'No need to get all feminist, *darling*,' he says, and a girl titters at his elbow.

'Oh, not *feminist*, Gareth. Be careful what you start, though,' I say, and move a little forward, adjusting my weight – so, the cleavage taking centre stage. Purple silk gown, like God, present in its absence, my body, present in its intimation – my body, always present, always real, always – and oh, of course he notices.

'Steady,' he says, like a jockey – like a jockey already harnessed.

Bunny has wandered. I watch him, at this *thing*, this ironic *xmas fest*, and I wonder how he can be with *me* with all these other gypsy girls, their curly hair and falling bustiers displayed towards him, and I think it is inevitable that he will leave – and *no* it's not anything to do with (*everyone dying*) – though of course, the bereavement counsellor would say that it has *everything* to do with that. I'm no fucking Holly Golightly, I think. I'm no flipperty gibbet, smoking with a holder, wearing kooky numbers, playing the guitar type girl. I'm a woman. With a thirty-six D bust that needs to be handled expertly at times. Bunny does that, and then I don't need him, because simply: love is over, love is past.

And there he is, old Bunny, little Bunny, Buns-a-go-go, charming that gorgeous girl who sat crying with me, the day I came back, sat there saying 'devastating' and 'blah blah' – I call it blah blah because those words are just words, words blah. And turns out she was crying because the guy, the *one* – you know, the one who is the inevitability, whose sperm will meet your egg, the one whose chemicals will turn your life into more life – he just upped and left, going blah fucking blah on her everything, just like the (*everyone dying*) thing.

He is so casually, brilliantly flirtatious. He is a triumph, my Bunny, placing his hand above her head on the pillar she's leaning against. Gareth is moving away, and I am sipping my drink and watching Bunny, and Gareth, I think, may have tried to pinch my arse, because the tittering girl has looked behind her in an annoyed way, and I see my reflection in her face, I see my full worth there: she's thinking 'over the hill' – she's thinking – bitch with feelings, she's thinking 'devastating' – and I raise my glass to her, and turn away.

We're at this *thing*, and again, the feeling of rootedness. It comes, when I'm not in the middle of it all, when I'm on the sidelines, and I'm sober or semi-sober, I suddenly feel how a tree feels. I suddenly feel – oh shit, I can't move, and I try, but my feet are just there, solid, lumpen rocks. Move forward, I tell them, and they do not. Stay still then, I say, and look about to find some help – would it be ridiculous to seek help? This time, at this thing, I am more canny. I lift my empty glass to a waiter, I look him in the eye, and he moves forward with the champagne, filling the glass, flirting with his eyes. Would I? Of course, I think I'd have him against the pillar now – be easy enough. There's no underwear. And if it made a baby, at least there'd be a baby, and I contemplate the whole making of a baby process, but in front of the boss, in front of the boss's wife, in front of my secretary Ann and the myriad others in this rainbow *thing*, all watching me fuck a waiter against a pillar, against the pillar Bunny leans against on the other side.

I laugh when I think of my face, the face Bunny complains about, the face that thinks of fucking but is dead. The face that cannot lie in the dark, the one Bunny kisses and kisses when it cries, this dead face, the one that died when *everyone died*.

Grey hair is suddenly here.

'Hello,' he says.

'Hello,' I reply. 'Have we met?' I want to be kind to him. He is still hunched.

'Yes, Claire. A long time ago, we were . . . friends.'

No, no. I do not want to know about a long time ago. 'Ah,' I say. Is it one of those times when I can say *everyone died*, you know?

'I was at Teddy Hall with . . .'

'Yes.' He was at the same college as Rob. That's all. Someone will have told him already, which is why he has been hesitant. I must remember to take for granted people's need to inform.

'You were at?'

'Somerville.'

'Yes. That's right. I remember. I remember you well.'

'I wish I could say the same,' I say, and I'm trying not to be angsty or rude, but am I? I question whether I really know what I'm trying for. Everything is out of my hands, everything is inevitably lost in that mist of death, that thing they call bereavement, where people are secretly alive and you hear children's voices in the house when you wake, you hear their laughter. Decisions are over there. The way you decide to say something, the way you play with words, or your glass or your hair or the way your toes shift or the way you fuck Bunny, it's all decided in that moment, that moment before you quite wake up, where you see the bulk next to you, and you put your hand on Bunny's back and think it's Rob – but silly, Rob never stayed in bed longer than you, so who is this, and you open your eyes, and beautiful Bunny face is there, his eyes shut like a child's, like a daughter's – all over there, the way you choose to smile.

'I'm Gwyn. I was Andy's friend.' Andy was our best man. I remember Gwyn and Andy, likely lads, lots of girlfriends, taking the piss out of Rob because he loved me, and I loved him, and we didn't hide being in love, but adored each other and spent days in bed worshipping each other.

'Oh, Gwyn. I remember now.' And I do remember now, which is a shame because I might cry, and I never cry. I never cry in front of people I work with. I never cry at all hardly, except maybe with Bunny, and even then, it's when I'm half asleep, so it's my brain doing it. Brave face, brave face, I say. Say the thing you say. 'You know *everyone died*,' I say.

Strangely, he pulls his shoulders back. He stands up taller. 'Yes,' he smiles, 'I know.' He sips at his glass, and I sip at mine. He moves sideways and stands next to me to let a waiter past. I like this man a little, because he stands shoulder to shoulder with me, yet says nothing, as if we are facing off the world, just for these few minutes. 'I was watching you,' he says.

'Yes, I saw you watching me. Was it because you remembered me?'

'Yes. But something more,' he says, and we are separated by a party of girls conga-ing towards the dance floor. The room is darkening, and the disco lights begin their sweeping search. He comes back. 'Something more,' he smiles.

We're at this *thing*, you see, and he tells me of me. He says: 'D'you remember that summer ball when Rob was in halls and the rest of us weren't? D'you remember that way we used to all say we need a sitting-out room, where we leave our coats, and where we can come back if we need to sit down or take a girl? And Rob said we could use his room?'

'Were Rob and I together . . .'

'Oh, yes. Of course. Of course . . .' he says, and he puts his drink down, guides my elbow so we stand nearer the door to the garden. It is quieter, although the bar is here, but only quiet voices. Bunny is forgotten. I don't want Bunny, I don't know Bunny. I want this voice; I want Gwyn to keep talking. 'Do you remember, Andy and I came first, and you were getting changed. You were in an emerald-green dress, and Andy said you looked like a leprechaun?'

I laugh. 'Bloody Andy.'

'Bloody Andy,' he agrees, and I see he is weighing words, balancing one against the other.

'What?' I say.

'Bloody Andy. You looked just near enough to fucking perfect anyone has ever looked, before or since.' I am silenced. He is silent.

'Gwyn,' I say. He smiles. I try to change the subject. 'Are you married?'

He laughs. 'No, this isn't one of those "I fell in love with you" stories, and have been hunting you down ever since, and here you are.' And I laugh now. 'But I did fall in love. In Oxford, everyone was in love with everyone else. We were all in love with each other, so I thought it no different. Oh, what the hell. It's only when I saw you, just now, that I realised that actually, well, you – in that dress – that *that* could have been one of those times . . . you know – *those times*.' And when he says it like that, I lean to him, as if he had dragged me there, I lean my chest on to his, and I kiss him. He is surprised. He doesn't back away, and his kiss back is clumsy and mistaken.

'I'm sorry, but I haven't known – I mean, I haven't felt,' I say, and he takes my elbow again and we are in the garden. It is a clear night, cold, moonless, black. He takes his jacket off. 'Little Gwyn,' I say.

'Little?' He is incredulous. 'I'm six foot,' he says, his Welsh accent only now coming through.

'Yes, but the other Gwyn was a prop forward or something, wasn't he?'

'Yes.' We sit on a bench, and he puts the jacket around me. 'How are you?' he asks.

'What, now? Or generally?'

'Whichever.'

'Oh. I don't really answer that usually. Only if my therapist asks. Let's see. I'm . . . starved,' I say, and I mean it. He goes to stand.

'I'll get you something,' he says.

'No, I mean: I feel hungry for *everything*. Life. Love. Sex. I'm desperate for *sex*.'

'But – what about . . .'

'Bunny? Yes, we have *sex* – but I mean – I want to have sex in my *head* – the way it was when I was married for twenty years – *that* sex. Are you married? Do you know what I mean?'

'No. I'm not married. Never wanted to be. I live alone. I have girlfriends. I remember my parents locking the door on Saturday afternoons. Every Saturday afternoon. I always wondered what that must have been like.'

'It's comfort and joy.'

We sit there for an hour or more, talking and not talking, and then his hand is on my thigh. I think, I like his hand on my thigh. Perhaps it will go higher. And it does, and he takes my hand and puts it on to his crotch, the hardness there, and in the dark, Gwyn could be Rob, and yes, in the dark, we put the jacket down and I lift my skirts, and in the dark, my face changes, because in the dark, there is the love, in my head, there is Rob and Gwyn mixed together, and my face smiles as he kisses my breasts, and my face smiles as he comes.

We're at this *thing*, I think. We're here, and we've fucked, and I feel the wetness, take his handkerchief to wipe it away, and I hear Bunny calling, and my hair is down.

'Do you remember,' he says, 'the day after the ball?'

'No,' I say. But suddenly I do.

After the ball, a June day slipped through our window –

Bunny shouts, 'Claire!'

And the windows were wide open, and I woke to the noises of scaffolding thrown down, the packing away of a marquee. Rob lying next to me in his single bed. We took our clothes off? No, we lay down on the bed, tired and drunk, and pulled the leftover coats over us, but as the sun had invaded the high ceiling, we had warmed and toasted, and I had pushed the coats from me, and with them my bustier dress. I had woken muzzily into sunshine on my face, on my neck, on my breasts. I woke, and now I remember –

'Oh, Claire,' Bunny says, as he sees Gwyn. And I hold closer, our diagonal bodies pull towards one another to deflect him –

I woke and Gwyn was there, and I lay next to Rob, naked, and he stood there.

'I've come for my coat,' he said.

'OK,' I said, and lay still, then reached down to pull my dress back up.

'Don't,' he whispered. I was embarrassed, ashamed.

'Go away, Gwyn,' I said.

'I'm sorry,' he whispered. Rob was drunk, heavily asleep. Gwyn did not leave, but looked at me still.

'Do you remember what I said?' Gwyn says.

He stepped closer. 'Claire,' he whispered.

'You said: I think I'm in love with you,' and I feel Gwyn's smile in the dark against my shoulder.

'Do you remember what you said?'

'No,' I say, because I don't want to remember.

'You said "in a different life, Gwyn",' and I pull myself away.

That June day I was angry: I hated his eyes, hated that he had eaten me with those eyes. But when the *thing* starts to break up, we go home together. In the morning I wake to an empty bed – but he is there, watching, waiting, and I scoop him back: I hold him, for the comfort, for the joy.

AT THE BARN DANCE

They had been sitting outside as the sky began to rest down on the crowd, its colours descending from pinks and peaches to every hue of blue and navy, like a dancer's tiered skirt. The trees thrust upwards as if to guard them from the inevitable night. The hall, overly lit by garish oranges that did not try to mimic the day but produced their own unique blend of the present and fashion, became the focal point for the two hundred people milling about the barbecue and salads. The woman sitting next to Preethi spoke.

'But it's a lovely name, it sounds like "Pretty",' and she patted Preethi's hand. Preethi had heard this summation of her name many times before, yet she smiled, laughed a little even: the woman meant well, and what was that, a small politeness to an old woman?

Preethi said, 'I didn't catch your name?' and the woman shook her head, as if shaking off the question and the need to answer. The music had begun to play, and a few of the younger secretaries whooped and laughed.

'Imagine,' said the woman, watching them, 'never having to rush home because children need to be picked up from school, or dinner needs to be made? Can *you* remember a time when you stayed late at work because you wanted to, and then went off to the pub?'

Preethi could remember it, in London, a long time ago. She looked at the girls in their tiny skirts and boots and cowboy hats, and she smiled wryly. They are half my age, she thought. They are getting drunk and acting stupid the way I did the year they were born.

A man's voice echoed out to them from the hall.

'This caller is very good. I've been to a wedding where they played. Exhausting!'

The woman laughed, her eyes turned up to the sky wearily. Preethi stood. She would find Simon. He promised not to leave her alone: she knew few people from his workplace, and although they were all pleasant, friendly people, she felt her status as an outsider. No one knew *her*. They knew the image she presented them on these occasions: this early summer barn dance or a Christmas ball, where she ladled on the diamonds and the kohl, rubbed her teeth nervously with a tissue for fear of lipstick smiles. She was not effete or fragrant. She did not groom like other wives. Preethi was rough and ready, calloused hands from her garden, earth staining her palms the colour of the rest of her skin. At Christmas, Simon's PA Emma had stared at Preethi's hands, with the fingernails uneven and unpainted, and she had been ashamed. Simon had teased her on the way home, and in the dark she had said coldly that he should stop. He had taken her literally and stopped the car.

'It isn't important,' he had said. '*She's* not important.'

'But it *is*,' Preethi had grumbled, not knowing why. She was never the first to point out her colour to anyone, never the one to shout 'racism' like it was a trigger to be pulled. She just felt it, the burden of Emma's stare. As Simon started the car, she had looked down at her hands in the dark, and even there, in her lap, they were the wrong colour, like an admonishment.

'She makes me feel I'm not good enough for you,' she said finally.

'Well you *are*, and she's a bitch,' he had said, pulling on to the dual carriageway. In the yellow blinks of fast motorway lamps, Preethi and Simon's colours had equalised to beige.

'Si!' a girl screeched, as Preethi walked into the hall. Simon did not turn from the person he was speaking to, but saw Preethi and raised his eyebrows. She knew he was annoyed. In the taxi on the way here, he had prudishly wished that the young ones would not get so drunk. At Christmas, some of the women had had to be carried into the coach.

'Si! Come and dance!' the girl shouted again. Simon did not look round, just waved his hand in the direction of the voice. Preethi looked towards the girl. She had no idea who she was. Why did she call Simon 'Si'? Could there be an intimacy there that Simon had hidden from her? He spoke very little of the office and the people there. And yet, she knew in her heart there was no one for Simon but *her*. She knew it. Ridiculous! How could she *know* it? We are all in the business of creating illusions, aren't we? Even the people we have slept next to for twenty-five years get up, go out and become something we have no understanding of.

Simon beckoned to her. 'Darling, this is Tony Stroud. Tony, this is my wife, Preethi.'

'Delighted,' the man slurred. He was already extremely drunk.

She smiled into his eyes, as the caller said, 'This is the Carolina Quickstep!' and the accordion, suddenly loud now she was inside, blasted through her, as she stepped towards Tony.

'Are you having a nice time?'

He did not hear, and put his hand to his ear. Simon had moved away from them both, towards his senior management men in the corner. She slipped to the side of Tony, and as she did, she noticed he seemed tremulous, and she put her hand lightly on his back and guided him away from the dancers, who had formed two circles and were walking in a large formation, their hands linked crosswise with their partners, women in the inner circle, men in the outer.

What am I to do now, she thought. She looked about and saw Emma standing nearby, a fixed grin on her face. Preethi smiled at her, but Emma looked through her, turning away. Next to her, his back turned, was a man Preethi knew. Preethi realised suddenly who it was. Prince Myshkin – Freddie. She could not countenance his presence, understand even. She circled the hall, stood at the furthest point away from him.

She watched Emma watch the younger girls striding through the arches made by the lead dancers, swirling their hips. Preethi let her eyes film over, and she heard the music and saw the dancers as if they were a murky dream. The colours were the blacks and greys and blues of denim and what she wanted to see were the rainbow colours of fairies, washed through with rain. She turned away from the dance and walked outside again. She remembered Emma's flawlessly made-up face at Christmas and how, when she talked to Simon, her small tongue poked through her teeth, so that the tip rested on her lower lip, and Preethi had to look away from the feeling of seeing something intimate.

Simon liked Emma, she thought. Preethi imagined them in congruence, floating in a balance of sex, a salsa of lovemaking. She imagined his too large feet and darkly haired legs supporting a laughing Emma, her head thrown back, the tip of her childish tongue peeping through her lips, and Preethi shuddered: in its truth, this tip became pornographic, dreadful, and she stood in the dark, and watched them, Simon and Emma, watched their eyes meet. She smiled. She laughed at the ridiculousness of it. The music of the last dance ended and people whooped and some laughed, and everyone clapped, outside and in. As she turned to walk out of the hall, more side doors were thrust open, and she glimpsed Emma walking away with Gary, her boyfriend, his kind face leaning into hers, his hand placed loosely around her shoulders. Once, Simon held Preethi in the same way, his arm about her shoulders, no space between them, as if the curves of their sides had melted.

She walked towards Freddie. It was an impulse, but she walked to his side and said, 'Hello, Freddie.'

'Hello,' he squinted down to her. He had not recognised her.

'It's me, Preethi,' she said. And still, she thought, he does not know me. But he did.

'I was going to marry you,' he said, laughing.

'And I you,' she said. It wasn't true, but no matter.

They moved out into the darkness, on to the grass. Others stood around and a few had blankets on which men lay sideways, and girls daintily tucked their legs under bottoms, and giggled. Freddie indicated chairs in a pool of shadow.

'Well,' he said.

'Let's not do that whole "so how many children do you have" thing.'

'Why not? How many do you have?'

'Two. Boy and a girl. But they're ancient now. All grown up.'

'Really? You don't look old enough. I have a daughter – she lives in Australia. It was an accident . . . well, not an accident. But something that happened at university. She's nearly twenty-five,' he said.

'Gosh.'

'Yes.'

They looked around as laughter erupted from under the trees. It was finally night.

'So, what are you doing here?' They both spoke at once.

Laughing, Preethi said 'I'm married to Simon.' She pointed in the direction of the hall.

'I'm just my sister's date. I'm visiting – Mum's got Alzheimer's, and . . .'

'Oh, I'm sorry,' she said, and already she was imagining the life she would have had. 'Where do you live, what do you do?'

'I'm a travel writer. I don't really live anywhere – I just move from one place to the next . . .'

'Gosh,' she said again.

'And you?'

'I'm a journalist,' she said, but she did not mention that it was on a local paper, trudging to magistrates' courts, and answering phones to anguished old ladies. Her children had been her life. Her children, and Simon.

'Well! Look at us. Using words to earn our daily crust, just as we said we would.'

'Well, it's hardly Dostoyevskian.'

Again, they paused to look towards the noise of the party. The music began again.

'Are you dancing?'

'No, absolutely not,' she said, waving both hands at him. 'Don't ask, don't drag me up. I won't go.'

'No fear of that. I don't dance either. So we're a pair.'

And now a leisurely silence. He tapped his thigh in time to the music.

'I wish,' he said.

'What?'

'I wish they had let me visit you, you know, after.'

'After I tried to kill myself, you mean?' She glanced down at the thin, silvered scars on her wrists. Even in the shadow, she could see him blush. 'Did you try to visit?'

'I wrote letters. I came to your house. They wouldn't let me in. I begged Rohan.'

'Lovely Rohan,' she said.

'How is he? Still a doctor? I Googled him once, to see if he was a consultant or . . .'

'He's in the States. He's a heart surgeon. Has a son. But he and his wife have split up. I think he just works and sleeps. It's sad, really – he should be happy, our Ro. What a family, eh?'

Freddie shrugged. She had meant – you were in love, and you wanted to marry me – what a lucky escape.

'It was a selfish thing to do,' he said.

'Yes. You mean trying to kill myself?'

'Yes.'

'But we were all selfish – children are selfish. I didn't know what else to do at the time. Are you asking for an explanation?'

'No. Not at all.' He paused. And then he looked into her eyes: 'You couldn't love me because I'm ugly. But I loved you *so* much.' It winded her.

'Did you? Can it have been love when we were so young?' From his eyes, she knew the answer.

'Shall I get another drink?' he asked.

'Why not?'

He got up and went in to the bar. She watched the dancers, the others sitting on the side at tables and standing around. Simon moved towards Emma now. Preethi saw him framed in the doorway. She sat backwards into the darkness a little further, so she could watch them undisturbed. He clinked his glass to Gary's, looked down at Emma, and Preethi watched Emma carefully as she smiled up into Simon's eyes. She could see Simon's face fully: did his eyes acknowledge Emma the way that his eyes acknowledged *her*? They did not. Simon put his hand in his pocket, and Preethi wondered if he was stopping himself from reaching forward and touching Emma. He walked on. Preethi turned around, away from the doors and looked into the dark, into the night. She stood, facing the trees, listening to the breeze and the snatches of conversation about her:

'. . . nah, he said he had to see his Ma in hospital . . .'

'. . . get us one, Chris . . .'

'. . . but I think roses are always best for weddings, so I said to her . . .'

She felt a nudge at her elbow. 'Did you dance?' It was the old lady.

'No. I watched. It looks exhausting.'

'Yes. *Exhausting*.' The woman looked around. 'I've lost Anthony.'

'Tony?'

'Oh, yes.'

'Does he work for them?'

'Well, of *course*. What else do retired politicians do? Just a little consultation, you see? He tips them a wink here and there, and they get the contracts.'

Preethi smiled. 'Is he very famous, your husband?'

'Oh, yes,' the lady said matter-of-factly. 'He did single-handedly win a war, you know. Well, at least, that's what he tells *us*. I don't know what's true and what's not. It's all men's work, boy's games. We're just here to shit out the next cannon fodder, love 'em till they're thirteen, ship 'em off to boarding school, officer's training, then the next bloody war. Feed 'em, wipe their arses, send 'em orff.' She paused to take another slurp of wine. She tilted in to Preethi's body, and Preethi felt her arm being taken, the unsteadiness of the other woman. 'What are *we* for, but to prop and hold and hope and fucking *save* 'em?'

Preethi smiled, but she realised the undying truth of this: how she had done the same. Brought Simon's children into the world, fed them from her body, and through the year obeyed the rhythms of the marital, familial dance. Women are ruled by the cycles of life, she thought, and whether we like it or not, we do it, we saraband around and around our days, our months, our years. Men blast through our patterns, sometimes, uprooting our even work with their sudden decisions and victories, and we steadily cast over the holes, knit them together with patience and silent bravery, obeying the patterns of our small routines. And the earth turns round and round, and we turn round with it. Preethi walked the woman into the hall, and sat her next to Anthony. They remained together against a wall, their glasses being filled by every passing drunk with a wine bottle, and they looked steadfastly ahead, at the dancers, at the band.

When Preethi was twenty-one, she had asked Simon to meet her in Trafalgar Square one Saturday afternoon. He was just finishing his articles in a pompous law firm in the City, and she knew if she flagged a CND march up beforehand, he would not have come. She told him which lion to stand by, told him it was important that she had been specific, and when the first speakers were in full throttle, he arrived, and she kissed him as if he had done a marvellous thing. In the event, they marched shoulder-to-shoulder, arms about each other. He had not resented the deceit. He had enjoyed the experience. His parents were Tories – there had never been a need for him to march against anything. Every political decision any government had made in his lifetime had been *for* him and people like him. Anthony, drunk in the corner, would have been a man with the power to detonate. She watched him now and marvelled at how small the world had become.

Simon waved at her from the other side of the hall. She raised her hand, and he mouthed, 'Dance?' She nodded assent. The accordion player arpeggio-ed through a chord, but the caller said, 'And now we will sing a song for you, before we take a small break.' There were muted cheers and someone shouted something from another corner of the room and people cheered again. Simon shrugged at Preethi and started to walk towards her, but the music started, and instead of crossing the empty dance floor, she watched him walk around the crowd, to make his way to her more discreetly. He was a cautious man.

'I know a girl that you don't know,' the singer started, 'little Liza Jane,' the rest joined in. The crowd began to clap. Preethi started to clap too, her hands automated, her feet more independent, tapping a different, faster rhythm. If Simon had walked across to her, placed his hand about her waist and swung her around, she would have danced with him, cheery and carefree.

'Oh, Eliza!' they sang, and she mouthed the words with them.

A young woman skirmished into the centre of the hall, hair hanging down in greasy spurts from under a full-brimmed hat. She wore a denim mini-skirt and a revealing shirt, her breasts threatening to gatecrash. On her legs she wore a pair of PVC cowboy chaps. She turned to her friends and beckoned them, but they shook their heads and shrugged.

'Ruthie!' one of them shouted, 'Get 'ere!' But she began to dance. It was not a fluid dance or a hopping-stamping movement. Ruthie put her hands out in front of her, as if to perform what the British think of as an Egyptian dance, straight arms sliding back and forth like a clock stuck at a quarter past three. Preethi was discomfited. She let her eyes film over, to transform the scene to the forest she wanted to see, of drunk locals in cotton shifts, their hair covered in roses and tumbling honeysuckle, curls of blonde and auburn grazing loose breasts, plumply tempting men in breeches. Her eyes glazed, and she saw a wise woman standing in the middle of the hall, beckoning people to come to her, summoning forth the evil of rain that would spoil the crop, dancing it away with sudden thrusts to the ceiling and the sky beyond. People around Preethi watched silently as the song continued and Ruthie's drunken swayings diminished her, until her legs began to give way, and she stumbled towards the floor, pulling at the chaps so that she made a drunken striptease which some men stood and watched and jeered at, and others turned from, ashamed that they had seen.

Freddie thrust a glass towards her.

'Thank you,' she said. Simon had been stopped by a colleague, a middle-aged woman, who was trying to convince him to dance. She watched him, and Freddie followed her eyes.

'Is that your husband?'

'Yes.'

'Looks nice.'

She laughed. 'What's nice? How can you tell?' It was strange, but despite the years, this boy, this man, seemed more familiar to her than Simon. She turned to look at him. 'Do you remember how earnest we were about everything?'

'Oh, yes. But that's every teenager, isn't it? Knowing everything. We would have made a funny pair, wouldn't we?'

'Do you think? I think – together – we could have conquered the world!'

He laughed. She had used a stock phrase, a journalist's cliché.

Simon reached his arm about Preethi as he halted at her side.

'Where have you been?' he asked her.

'Outside. I met a friend. This is Freddie.'

'Hello, Freddie. Now, who are you married to?'

And she watched her husband charm Freddie, holding the handshake a little longer than necessary, looking up into his eyes. He turned to her: 'Look, I need to go and talk to other people. Are you all right here? When do you want to go?' he asked, and she heard the new note that had chilled his voice towards her recently. The children were older, their youngest almost sixteen. Perhaps, oh, God, perhaps he has someone else, she thought.

'No, not go. Just spend some time together?'

'Fine,' he said. 'Come and talk to George. He's been asking after you.'

'No. Time, just you and me.'

'At a barn dance?' His eyebrows raised.

'Yes, at a barn dance.'

He turned as someone tapped his shoulder. She turned to Freddie, and began talking again. But soon, his sister came and claimed him, took him away. Simon took her hand and they walked purposefully through the crowd. He took her to the bar, and when they were given two glasses of red, he clinked their glasses. He turned to face her, and smiled, so he was completely hers. There was no malice that she could detect in his face.

'Do you still love me?' she asked. It was not a sudden question, she thought, just a curiosity, now that she was drinking her third glass of red.

He looked astonished. 'Why even ask? Of course I do. I could not love you more if I tried!'

She laughed. 'What an unfortunate turn of phrase,' she drawled, and turned away from their introspection. 'Who was that girl, Ruth?'

'Why did you ask me?'

'About Ruth?'

'*No.* About loving you? Of course I love you. There's no one else for me.'

'Fine. Why did they let her dance all by herself?'

'Oh, she's just one of those girls that always gets drunk. Look, do you doubt me?'

'No. Well, I . . . no. No, I don't doubt you. At least – it's different here. Different with these people. I need the loo, Simon. Why does someone keep shouting "Si" at you?'

'They think it's funny. Look, the loos are that way. Come on,' he said, and pulled her hand. He led her into an atrium to the side of the hall. There they parted, he to the Mens, she to the Ladies. When Preethi emerged, Simon had vanished. She looked about the atrium, and where there had been people walking to and fro, there was no one. Not one person. The toilets had been empty, and when she emerged from the smelly sterility, she felt transformed, as if she had travelled into another time, another place. There were no sounds, no noises at all. She stood and waited. And then she heard hurried footsteps, a man's feet coming towards her from the gravel outside.

A fat man in a white shirt and white trousers stepped through the doorway.

'Where are we?' he asked. He fanned his face with a straw hat.

'I . . . I don't know. I – well, I don't live around here,' Preethi said.

'Nay, lass. What's the village? What's the nearest town, then?'

She smiled at him, dumb, listened for the noise of the crowd, for the racket of the playing band or the child-adults shouting. Nothing. Just her, and this man. He looked about him, gazed at her blank, tipsy face. He strode towards the hall, grasped the double doors, and suddenly sound entered her vacuum and the buzz and flow of the dance came out to the atrium, and the man walked into it and away from her. He walked across the dance floor and to the band and the caller clapped him on the back. The man threw his hat to the ground and moved behind the band, picked up a guitar, nodding his head again and again as the band teased him. Preethi watched him from where she stood. She had been certain; she had been afraid, but certain that she was the only one here, in this building, and that the fairies she was so sure she would see had finally arrived.

George said, 'Come now, you haven't danced *one* dance.'

'Are you asking me to dance, George?' Preethi said, smiling sweetly.

'Well, would you dance with me if I asked?'

'No. You're a bloody awful dancer.' He laughed rowdily.

'Thing is, Preethi, I thought when I said "barn dance" that people would understand that I meant, you know, *English* country dancing. But look, they've all got these bloody cowboy hats, and they're "yee-ha-ing" as if they were from Texas or something.'

She was suddenly animated. 'I know! I don't understand. I was expecting a clear demonstration of Englishness. I was expecting chocolate-box Englishness. I was expecting to watch, like a tourist; I was expecting . . .'

'But you're not a tourist, are you?' George pointed out. 'You're from England. You were born in London, I remember you telling me.'

'Yes. But . . .' but he had wrong-footed her. Yes, she was *from* England, by birth. She was *from* England the way she certainly was not *from* Sri Lanka. Her demands of Sri Lanka were as stringent as her demands of England. She had an impression of the way countries should be, the way their inhabitants should behave, the way everything should be.

'I know what you mean, though,' George sighed. 'These idiots don't know they're born. They have so much that's good here. They're surrounded by countryside and tradition, good food, the land, and what do they do? Sit at home and watch American crap on the telly.'

Simon had joined them. 'Not all of them, George. The rest of them are out getting legless.'

'Well, at least *that's* a good British tradition,' George said, and he and Preethi giggled, but Simon looked out at the crowd, and Preethi noticed his jaw twitch.

Anthony and his wife were walking unsteadily towards them. She held his arm by the sleeve, at the elbow, like a nanny leading a child. They came to a stop in front of George, Preethi and Simon.

'Well, boss,' Anthony slurred, 'it's been a fine party. A fine, *dance* you have led me!'

'Thanks, Anthony. Have you had a nice time, Beatrice?'

And as they conversed with Simon, George said softly to Preethi, 'Drink like a fish, both do, since they lost their son in Iraq,' and he smiled kindly at them. 'Have you met Simon's wife?'

'Oh, Pretty,' Beatrice said. 'Yes, we met outside. We talked about bringing up children and how it ruins our lives.'

George laughed, and dug Preethi's ribs with his elbow. 'You turning Beatrice into a fucking feminist?'

Preethi smiled. She thought of her days, the rhythms of her days. The back and forth walks to schools, the buying of food, the preparation of meals. She thought of the years and years of PE kits, and music lessons, chess clubs and drama productions. She thought of Simon's daily arrivals home, how she would tease their daughter that she would be taken to the Beast's house because she was always the first to greet her father at the gate, and how latterly it was only a dog who waited patiently for his car door to slam. She thought of her garden, and the beans and courgettes that magically appeared every summer from seeds she had planted, and the vines that climbed her golden-bricked house, and the marigolds that dotted the beds orange so that from heaven it would look like the sun had shattered and sprinkled itself all over their land. Her children walked in sunshine; her children danced in sunshine. She had never claimed it had ruined her life. She and Simon had had a good life, and if it were to end today, or tomorrow, it would have been as good as it possibly could have been.

George had his arm about Anthony's shoulder, and Simon on the other side held Beatrice about the waist. Preethi put her arm about George's shoulder, and there they stood, she thought, like she and Simon had stood at the CND march, with the politician who had won the war. The caller shouted 'Last dance, everyone, last dance!'

Simon escorted Beatrice to a chair, and George walked Anthony to the chair next to her. Simon turned to Preethi.

'Will you dance with me, my love?' he asked. She took his arm, and they walked to the centre of the hall.

'This one's an easy one,' the caller said. 'No circles or moving on or anything. Just promenade about the hall, and when I say spin your partner, then promenade again. See – easy!'

And then she and Simon were walking together, arms linked, as if they were an old couple taking a daily stroll, or a newly married couple walking up an aisle, or a couple in love absorbed in each other, or they were just themselves, just Simon and Preethi, the golden ones, who walked in sunshine their lives through. When the caller shouted 'Spin!' she took his hands and they spun, with only their eyes on each other, and she laughed and she gurned, her face distorted and excited.

Simon's face was the same each time, though, a smile, passive and unafraid. On their last spin, he let go too soon. She fell, but he leant over her, right down, and holding her arm lifted her so that to anyone else who watched, they looked as if she had made a low curtsy, and he had pulled her up into a twirl. When she glanced about, embarrassed, she noticed that Emma stood alone, at the side, watching them. Her face was sullen and Preethi smiled, walked forwards to break the silence between them, but Emma had been watching Simon. Preethi looked back to Simon too. He smiled at Preethi only, and they linked arms again and walked away. Emma was only at the beginning of her dance, Preethi thought, and they were at the end. And we have done it well. They walked back to the open door, to where George stood with Anthony and Beatrice.

The caller said: 'Before we finish, we'd like to sing a last song for you. It is called "Rolling Home".' He played a chord on his accordion. The man all in white – my Fairy, Preethi thought – sang the first verse as a solo:

Round goes the wheel of fortune,
don't be afraid to ride.
There's a land of milk and honey,
waits on the other side.
There'll be peace and there'll be plenty,
you'll never need to roam.
When we go rolling home, when we go rolling, home . . .

And as each of the tenor harmonies joined one by one, the crowd grew silent, until only the voices took off into the night, like elfin wings. Preethi looked up at Simon, and above his head a single moth flew idly, its lassitude echoing the men's voices as they sang about ploughing and hedgerows and the labourers. As they entered the last chorus and the Fairy-man sang the first verse again, Freddie came to say goodbye.

She looked up to his face, his now broad shoulders, the greying brown hair, still wavy about the temples. And he looked down to her.

'If we had married, it would have been an entirely different world we lived in,' he said.

She stepped to him, put her body against his, her arms high above her head about his neck, and placed her ear against his chest. She heard his heart beating steadily: she thought of Rohan, she didn't know why. 'Oh, Freddie,' she said. Tears had come to her eyes, and when she looked up, his eyes too had dulled. They did not exchange email addresses or mobile numbers. But as she turned to go, he caught her hand, held it, and she turned back to him and walked away backwards, letting go of him at the very last moment.

Later, as the taxi drove them through the winding roads of the forest, Preethi thought: I don't want it all to end tonight. I want to try, and keep trying. I want to understand, I want to *know* the things I just imagine, the things I expect. She thought about Emma, and about the people in the cowboy hats, and about Beatrice's quiet dignity and Anthony's grief. She wanted to understand what people wanted. But she did understand, for when Simon's head lolled on to her shoulder, she held it there, feeling its weight, and kissing his temple, she whispered, 'I love you' into his dreams.

RESEARCH

When the poet, Margaret, asked her for her name, she said 'Lolly', as if a child again. And then she corrected herself: 'I mean, it's Louisa. I couldn't say Louisa when I was small . . .'

'So you said Lolly, and the family allowed that name. They petted you and patronised you with it, and you cannot help but feel a little patronised and petted by *me*, so you – reverted?' replied Margaret.

Louisa – for that is what she infinitely preferred – said, 'Yes,' simply, and with that yes a number of other questions were answered. Questions made with flashing eyes and meaningful smiles. Margaret, who kissed her later and allowed Louisa to drunkenly search about her well-worn décolletage, never allowed the name Lolly to be used. Not even by Louisa's sister Deirdre, or Shamini, her mother.

Margaret became as near to a partner as Louisa had had: many glorious weekend days of walks by the sea and evenings in bed. And then, as suddenly as she appeared in Louisa's life, she disappeared. Her breasts, glorious, tanned and heavy, harboured a killer of such great proportion that nothing could save her from the lack of hair and the double slicing away, the ghostly march so many of her friends had fallen into. Margaret made little of it, not even poems; the radio waves of her life force seemed palpable in the room, and her concentrating face towed, drained, channelled them until one day it was as if she had forgotten to make the superhuman effort to keep living. Louisa watched her wane, her last few minutes painful and bitter, and then Margaret was gone. Louisa, who had taught herself to share her life, where she had been used to being alone, grew used to it again. It was a hardship she felt dimly, like hunger pangs at eleven in the morning, to be got over with work. She buried herself in the vaults at the library, never believing that the physicality of her grief was anything more than a daily routine of pain, like the limp of an amputee.

A year later, as if emerging from a sleep, Louisa stood up from her desk, removed her glasses from her weary eyes, and answering the phone, managed a smile when the enquiries desk reported a visitor.

'It's a Mr Harrison,' they said. 'He asked to speak specifically to *you*.'

His name made her smile. Margaret's name was Harrison. A coincidence on a spring day, and as she walked up the stairs to the ground floor, she noticed that tears did not come when she thought of spring: it was a year and a few weeks since Margaret had died, days before blossom appeared on trees and baby birds surfaced from cocoon-like nests, and the young people on campus held hands and kissed, their eyes closed against the sudden brightness of the sky. Her days were still spent in the vaults, but she ventured out sometimes to witness the world going on, to watch with pleasure the everyday, fascinating lives of others.

He stood with his back to her, very still. But she knew already, the way he stood, perhaps the colour of his hair, she knew.

'Hello,' she said to his back, 'I am Louisa, the archivist.'

He swivelled slowly on one heel, as if on a turntable, as if required to reveal himself gradually. She stepped back. Her hand, outstretched to take his, curled back to her side.

'Hello,' he said. 'I'm Tony. I . . . I have something for you. My mother . . .'

But he started to cry. She stepped towards him, looked at his crying face, and then holding his arm, guided him towards an office behind the enquiry desk. He was young, maybe twenty-five, thirty at the most. His hair was the colour and texture of his mother's hair, an auburn brown, multifarious in its tones and curly, as though it had been teased and pronged and tied into its complex of tangles, and as he sobbed into the broken tissue she found in her pocket, he grabbed at his hair and messed it backwards, much as his mother had done when Louisa made love to her. And Louisa, thinking this, took a step away from him again, worried that proximity would betray her.

'Can I bring you a cup of tea?' she asked.

'No, God no! I am so sorry,' he said, and roughly drawing back a chair, sat down at the desk awkwardly, his long legs thrusting under it, until he became the interviewer, and she the nervous interviewee. 'Look, my mother left you – I mean the university – her papers. But with the proviso that *you* – I mean *you* – take care of them.'

'Oh.'

He smiled up at her. 'Yes. "Oh" is what I thought too.' He waited for Louisa's response. She stepped backwards again. He smiled, uncannily the smile that Louisa thought of every morning the moment after she woke and reminded herself of the things she had lost. 'Cup of tea,' he said. 'That's our answer to everything, isn't it?' He sniffed, wiping his nose on his sleeve.

'I had no idea she had a son.'

'No. She didn't tell people.'

'We were close.'

'She gave me to Dad. I only saw her once a year – well, more, when I was grown up, but not so much in her last months. I don't know why. I think she may have wanted to . . . shield me.'

'Yes.' But Louisa blamed herself. Margaret's last months had belonged to Louisa, completely.

He stood. 'Tea,' he said, clapping his hands together. 'Tea. Always a good idea. Come on. You look as if you've had a shock too. Were you close then?' he asked, unnecessarily repeating her, looking at her sideways as he reached for the door handle behind her. Louisa flinched away, but she smiled too, and made the decision not to tell him.

It was a good decision, for his powers of persuasion were as strong as his mother's, and soon, three or four months after their first meeting, they were holding hands in the late spring, as though holding hands was the camouflage of campus. In the summer, as the undergraduates began to pile their boxes into the backs of their parents' cars, they were quiet lovers, and come the autumn term, he had signed up for an MA, and had moved into her flat and her bed, overwhelming and stabilising her, in much the same way his mother had two years before.

Louisa's work continued. She noted and sifted collections of manuscripts, photographs, pamphlets, diaries, newspapers, maps. She negotiated with depositors of collections, stepping gently in the dance around their loved one's very real remains, carting away papers in boxes and sometimes black bags, closing the door of her car quietly as the wife or husband or child stood listening for that sound of one final goodbye. She made grant applications, to somehow fund the cataloguing. She negotiated her own terms with the university, all the time justifying to them that the collection she was building was worth keeping for the hundreds of years she was planning for. She gave each piece of paper its own importance, and a place in her democracy: assigning it a reference in her register, a cream, acid-free envelope in which to lie, and a grey, acid-free box, in which it was held, in air-conditioned stasis, each piece like an embalmed body in its coffin, never to feel the weight of earth and start its natural process of descent to crumbled soil.

At their first meeting, when they had had their tea, Tony had brought her two document boxes filled with Margaret's papers.

'She willed them to the university,' he said, 'for the establishment of the Margaret Harrison collection.'

It was a strange business, she thought, this delving into the past. To her, the past was just an impersonal town of comings and goings, a glossy history book full of famous white people who had nothing to do with *her*, Louisa. Margaret, the love of her life, was in the boxes Tony had handed to her – but it was Margaret's working self, her everyday drudge of a self, separate from the Sunday husband she had been for Louisa. To settle her words into their new resting places was Louisa's job, and this is what she set out to do. Taking the boxes down to the archives, she gleefully announced their new bounty to her colleagues, but Margaret had not been hugely well known, and people were only mildly impressed, and actually annoyed because it was yet another collection that would have to wait to be catalogued: there was no monetary gift that supported it.

None of them could foresee an academic who would be attending the reading room on a regular basis to examine the diaries of a northern, latterly militant, lesbian poet. No one could imagine even one thesis being written about her rhyming schemes. Margaret's addition to their collection was as important as the addition of her bones to the ground.

Consequently, Louisa, over a number of weeks of falling in love with Tony, put Margaret away, chronologically, then by subject, assigning her manuscripts reference letters and numbers, significant, it seemed to Louisa, only to herself. She would occasionally flick open a page – carefully, with immense respect – and there would be words, and names and ideas that were nothing to do with *her* or Tony, for that matter, and she would close the page again, stroking it down, understanding its texture and substance more than she understood its previous owner, who had once been the centre and the meaning of her world.

A year later, when they were discussing marriage, and having a child to share their life, Tony said, 'Why were you and my mother so close? How did you know her? You've never explained.'

'We were friends. I went to one of her readings, and we saw each other after that.'

'Saw each other?' he said, turning from the sink, his hands still wet. The sun glinted on the auburn curls, and he reached and wiped his hands on the cloth she held the last dish in.

'Yes. You know. Coffee, drinks, that sort of thing.' She knew how to lie. Her grown-up life had started when she was eight and crawled up her bed, higher, higher, away from Kumar, imagining she was climbing a mountain as she reached her hands up the wall towards her bookshelf, so her fingers did not touch where he tried to guide them. Lies were what she repeated to herself in order to forget him, and lies were what she told other people so they would not know she was the nasty, guilty, dirty child, always eight inside. Except when Margaret loved her. Except now that Tony loved her.

'Tell me?'

'Tell you what? What is there? We talked – about art and poetry and we made jokes, and laughed.'

'But what did you laugh about? Why won't you tell me?'

'Of course I'll tell you. It's just hard . . . I really loved her. I mean, as a friend. And . . .'

'You loved her? I wish I had known her. I wish I had had the opportunity to love her properly . . .'

His eyes filled with tears; hers remained dry. 'My father,' she said, changing the subject quickly, '. . . he left my mother when I was six or seven. I remember him really well. He just went back to Sri Lanka and never came back. And my mother was so angry with him that she stopped all contact. I would have loved to have known him.'

'Did he . . . ?'

'Die, you mean? You're going to think I'm crazy, but I don't know.'

He pulled a face like his mother's, a grimace of impatient intelligence. 'Did you never want to know?'

'Well, he left. He left and he didn't come back or try to contact us, so . . .'

'But maybe he did. Maybe he did but your mother didn't want you to know.'

She had never thought that her mother could deceive her in that way. She did not know her mother, really. Shamini had stopped understanding Louisa when she was eight, and Louisa empathised with her mother. A remarkably intuitive child, she had been able to look at herself and see what her mother saw: a solemn sadness, an unwillingness to speak or to laugh, to hug or to kiss. She had been a burden to her mother and her sister Deirdre and when she had left home, she knew they had both been relieved. It was useless to think of her mother deceiving her about her father, because it was not the point. What she owed her mother was her childhood; what her mother owed her, she did not know nor cared to know.

'It's not important. He left. I never questioned it.'

'But don't you question it now? I mean, now we're talking about having children, and marriage and everything. I question my mother's motivation all the time. I wonder why she didn't want me.' He looked out over rooftops at the setting summer sun reflected over the calm ocean. Louisa could not comfort him, could not say – perhaps she *did* want you – the way normal people would. Margaret had emphatically told her that she had no children, nor had she ever wanted children.

'Now that her papers are part of the university,' he said, as if it were an idea that had only just occurred, 'I could read her diaries.'

'No,' Louisa said. 'I don't think that would be a good idea.' They looked at each other, and she knew that he would do it, and he had every right to do it. She recognised that the whole conversation had been leading up to this; he had been looking for a way to ask. Perhaps signing up for the MA, perhaps even his relationship with *her*, was simply for this. She had not read the diaries – never wanted to know Margaret's feelings about her. But now, she cared.

'Mum?' she said.

'Lolly! Has something happened? Why are you calling? You are lucky – I *just* returned from the supermarket, and then Deirdre is expecting me to go and look after the little man, *my*, he is *so sweet*. Such an *angel*! *Why* can't you and that boy get married? And have children, for goodness' sake, child, you're in your thirties already!'

'Mum, look, I'm on lunch and . . .'

'Oh, that job is so *dull*. Hiding away in a crypt full of *dead* people when you could be *anything*! How many girls become librarians when they have a Masters in History?'

'Mum!' But Shamini launched into another story.

'. . . the little man said something *so funny* the other day. He is *so* intelligent. Who knows, he may become the first doctor in the family!'

'Will you stop for a minute? I need to ask you something . . .'

'Let me finish, will you? It is *so funny*.'

'Mum – what happened to Dad? I mean, I've never asked you. Has Deirdre ever asked you?' She heard Shamini pause, take a breath.

'Of course she hasn't asked me, because she is my *daughter*, who *cares* about my *feelings*!'

'Oh, Ma. Don't start, now.'

'How is Tony?' Shamini asked, with a sniff.

'Don't change the subject. Did he die?'

'Did he die? Did he *die*?! Don't you think I would have told you?'

'You haven't told me anything. And Tony is the reason I'm calling.'

'He's asked you to marry him, hasn't he?' Suddenly she was elated. 'You can get married in the university chapel. There is a chapel there, isn't there?'

'Ma, I've got to go . . .'

'And then I won't hear from you for another three months. I'm getting old, darling. What if I were to just roll over and die one morning? I know who I would call – Deirdre. *That's* who.'

'So if he didn't die, why did he not contact us? Why have we just got on with everything, without him?'

'Because it is better that way.'

'What is? Life? My life? Deirdre's life? Your life? I think I have a right to know my own father.'

'Hoity toity, little Lolly,' she chanted, something she had started to do in those grim months after her cousin had been arrested.

'Don't, Mum. I need his address then.'

'Why? What will you do?' She sounded panicked, perhaps even afraid.

'I'll write to him, and then Tony and I will go and see him.'

'No. I refuse to give you his address.'

'Don't be stupid, Ma.'

'You use *this* language to me? Wait till I tell Deirdre . . .'

'Just give me the address.'

When she was six, her father had taken her to Sri Lanka. He had taken her by herself, and she remembered the glory of being completely his, and he being completely hers. She did not remember why he had chosen her, and why he had left Deirdre behind. They had taken two planes, landing in Bombay at dawn: she remembered him carrying her off the plane, and raising her head from his shoulder to show her the sunrise. She remembered his camera, a Leica, which he carried as close to his chest as he carried her: he put her down on the tarmac, and took a photo of the rising sun. He turned to her and said – what was it he said? He said, 'For you to remember.' She had never been somewhere so hot or been awake so early in the morning. Of that trip, all she remembered were scattered moments of joy: meeting cousins who played and laughed in just the same way as her friends at school, yet who sounded more true, more real, and who looked beautiful, despite being brown. At school, her friends said, 'You have to be the clever one – you can't be the pretty one, because you're coloured.' In Sri Lanka there were beauty queens and ugly beggars with leprosy on the street and grandmothers and schoolchildren and Buddhist priests and market tradesmen and great-aunts who were troublesome, and uncles who could do tricks with slim silver coins – and all of their faces were varying shades of brown – from tan to blue-black-brown – and Louisa stood among them and not apart from them.

Her father was the same shade as her, what her friends called 'red Indian colour' and when her aunts stroked her cheeks, they looked at her fondly and said, 'She is so fair! So beautiful!' Her father, she remembered, was good-looking, with the wide eyes and aquiline nose of a Westerner or an Indian film star. If she was not playing with her cousins that summer, she would sit on her father's lap, as he lounged in a planter's chair on the veranda of his parents' old colonial house on the Galle Road just outside Colombo. The fan would be brought out for 'baby' as the old servants called her, and sometimes she would read as she listened to her father and his father talking in their peculiar mix of Sinhala and English. And sometimes she would doze off and wake to find the light already dimming at five, and her father heaving her into the arms of her grandmother, who would take her to the bathroom to douse her awake with a cold-water shower. Then off they would go again, into the evening's heat in her grandfather's old Austin, to visit more friends or cousins, uncles or aunts, or to eat in restaurants that looked out to an always-raging sea.

One night, they were coming home late, and she was talking to him, she remembered, but he was quiet, and he listened and laughed at whatever silliness she was saying. She was holding his hand, and she traced the veins on the back of it, knowing that he belonged only to her. He said, 'Do you like it here?' He said, 'Little Lolly?' No, he never called her Lolly, nor did he call her Louisa. What did he call her? She could not remember. He looked out of the window into the dark night, and he cried out suddenly. They were driving up from Matara along dark, unmade country roads, and the driver swerved and stopped. Her father told the driver to stop, and he leapt out of the car. And this is what Louisa remembers most clearly, her father's face as he looked back into the car at her, his hand outstretched to her, and she knew that hand would always be there as an offering, as an assurance. 'Come, darling,' he said, and she slid against the sweaty, leather seat, out into the dark.

All around her, dancing about her head and shoulders were fairy lights. Fairy lights, which flew around and around. Her eyes stilled themselves so that she saw only them and the whites of her father's eyes. 'See if you can catch them, darling!' he shouted, laughing and dancing about her, as he cupped his hands and lunged. Here, she loved him, here. This moment was in a cream envelope, in stasis. The glow-worms fly around, and around, inside that cream envelope, and she had not opened it, had left it on a shelf behind a strong door, in case – his hand had never been there – in case, in the interim years, the glow-worms flew away.

The librarian phoned down from the reading room.

'Tony's here. He says he made an appointment, but he's not in the book.' Louisa sat back in her chair, looked about her office, at its shelves full of accession registers and the dog-eared poster of common paper-eating insects taped to the filing cabinet, the old rattling radiator.

‘Ask him where he wants to start,’ she said. She heard her question relayed to Tony.

‘He says – at the beginning.’

She took her bunch of keys and went across the corridor to the locked storeroom: her domain, with its stale smell of dust and creaky leather and the bad breath of dead paper and ink. Margaret sat nearest to the door, the newest collection, not catalogued but in perfect chronological order. Margaret had been easy to organise: she was a meticulous writer, keeping working notes with her daily diaries, letters too within the day in the diary when it was received. She had even marked envelopes with ‘important’ or ‘should throw away’. It had been easy for Louisa to package up the papers and notebooks and diaries, pencilling dates on to the envelopes and then on to the boxes, before she put each on top of the other, the layers the strata of a poet.

The first box contained Margaret’s teenage years. This would not be what Tony wanted to read about, Louisa was certain. After all, he was born when Margaret was twenty-five: surely he would want those diaries? But she took him at his word, and brought out the first envelope, her diary for her fourteenth year. He wanted to start at the beginning.

She took the envelope up to the reading room herself. She held it the way she held all scripts that came from the vaults, her left hand a tray under the envelope, her right hand resting on top. She walked slowly up the stairs, passing a boy with his earplugs in and a girl shouting directions into her phone. She walked slowly, ploddingly. Reaching the top of the stairs, she smiled bravely, but suddenly she kissed the envelope, as if it were a child fostered in her care and now to be handed over to its real parent. She pushed open the door of the reading room, and there he stood, awkwardly, like a stranger, the man who brought her a cup of tea this morning, the man whose easy nakedness was comical in his strides about her attic flat, his head grazing against sloping ceilings, his discordant singing filling the quiet spaces of her life. She handed the envelope to him as though he were any other reader with an appointment. Tony took it as if he were any other reader, too. He nodded, and sat at a table, his hands reaching eagerly into the envelope, extracting the diary, his head sinking towards it, as though the tiniest invisible hairs on his face were ashy filaments of iron pulled by his mother's words. Louisa turned away, and went back down to her office.

Louisa walked about her mother's house with her naked feet sloshing. The pregnancy had been relatively trouble-free: except now, in the heat, water swam under her skin. Her feet were swollen into a caricature of themselves, the lines on her normally elegant toes had almost all disappeared, and the toes laughed up at her like ten swollen Buddhas. In the distension of her body, there was a calm rhythmical verse, she thought, and the words that made it were limbs, hands, face, head, cord: all her daughter, all her secret. She called her Margaret already, and the child was as much the outcome of the love Louisa bore for her grandmother as for her father. She balanced, head nestled into Louisa's cervix, ready to be pushed forth, and every now and then, Louisa would feel the muscles tighten, and she breathed slowly out, allowing the air to hiss away. Tony would glance up then, smile, watch her in her compact, private world.

He was looking through an album of photographs. It was Louisa's childhood, just one album. Faded photographs of Deirdre and Louisa in matching crimplene frocks at a Sri Lankan wedding, another of Louisa by herself peering upwards, through a curtain of hair on one side, hands behind her back, in a skirt that was too short, her knees dirty and socks around her ankles. Deirdre always smiled. Often Louisa looked to the side, as if looking for someone behind the camera. No smile for Lolly, Louisa thought. She paused in her walk about her mother's living room to look over Tony's shoulder.

'Why did I never smile?' she asked no one in particular. At the moment she never stopped smiling. Tony and she just had to look at each other, and she would grin, dance with the knowledge of what she carried. A child! Her child!

'Oh, you. You were miserable. Never smiled, always moody,' her mother said. Shamini shifted in her seat, to pull herself up to look at the pictures more clearly. Tony looked back and winked at Louisa. She did not mind her mother. It did not matter. She walked on. The room no longer bothered her: for years, the chaos of boxes and magazines, the old furniture in disrepair, the dirty yellow carpets, the piles and piles of books, unsorted on shelves and stacked on the floor, would have ruined a visit to her mother's. She would have started to clear small pockets, putting black bags of ten-year-old Sunday-supplement magazines out to be recycled, taking Deirdre's broken Barbies to the charity shop, while Shamini would sit impassively in the middle of the room telling her how unnecessary her actions were: 'I can never find anything when you have visited,' she would say. And of course, when Louisa returned, fresh chaos would await, to scold her and make her feel lost within it. Now her feet splashed about the puddles of magazines and books and albums and unfinished knitting, and she cared very little about any of it, for somehow the space between her mother and herself was no longer filled with yearning or pain. The space was filled with flesh growing inside her, flesh that could be given time and love and protection and the kindness that had somehow passed the child Lolly by.

'Who is this?' Tony asked, almost too eagerly. Louisa walked back and stopped. Over his shoulder, she saw a picture of Kumar. Even *he* could not stop her smile.

'*That* is my cousin,' replied Shamini. 'He is dead now. He lived with us for a few months, and then he was imprisoned for a crime he did not commit – do you know, these "miscarriages of justice", they are a terrible thing. But now, you see, he is dead anyway. I never liked him though, filthy habits. Never washed. And he was a drunk . . .'

Louisa said, 'You never told me he died.'

'Why should you want to know?'

'So I could dance on his grave.'

Shamini looked around quickly. 'Why would you say that? What a strange thing to say.'

'I hated him, Ma.'

'Why? What harm did he do to you?' And then, Louisa's mother understood. She understood her daughter's eyes, understood the years of hurt: she had known already. Louisa could see. She had known, but had put it aside, and Louisa recognised herself in her mother's pursed lips. 'No, they cleared him – ten years later, they cleared him,' Shamini said.

'Yes,' Louisa said, and she started her journey back towards the French doors, deciding to step into the sunny garden beyond, and leave it all behind. But then she stopped.

'How did he die? I wonder if it hurt?'

'Oh, well, you may as well know. He was strangled and someone threw him down a well.'

Tony laughed. Louisa turned back and laughed too.

'It is no laughing matter, child! It's a family secret, you know?'

'Whose family? *Our* family? Why didn't you tell me?'

'Because you never asked about him. Deirdre asked about him, and I told her. But you never ask about anything.'

'I asked about my father – almost a year ago, and you wouldn't give me the address.'

'I was upset.'

'Someone threw him down a well?' Tony said, incredulous and brave at last. 'Louisa's uncle was strangled, and they threw him down a well?' And then he laughed again.

'These things happen,' Shamini said expansively. 'Now that you . . . I am glad of it,' she said finally, patting Louisa's hand. 'Come, let's go and eat. I made chicken curry. And *Vambuttu* the way you like it.' She got unsteadily to her feet and pulled herself this way and that, loosening her arthritic hips. 'If you would have told me, Lolly, *I* would have killed him myself.' She turned to Louisa and affectionately pulled her daughter's bulk to her chest, hooking her arms about her neck. 'Poor little Lolly,' she said.

In the car, Tony was silent. Louisa, weary and lacking the physical strength to think, closed her eyes and leant back.

'You shut everything away,' he said into the dark. She opened her eyes, saw his face light up with the motorway lamp-posts, then close into the night. Her eyes drooped again, and she placed her hand on the hand or foot which waved across her abdomen.

'I . . . don't know what to say,' she said. 'It was something private that happened. Something that was – done – to me. It isn't something I should have to explain. Things are *done*, and we learn to just forget, to stop remembering, stop holding on to it all, because it hurts too much.'

'But it seems to me that it is so integral to your growing up – it is all so huge. And your father not being there. And your mother being mad . . .' She laughed. She made the same sort of jokes.

'Having a mad mother has actually saved me, I think. When you're a child and things happen, you just get on with it, don't you? Why we are like we are – well, it is not something we should stop and fathom. I mean it isn't just one thing, or two or even three things. Being the child you were, without a mother I mean, is not why you are who you are, is it?'

'No.' He was terse. She put her head back again, closed her eyes.

'What's the matter?' she asked.

'You. You and my mother.' She felt the coldness from him.

'She was such a good friend,' she started.

'No,' he said into the darkness. 'I know you must be "L" in her diary.'

'Yes? And?'

'She describes her love for you. She *loved* you, for Christ's sake. But you didn't tell me about that either. You just put things away, and you don't analyse, and you don't try and understand how other people feel, and . . .'

'Oh, stop,' she said. They drove on in silence. She dozed

and woke into a murky, post-prandial evening, with a dry mouth and an ache in her lower back. The sounds of his driving gave her pleasure, the ticking of the indicator louder than she remembered it from before her sleep. He was still here, in the car, driving, even though she had dreamt he had left the car during the journey, and put her in the care of a faceless man who unquestioningly drove her home.

'Tony,' she said. 'I love you.'

'I love you too,' he said, and his steady driving pushed and pulled them along, towards their little flat, full of their sturdy life.

From the start of her, her very conception, Louisa noted Meg down in a little book. The pregnancy test, its blue line, was taped into the front, and then the black and white scan, its white fairy form stark and clear on the black background, Meg's stubby nose already like Louisa's own. And when she was born, Louisa began to write, clear descriptions of love for her child. It was an opening up, a discovery of a life that had been parallel to her for all these years. Post-natal elation, she thought, and the rest of her life before this had been the depression. So Meg gave Louisa life. It was a fine discovery and if she were to choose the happiest day in her life, she could have chosen any day after Meg was born: she could have chosen every day.

She chose one of these days, filled with nappy changing and feeds, to write to her father. Tony was fascinated by this last piece, this final person that made up Meg. So, she wrote. She did not say very much – *I have a child now. She is called Meg after her paternal grandmother (and Shamini to please Mum) and she is beautiful, with skin like a coral mermaid's and curly red-brown hair. Did you stop the car when I was six, so we could chase glow-worms? I can't remember what you used to call me. Why did you leave me? I miss you* – and she added, rashly (but she was happy) – *I think I always did.* When Meg woke, she walked down to the post office and sent the letter off, with the photo they were sending to everyone, of the three of them, lying on their bed in their attic nest.

He phoned her five days later. It was almost normal, she thought afterwards, to pick up the phone and hear him say, 'Hello?' in his quavery, uncertain voice, clearing his throat, and then saying, 'Louisa? Is that Louisa?'

'Yes,' she said. 'Is that . . . *you*?' She sat down on to the side of the bed, next to the cot where Meg lay sleeping.

'Yes,' he said. She could hear an echo of his voice coming down the line from Sri Lanka, as if he were talking from the past. 'You know, I used to call you Lulu. You were my little Lulu. There was that pop star when you were little – and you were dazzling, like a pop star, you know. You were . . .' and his voice broke, and he coughed again.

'Dad. It's you,' she said.

'Yes. We *did* try and catch glow-worms! We *did*! I am so *glad* that you remember! Oh, my little Lulu!'

She laughed out loud into the quiet room full of its settling dust. The child's arms jumped sideways, but she sighed and slept on. They talked for a long time, Louisa thought, but it was only twenty minutes. He said he would send her a letter. 'And when will you come here? When can I meet my granddaughter?'

'Not for a little while. It's too early for her to travel,' Louisa said preciously. 'But soon. Can you come here?'

'No, darling. I am ill. I cannot leave the country. My doctors will be very angry.'

That came hard, and she started to cry. 'Oh, Dad, I didn't know. Why didn't Ma tell me? Why wouldn't she let me have anything about you?'

'Louisa, she was protecting you. She has always said you were the vulnerable one.' This was shocking.

'No, she never behaved that way,' she interrupted.

'She was trying to make you stronger.'

'Why are you defending her?'

'Because I'm old, child. And tired, and possibly, I might be dying. Oh, Lulu, don't cry. You know,' he said in a sort of whisper, 'we try our best. I failed, because, well, because your mother and I could not love each other and could not agree on anything. I wanted you. I wanted to bring you here. That is why I brought you on that holiday. That night – the glow-worms night – I asked you if you would like to stay, and you said Yes. So, I thought – that's it, I will just keep her here, with me. We won't go back to England. We will forget the other side of the family. And then, that night, I put you to bed and you had a nightmare – and you called out for your mother, and you called out for Deirdre. So I knew: it would be better to take you home. I thought that someone had to make the hard decisions.'

'You made the wrong decision,' she said, through her sobs.

'Well.' He waited for her to stop. 'Every day, I think how I wish I had known more about children and how they can get over anything.'

She said nothing more. He promised to write soon, told her to call whenever she wanted to call. Meg woke, and she put her in the pram and walked down to meet Tony for lunch.

In October Tony noticed a growth at the base of his spine. He continued with his work, and with the cataloguing of his mother's papers. At first, she treated the growth with as much light-hearted disdain as he did, but she remembered his mother's dying months, the way she dimmed, diminished. He refused to go to the doctor, and then, when he finally did, it was too late. They amputated a leg, and this seemed to him an easy bargain to make for his life.

When he was ready to come home, it was clear that he could not return to the flat, so they moved in with his father, Jim. Tony spent his final year sitting in the garden of his father's sprawling country house, watching his daughter crawl, totter, then walk about in his father's footsteps, while Louisa sat next to him learning to knit. They talked and loved each other quietly, and gradually came to a peace. One night, after she had helped him into his bed in his father's study, and bathed Meg, she sat at the kitchen table with Jim.

'Are you tired?' Jim asked.

'Only a little.'

'I don't know how I would get through this if you and Meg weren't here.'

She shrugged. She was no good at speculating. She was here, and Meg was here, and that was the only way it could be.

'I mean – well, Tony and I – we're really lucky to have you, dear.' He was an old man, maybe seventy or so, she thought. He stooped when he walked, and he had lost most of his hair. Tony had inherited his kind eyes, which smiled at her now. Meg had inherited his dog-like smile: an immense swipe across their faces, toothy and honest. He broke down, making a gritty sound and sniffing loudly. She remembered Tony crying the first time she met him. 'I suppose, well, you've been given a gift,' he said. 'You understand people. You know how to . . .'

'Tony says I shut things away. But I don't. I just know that my feelings aren't as important as his at the moment. I'm not as important . . .'

'No. Well, you know that's not true.'

'Yes. But it's useful. It's what I do.'

'I just wanted to say . . .'

'No, don't,' she said, embarrassed, upset. She would just like to hold them all, there, in their small, significant space, before Tony was taken, before everything was taken away again.

Louisa woke up. It was the middle of the night. She was holding Meg tight to her belly, and could hear Tony's shouting. She thought – 'the morphine dose', and immediately rose, her head dizzy, her arms aching from holding the heavy child. But she could hear Jim's voice too. She could hear him talking calmly, saying, 'No, darling, no.'

She sat up, placing Meg's head on to the pillow. When people die, she thought, it is like waiting for a baby. No one will tell you when. They come, they go.

Tony shouted again: 'I hate her!' and she knew, somehow, he would die soon. It was like Margaret: how she got bitter and angry. When she saw her life drift beyond her reach, she turned on Louisa. She said, 'Little Lolly, so sweet and fragile. You *do* nothing! Slavish Lolly, stupid Lolly, dour Lolly, sallow Lolly. Lolly the Dolly. I want to – slam you against a wall and take your life! I want to fill it up with mine! I would live your life better! I would BE!' Her last poem, Louisa thought. And Louisa had taken a cloth and wiped the sweat away, kissed Maggie's head, stroked her hands and arms, swaying back and forth all the while.

'No!' she heard Tony shout, and Jim's calm voice all about him. Meg stirred, and Louisa pulled herself away from her baby, reaching for Tony's old sweater on the end of the bed. She put it on and tiptoed down the stairs. She stood by the door of Jim's study which Tony had inhabited since the illness had crept to his liver and spleen. The violet smell of morphine and sweaty skin seeped out of the crack in the door, and she looked beyond it at Tony crying. He did not feel sorry for himself: it was not in him, it was something else.

Jim said, 'There's no reason to talk to her. If this is it, son,' and his voice broke, and she saw the gore of snot and tears and grief drip, 'then it's up to us to be the brave ones, isn't it? She's here, isn't she? She had Meg for you, didn't she?'

'Fuck it, Dad!' Tony shouted again. 'I love her! And she doesn't me! She used me! She's never wanted *me*. She's never said it – never demanded: *me*. I wanted her to look up and only see *me*. But she saw Mum and me. She saw more than *just me*. She *loved* more than just *me*.' And then he cried. Louisa turned. She tiptoed back. She walked towards the stairs and at the top stood Meg.

'Dadda crying,' the baby said.

Louisa nodded.

'Dadda want me. Dadda want me.'

'You want to see Dadda?' Louisa asked through her tears.

The baby nodded.

Louisa carried Meg into the room, their arms about each other, scared and shy and knowing.

'Dadda want me,' Meg said loudly confident to Jim.

Jim sobbed.

'Why you laugh at me, Grampy? Lulu, Grampy not laugh at me want Dadda.'

'I want you, Meggie,' Tony said.

Louisa carried Meg to the double bed, and laid her in the middle so that Meg could lie on her side and look Tony in the eye. They stared at each other, and Louisa tucked the end of the sheet and quilt over the child's feet and legs. She was soon asleep again.

Louisa sat in a chair next to the drip, next to Tony. 'It hurts,' he said, before he too drifted into sleep. Meg woke in the morning when the birds began to sing. She turned to her father and kissed his face, but he was gone.

The package her father sent to Louisa contained slide transparencies. There were pictures of their holiday when she was six, the picture of the sunrise at the airport in Bombay, the glow-worms too, faded lines of light across her small Meg-like face, slides of her in nappies, sitting at tables with pens scrawling, and the detritus in the background of early toys, ornaments, shoes and coats, like piles of dusty gold to Louisa. Pictures she had never seen of her life before a darkness had fallen and she had lost herself. And in every picture, she smiled or laughed or fell over with guffaws.

Louisa took the envelope back to the library. A single cream envelope with a few poems by Margaret, and a diary of the fledgling days of Margaret's love for her. It was in this envelope that she discovered the poem about love, the one that became famous: the one that said '*we search, and re-search, and sometimes, we find what we are looking for*'. She burnt the diary, of course, and she knew it was a shame, a pity. But what was there to do? No one – not Meg, or anyone else – should know about Margaret's feelings for her. They belonged to her. And putting them away in an envelope for others to discover, was something that she could not do.

THE TERRORIST'S FOSTER GRANDMOTHER

Gertie got on the bus at ten past nine, on her way to see Nandini. Gertie was used to being a widow: it had been over thirty years since her husband had died. Nandini had lost Victor so recently, the rawness of it was in every word she spoke, every smile that failed. Gertie took three buses there and three buses back, twice a week, in order to sit quietly with Nandini in her kitchen and sip tea. Her arthritis was playing up today, her bad hip aching. The world seemed in pain this morning, jittery. People fluttered on and off the bus, the voices more urgent than usual.

Since coming to England in the sixties, Gertie had always used buses. Sometimes trains, never the tube. So, there had been many bus journeys, too many to even estimate. There were a few memorable ones: with Reggie, when he had his heart attack, and with her foster child, May. May was still there, in her mind's eye, forlorn and afraid, begging, 'But why? Why?' She was twelve years old on that journey back to her mother, and every day Gertie took a bus, she remembered her. Occasionally she surveyed the crowds from her perch on the back seat, looking for a grown-up face that could be May. Sometimes she would see a beautiful half-black girl with cream skin painted just so with foundation, the eyes blackened with eyeliner, and she would wonder. She would smile, nod from her seat, try to catch the girl's eye, hoping that May would recognise her, move to her, sit with her as she used to. It was an unrequited passion, a love lost but always hoped for.

Mumtaz entered the bus at twenty past nine, at Euston. The confusion outside, the sirens: it was a quiet haven inside. He remembered London buses, rides with his mum. It was not his first time back to London – he came with his uncle a few years ago, to a solicitors', to talk about his parents and his uncle becoming his proper father. It seemed a long time ago now. Mumtaz still dreamt of his mum sometimes, although there was nothing of her face: just the touch of her, an essence, a smile. And when he daydreamt, he imagined being married, like some of his friends, and having a little girl called May.

His backpack was heavy. He reminded himself: he was a soldier for Allah, like a sixth-century man, brave and upright, his purpose clear, robustly fervent. He thought of Faisal's preaching, and instead of making him breathe deeper, stand stronger, he felt dismayed.

'Bomb Indian businesses,' Faisal had said. 'As for Jews – you kill them physically.' All spoken in the warm Jamaican accent of his old London friends' parents. Indian businesses: but Uncle's shop was the same as any Indian's. He had never met a Jew, but were they so different from everyone else?

Mumtaz moved to the back of the bus, hoping to take two seats so he could rest his backpack. He sat down next to an old smiling woman, who nodded her head as he lowered himself into the seat. He turned to the window, away from her.

❂

A few days before she took May back, Gertie asked the girl if she remembered how she had been abandoned. She was not supposed to have asked a question as bald as this. No going back to the past, the social worker said. Only positive ways into the future! It upset her, the idea that her history, the generations who had gone before her, could be whitewashed away. What anger she would boil with if she did not know the name of her grandmother, her great-grandmother, the acreages of land in Sri Lanka that had belonged to her family, and had been lost in debts or sold. This knowledge of land and people far away was what made her. May knew nothing, her mother had never told her, so Gertie told May *her* history, gave it to her over the four years they lived together. It seemed only fair to ask: tell me your minuscule moments, tell me about before I was in your life. Tell me it all.

May had told of a bus journey. A simple one, that haunted Gertie for years, but now only disappointed, as if the retelling of it diminished her memories of the child.

'I remember the colour of the bus was green and the seats were scratchy,' she had started. Gertie's consternation was already rising, but she said nothing, simply nodded. An innocuous beginning. 'They said it was a surprise,' May had continued. On the bus now, Gertie could see the small twelve-year-old, her hand resting by Gertie's own on the same brown velvet settee, in her sitting room in Poplar.

'They?' Gertie had asked.

'My mummy and her friend, Jim. They both took me. They said we were going to have a picnic, but they didn't take any food. We went to the very end. You know?'

'To the bus depot?'

'Sort of. It was in the country. There were no buildings or people. Just trees. And then we walked, and I held their hands.'

Gertie could imagine her little eight-year-old legs, thin as a bird's, skipping perhaps: May had always skipped in the park when *she* took her. Skipping between them.

'And then they opened a gate. I remember the gate, it was really big and there was a metal bar that you pulled to open it, and Jim pulled it hard – he used both hands and pulled. And we went into the field, and Mum said to be careful to look out for bulls, to Jim, I mean. But there weren't any bulls.' Gertie remembers the little shrug, the small smile.

'And then?'

'Mummy told me to be a good girl and stay in the field where they said.'

Gertie knew the rest. They had walked away from the field, got back on to the bus, which, she imagined, had waited long enough for the driver and conductor to have a cup of tea and a fag. And they had driven back to town, to their reality without May. As it was Sunday, they had waited until the next morning to use the phone box opposite their flat to phone the adoption agency to tell them where May was. Gertie did not push the child to say more. But May had continued: 'A farmer found me in the morning. He put his coat around me. It was lovely and warm. They had puppies in their kitchen, and I thought I would stay there for ever. But they didn't want me. Nobody but you wanted me,' Gertie remembered her saying. And Gertie had clucked at her, and got up to turn the light on because it was evening.

The bus juddered suddenly and Gertie was thrown forward. The lady in front turned and smiled embarrassedly, and the Muslim man next to her flung himself sideways on to his large bag.

'What's happened?' he said hoarsely.

'Happened? Happened – nothing has happened, has it?' Gertie asked the lady in front of her. The lady nodded, pointed out towards the front of the bus where a stream of people were walking. Some were running. One person seemed to have soot on his face.

'What is it?' Gertie said to both her neighbours. Further down the bus, people were fumbling with their mobile phones. The man next to her said nothing, sitting up and righting his bag carefully, checking something in it, and then placing his hands in his lap. He stared ahead at the people.

'Something has happened,' Gertie said, and she realised her voice carried through to everyone, as instantly the bus filled with noise of people trying to talk on their mobiles and to each other.

Mumtaz heard someone say, 'It's a power surge, they're saying on the BBC – my mum says. A power surge on the tube lines. Six stations, apparently.'

The woman next to him was old, her white hair in a bun. She looked about her for help, he thought, and he looked steadily ahead. He didn't want to get involved, or start talking. He needed to get to his destination as quickly as possible, as agreed. He could not be looking after stray old ladies. But he stole a glance at her: the white bun was collapsing around her ears, and her broad dark brown face, although concentrating now, seemed kind and jolly. When she spoke, her peggy teeth caught on her upper lip. She sat with her hands folded on her belly-chest. She looked like a grandmother in a story.

You and your stories, his friends would say. For every moment of truth, of disappointment or disaster, there was a story he could tell. For every rule, for every statement made at his group, there was – in his head – a dream of associated words turned into flesh.

'We're a generation of Muslims who have woken up,' a leader at a meeting said, and when he thought of the Muslim young men waking up to perform the great Jihad, so that *we* will rule the whole world, Mumtaz remembered a story from school. He remembered Arthur and his thousand soldiers, buried under a Welsh mountain, waiting for someone to ring the bell that would awaken and summon forth their might. When he first heard the story, it had kept him awake that night: the idea that there were men, real men, asleep but ready, men who had given up life, and given up their death too, for the cause of what? Their king, their country. It had scared him, but made him long for the same purpose. To be *part* of something. More than anything, that was what he wanted.

The bus started again. It had let some passengers on, and consequently people had walked to the back, were trying to squeeze in next to him and the old lady. He moved his backpack out of the seating and into the aisle, placed it between his knees. He looked around at the old lady, and she gave him a smile, a sideways shake of the head.

Renee Chatterjee had told Gertie about the tribes of Britain. She remembered a few of them: Iceni, the tribe of Boudicaa, Caledones, the Parisii of Yorkshire. When she looked at crowds of white faces, she thought of them as descendants of these tribes. Sometimes, there would be a face that Rembrandt had painted, or Irish blue eyes, and it gave her satisfaction to place them. They were geographically classed, and this pleased her. We are all products of our geography, Renee would say, and more than any religion, *this* had made sense. Culturally, we are made by the mountains or the streams that we live upon, and our composition was as much a product of these natural influences as our genes. Her friendship with Renee had given Gertie longevity, for it had given her a purpose. Travel became her passion, and soon she embarked on package tours to African deserts and waterfalls, basking in their alien sun, and swallowing their cultural mysteries whole, laughing with their laughter. When she travelled in Sri Lanka, it was easy to understand people in just one look: this one comes from the hill country, that one from Jaffna, this one is fisherman caste – each one classed, clearly defined, knowing their place. In Britain, it was more difficult. When people got on the bus now, she thought of the modern tribes, the different Asian countries all represented in this crowd, the people from African countries, West Indians, and Europeans. She played a game as they waited in the chaotic traffic for police and ambulances to go by, guessing, guessing.

She turned to the Muslim boy to her left. After some study of him, she could not place him. The structure of his face was Western. He was brown, yet white. His face was sallow in the way May's had been; his hair was silkier than hers, though, and darker. He wore it short, with a long, thin beard and moustache. He wore a Kufi hat, and the customary long shirt, like her father's pyjamas. He was a devout Muslim, no doubt. Strange, she thought, how much these people had become the main complaint for everyone in Britain, even her own people. They made it difficult for the rest of us, imposing their rules, making people believe that they were *all* brown immigrants. She tutted to herself. What are we to do, if a war is fought between Muslims and white people? Where would *we* be? She would ask Renee next time she saw her.

Mumtaz looked at his watch. It was nine-thirty. The bus had been diverted, apparently. He could hear people talking on their phones. Some said the signals were jammed, they couldn't get through. He thought of calling Uncle, to tell him he was OK. But then Uncle would have his new number; he had said his final goodbye, he was now a grown-up, eighteen, in the world. It would be mad to phone, just because other people were. But Uncle would worry, because Uncle was always anxious, if he was even ten minutes late.

'I worry you'll be knifed,' he said once. *In Bradford?* Mumtaz wanted to say. He still didn't speak much, didn't say out loud the things that came to his head – he just couldn't say them in case they were wrong. Learning to speak again had been like speaking in a foreign language. He was still a mute in some ways: he never spoke of his feelings, of his mother, of his life before this life. He never told anyone the truth of himself. The stories he spoke *were* him. When he had started to tell stories, he had no longer any need to mime his feelings, and Charlie Chaplin, his muse, had been left at home, as if there were a too small suit, too large shoes and a bowler hat and cane neatly hanging in his wardrobe next to his black puffer jacket and his grey hoodie. He had given up his past, and since Uncle took him to see Faisal, he knew what he belonged to, knew that Jihad meant that he would end in paradise, that his reward would be there. Everything in his life would be linked back to Allah, and the great prophet, but . . . always *but*.

When he thought of paradise, he thought of arriving in a sunny place, like his mum had told him it would be. She had said it would be like that story book from the library, *The Green Children*.

'We're like them, Mumtaz. We're always looking for our realness, where everyone is like us. And one day, one day, you'll climb up, through a cave, and the sun will shine, and everyone will look like you and me, they'll all be *us*.'

And he had said, 'Will they all be green, like *us*?' And she had laughed. He remembered her laughter, not the sadness later, not the way his father had killed her. When he woke from nightmares of the noises of her windpipe being pressed upon, the gurgling last breaths, he had learnt to think of her laughter and her voice as she sang him to sleep. She was so young, his mum, barely sixteen when she had him, only twenty-two when she died.

'Oh, Mum,' he whispered, and Gertie looked at him sharply.

'You are scared?' she said to him quietly.

Mumtaz looked back steadily. 'No, not scared,' he said.

He pulled his backpack closer to him, tried to heft it on to his lap, then let it fall gently to the floor. The only connection to his old life was in his jacket pocket: his torn picture of his mother as a little girl, with her scrawl 'MAY' on the back. She was a talisman. She and her baby were waiting in paradise. Everything else was in the backpack. Everything that would deliver him to paradise.

Gertie thought of her house in Poplar, the back garden where the wooden swing still swayed desolately in the wind. She had had it installed for May, but that was years and years ago, in the early eighties. It was eaten up by brambles now, at the end of the garden where foxes prowled and the neighbours' cats fought for territory. She loved her home. She loved its neatness: everything had its own place, simple and calm. She loved the two chairs in the living room: Reggie's high-backed, winged easy chair, so underused, and her slovenly low chair, grey and worn, a dent in the cushion shaped like her bottom. The pile of children's books on the corner shelf, bought for May. She loved the barred electric fire, and the green and gold floral carpet. All of it paid for with hard work, and Reggie's life insurance. She was worth a pretty penny now, and no one to give it to. If she could find May she would give it to *her*, but she had never tried to contact her. The social worker had told her that that would be out of the question. It would be up to May to find Gertie, if she wanted contact. But May had never written or turned up at her door. How could this little girl be so important, and then disappear? It was as if the child that she had been was a ghost above Gertie, around her, and the grown-up that she now must be existed in a different time. The grown-up who had never knocked on Gertie's front door.

The bus was taking a very strange route, around squares and through side streets she had never driven down. She stared through the window at people standing on street corners.

'What a strange day,' she said to no one.

'Yes,' the Muslim boy answered.

'Do you think it might be terrorists?'

'P'raps.'

'Are you from the north?' she asked.

'Yeah, Leeds.'

'Ah. Were you born there?'

'No. Peckham, actually.'

The bus stopped as more police motorbikes drove past.

'But you were brought up there?'

'Yeah.'

'And what are you doing here?'

'I've come . . .' But he didn't finish his sentence.

He had seen someone on a bus passing in the opposite direction. He was certain he had seen Hasib, one of his friends from the study group. The buses stood side by side. Was it Hasib? But it couldn't be – his beard and moustache were short and Western-looking, he wore jeans, a polo T-shirt, a normal jacket and a rucksack. No, he was mistaken, Mumtaz thought, Hasib was devout. He wouldn't have changed so much, so quickly.

The bus pulled away, and Mumtaz turned back to Gertie.

'Where d'you think we're going?' he asked her.

'I don't know,' she said, and she smiled her toothy smile.

He wanted to laugh. Her hair had come right down at the back.

He didn't know why he was on a bus. He was supposed to have met someone an hour before. Now he was away from home, everything they had taught him seemed watered down. He was like a glass, and Jihad was Ribena, and London was a tap, and its air the water flowing in. Silly, the ideas he had. Ribena, for goodness' sake! But that purpley liquid was the right colour, he thought: the countries of the world were like a cloth, and Jihad was like a purple-coloured stain seeping across the cloth, until all the countries were the same pink colour. And everyone will be bloodied by it, and it scared him.

He needed a piss. More people had got on the bus, and more people were milling outside. They were at a standstill again. Someone was crying at the front, he could hear the noise, muffled into someone else's coat. The grandmother next to him looked like she had nodded off. Or was she dead? He was startled. What if she were dead? What would he have to do then? He fidgeted deliberately so that his elbow caught her, and her head jerked up. She took a tissue from her sleeve and dabbed the spit at the side of her mouth.

'I need the toilet,' she said to him. 'What to do? I will have to hold it.'

Gertie liked the look of the boy next to her. No, she liked his demeanour: quiet, slow, thoughtful. He had eyes that seemed to have pain behind them, that private pain of those who have experienced death. The pain that our brief moments of madness stem from. But his dress: this was odd. When she arrived in England in 1961 with nothing but a bag of sarees and blouses, a cardigan bought in the department store in Colombo and a pair of shoes, she felt like a foreigner. She and Reggie had gone to Oxford Street, bought clothes – the best, from Dickins and Jones, John Lewis. *When in Rome*, Reggie said. But it had become more than that: in Sri Lanka she still dressed in her skirts and jeans, hip-length kaftan tops and twin sets. She was all mod cons, as Reggie said. When she saw the Muslim girls about, in their scarves and their black coverings, she worried for them. How would they learn about the world, shut away from it? If you could not see their faces, how were you to place them within the world? Or was that it? Were you supposed to define them *only* as Muslim: was Islam the only world they could belong to? But, they are women, Gertie thought. Women were the world.

She turned to her neighbour: 'Does your mother wear hijab?' she asked politely.

The boy shook his head. 'Nah, my mum's dead.'

'Oh. I am sorry. Do all the women in your community wear the headscarf?' she persisted.

'Why?'

She could see it was annoying him. She looked out of the window. Suddenly, a booming noise, so loud, so near, a ghastly, sickening sound, metal screaming against rock. She jumped, put her hand towards the man. He too reached inadvertently, outwards, towards her. There were screams in the bus, and then people running outside, and the noise immediately of sirens.

'What is it,' people were saying, 'what was that?'

'An explosion,' Gertie said to the boy. She took his hand and held it. It was shaking. 'It is all right. We are safe still. It wasn't us,' she said kindly. She had been in Colombo when the Tigers had blown up a bus, not so long ago. Her cousin, a minister in the government in the eighties, had been killed by a suicide attack. She was fatalistic now, when in Sri Lanka. And she realised that perhaps she would have to extend that fatalism to her days in her own country, in her own town, this centre of the world, this safe haven for all.

The bus drove away towards the west of the capital. They were let down at Marble Arch, and it was Gertie who suggested they go in search of toilets and hot tea. She asked him where he was going.

'To the airport. But I think I must have missed my flight.'

'Oh! I love to travel. Where were you going?'

'To Pakistan. I was meeting someone, and we were going to Pakistan together.'

'What? You have relatives there?'

'No. It were a course, you know?'

But she had no idea.

They found an old-fashioned café in the backstreets. Suddenly, he felt conspicuous, as they sat and watched the television, watched people with terrible injuries being stretchered into ambulances, a woman with a burnt face being guided across the road. They were there, they were part of it.

'Would you like sugar?' she asked him kindly. He had showed her to the toilets, leaving his bag at the counter, telling them he was just there, just over here, going to the bog. He removed his Kufi when he got off the bus, and now he didn't know where he was, who he was.

'Why did you ask me about my mum wearing hijab?' he said.

'I was thinking about it all,' Gertie said, waving her hand generally at the television they were watching and the people walking beyond the windows of the café.

'Yeah, but, what? What's hijab got to do with it?'

'Women,' she said.

'What?'

'Young man, I do not want to have a fight with you. We have all had a shock, isn't it? But . . .'

He could tell what was coming.

'Nah, man. You're saying, right, that modest dress in women is to blame? For all this? Nah, man.'

'Yes,' she said emphatically. 'Yes, man. If women were given freedom, if they were given the same as men – if they had power, if they were allowed to follow their hearts – *then* . . .' but Gertie drifted off, into a reverie. She watched the first pictures of the bus with its roof blown off. 'That could have been us,' she said to Mumtaz.

'Yeah, I know.'

She struggled with her bag. 'I should call Nandini. She is expecting me. You should phone your friend, and your family. Your family will be worried.'

She took her glasses and an ancient mobile phone from her bag. Then, licking her finger, she thumbed through a small brown address book slowly, with the glasses balancing on the end of her nose. Again, he wanted to laugh at her natural comedy. She glanced up at him.

'You don't have a phone?' She picked hers up and pushed it into his hand. 'I haven't found the number yet. You call. Call!' she commanded.

Mumtaz had left his phone in Leeds, with a note to his uncle telling him where he had gone. Telling him he would see him in the next life.

'I can't,' he said.

'Don't worry about the expense. I'm a rich old lady,' she said, striking her belly. This time he laughed. 'Ah, ah! I make you laugh, now? *Very* nice,' she said, teasing him.

He took the phone and dialled his uncle's mobile.

'It's me,' he said. At the other end of the phone he heard his uncle sob.

Still in the café, much later, after tea and lunch and cakes and coffee, Gertie said, 'Well, I am going to go home. Where will you go tonight?'

'I'll go home too,' he said.

'I was not arguing with you,' she said suddenly. 'Sometimes, because I am old, I see things. I'm fat, and I'm old, and I'm going deaf. But I see *things*.' This last word, she elongated. 'If we were allowed to own our own land and till our own soil – and never have a man tell us what and what not we are allowed to do . . .'

'I see what you're saying, but . . .' and here the need, the passion for Jihad left him, because if it weren't for his dad, his mum would still be alive. Even now, she and the baby floated above him, saying *up here, they're all green, Mumtaz!* And laughing that laugh, that mocked him and caught him in love all at once. Tears sprang to his eyes.

'Oh, you are tired,' Gertie said. She watched him. 'Tell me,' she said, 'how did your mother die?'

For the first, and last time, in his life, Mumtaz told the one person who would care how it had happened. And when the words were out there, between them, May was between them, sitting in the café, a small girl stroking Gertie's hand, a young mother tussling Mumtaz's hair.

⚬

They said goodbye, and Mumtaz promised to text Gertie to tell her he had arrived home safely. He went back to Euston and got on one train and then another – a trail of trains back to the safety of his uncle and his life. Gertie went home to Poplar and sat in her chair opposite Reggie's. She would go to see Nandini later in the week, she thought. She had so much to tell her.

TEST

Sometimes, at night, Rohan forgot to breathe. Since Victor died, heart palpitations would come upon him as he finally let go into the first moments of sleep, and he would startle awake like a fat man with an apnoea. He lay there, holding his left pulse with his right forefingers, chanting the cardiac cycle: *Diastole, Atrial Systole, Ventricular Systole, Diastole*. That word, *Diastole*, became a mantra, meaningless on its own, but a word to calm him, make the racing beats stop within him.

Rationally, he knew it was Victor's death that caused it.

At breakfast, chewing oatmeal and fresh fruit, drinking green tea, he knew there were no outside influences, nothing to make this happen, but fear of death, but the freefall of no longer having his father in the world. It never occurred to him that the death could mean freedom. That it could mean claiming for himself a life that no one would judge.

Diastole, Atrial Systole, Ventricular Systole, Diastole, he whispered at night, trying to hold a human heart, trying to stop the skipping, the flailing about of the air coming in going out: yes, trying to hold a human heart.

o

He was at the Oval for a cricket match, with Carl. He had driven into London from the airport the night before in a hire car. He had been late, and Deirdre had hardly spoken as she handed Carl's things to him in a neat little case. They had slept late, in a double bed together in a hotel, he and this strange nearly seven-year-old creature who at some point in the night had pushed his back against Rohan's back, and Rohan had remained awake, worried, frightened even, of waking him, of causing an emotional explosion. The child was his, was used to the *idea* of him, off-handedly called him 'Dad' in the car on the way to the ground. He was *his.* In the car Carl had said, 'So, do you understand cricket?'

'Yes, I understand it. Do you?'

'Of course. Papa told me.' Papa was Victor, and Rohan had a pang of jealousy for the relationship that had been dependent on his absence.

'Have you seen a match before?' he asked the boy.

'Only on telly. It's boring when it goes on all day.' And then he looked out of the window at the cars. He began to sing-song the colour of the cars, shouting 'GREEN' if there was a green car. Other colours were almost whispered. How to understand this, Rohan wondered?

o

He had read paper after paper in his work. All of what he did every day was logical. He started at the beginning of a problem and using straightforward methods he thought through ideas based on scientific summation, and found a solution. And if not a straightforward solution, a way through the problem, a compromise perhaps, or a different way through, using a new method. It was exciting, and also thoroughly reliable. Like digging for gold. Sitting at his desk, or in consults, there was his stethoscope, as reliable as a spade. And in theatre, there were his catheters, his wires, his reliable needles, so strong and beautiful – he could almost hear the tingle of their worth. He smiled at the boy in their seats in a half-empty stadium. He had no weaponry to tackle this. He felt love, sure, but my goodness, how can that be enough?

'When are they coming on?'

'Not yet.' He looked up at the sky. 'Still, look, the sun's come out, Carl. That's good.'

'What'll we do?'

'Nothing.' They sat still. Rohan looked about him. There were a few Sri Lankans below them, in dark-coloured jackets, a couple of royal blue T-shirts between them. No one he would know. He was out of touch with his parents' friends. At his father's funeral, there had been very few people he recognised.

'Shall we go and get a hot chocolate for you?'

'No,' Carl said. Rohan remained where he was. Carl stared steadily ahead. 'After Papa's funeral, you said that we would have fun,' he said. Rohan looked at him.

'I need some tea. Come,' Rohan said. They climbed down from the high terrace where they had been sitting, and joined the queue for the drinks van.

When he married Deirdre, Rohan had made it clear to her that sex was for making children only. It was a function with a purpose, and being a doctor made it easy to take temperatures, plot graphically her fertile days. If he could have given her a cup of sperm and a syringe, it would have made it easier. But into her he came, while wanting to cry, and instead crying out quickly, efficiently, for he knew the unfairness of both their lives was equitable and Deirdre's suffering must be minimised.

She became fat with pregnancy, and remained fat way after the baby grew long limbs and climbed trees. Her demands of him were only material, which suited him well. He worked hard through his residencies, transferring to a hospital in New York for the cardiothoracic surgical residency, thus creating a crisis in the family: to move Deirdre and Carl with him, or to leave them in London, with Shamini and his own parents. It seemed natural to take them. He loved Carl, loved the idea that Carl would be something different, something *other*, with an American accent. It would have been perfect to come home to the child and his mother; to walk through his busy days and nights, through corridors at hospitals, down subways and up through tunnelling streets and arrive into a centre of something he had created, warmth, safety, home.

But it didn't work, he and Deirdre, despite the good wage, despite the promises, and despite being the perfect husband. He was attentive, kind, undemanding. He loved the movies she loved, bought DVD box sets of *Sex and the City* to show her what she would be missing if she did not come to New York, and what's more, sat and watched them with her, commenting on the fashion, enjoying the shoes. He was a social being, to all intents the light that people followed: he was the energy, the laughter, the taut-bodied being in the middle of every social situation, knowing everyone by name, pouring the drinks. He was the one people asked to dinner, not Deirdre, and he was afraid that Deirdre knew this. Poor Deirdre was ten years younger than him, pudgy and not as bright as her sister Louisa. Nandini once said, 'You married the wrong sister,' but she said it quietly, while holding the baby Carl on her lap as Deirdre thumped and bumped around their kitchen, pausing to stuff food into her mouth. He had looked up from his newspaper and sighed. His mother didn't understand his relationship with Deirdre; but nor did he, unless it was mediated by his parents' expectations. Preethi had been kinder, trying in a roundabout way to advise him on sex. He had laughed. He was much clearer in his understanding of other people's marriages, and that one was doomed, he could see. He thought when she talked of 'sexual healing' it would be unkind to mention that he suspected Simon was being healed elsewhere.

He had left when Carl was two. And had remained in New York, being sucked into his work, and his friendships, the parties, the human stories of his patients, the everyday routines of running in Central Park, and drinking in Manhattan bars that he expected Samantha or Carrie or Miranda or Charlotte to walk into any day – and put their arms about his shoulders and show him how to come out and be their new – celibate – gay best friend.

Deirdre had remained in England, living on his earnings quite happily, bringing up their son to hate Rohan (he imagined), and to speak like a south Londoner. He was taxi-ed between his grandparents. Shamini on the one hand, supporting her daughter in her project of depending on and reviling her son-in-law in equal measure, and Nandini and Victor spoiling him and loving him and recognising their son in him in a myriad of ways, except the most worrying way. He just wasn't like Rohan was at the same age – and that made them love Carl even more.

Rohan realised that the giving up of things was the key to living a good and safe life. He had been a vegan now for two years. Alcohol was a problem, so he gave it up. He was too reliant on coffee and that too went. Sex had gone years ago. In fact what he had done to Deirdre to create Carl had been the only penetration since his twenties. He was now forty-one. He was closed down, shut down, his whole body ascetic and pure. He was thin, yes, but good-looking thin – not anorexic thin. At bars he was still hit on. He liked to flirt. It just didn't go anywhere. It was the key to living, this giving up of things. To be tested all the time meant that you learnt about yourself every day, that you understood yourself anew.

Yes, he had slips, spectacular ones sometimes. When Preethi called to say his father had died – he had just come out of theatre, after performing a very straightforward valve replacement, he remembered the time before she called so clearly – he had gone straight to a bar with his friend (and regular anaesthetist) Noah, and they had got trashed. Noah drank beer with Tequila chasers. Rohan had stuck to red wine. Nearly one bottle – he was thin, it didn't take much – and then they'd hailed a cab, gone home to his apartment, and fallen into bed together. Noah held him as he cried. That was all. The slip was the alcohol. Noah was there the next morning, and when they had drunk three or four cups of coffee to clear their heads, Noah had said goodbye and gently kissed him, on the cheek. It was nothing. But after, Rohan had been left with real and passionate yearning – not just for Noah, but for love itself. Or maybe it was just for Noah.

They were friends. It was now exactly a year since Rohan's father had died. In that year, he had steadily distanced himself from Noah, and Noah had taken the hint. In theatre, they were a formidable team, Rohan performing the PAVRs, with Noah clowning about in the prep room, playing music, telling jokes and talking about sport, teasing nurses, generally being a perfect foil to Rohan. And yet, when they happened to be alone, in an elevator or in the scrub room, they said nothing. It was fine though. It was a tender silence.

At the cricket match, Rohan thought of Noah, as he looked at his child, and the tenderness of everything in Noah made him suddenly ache for the man. Noah was olive-skinned, pale-eyed – were they green or hazel? – dark-haired, always stubble-chinned. He had wiry forearms, something that Rohan continued to turn his gaze away from.

He and Carl had brought their drinks back to their seats. The stadium had begun to fill up. The pitch looked white, and the two teams were now in the outfield throwing balls to one another.

'Who's that?' Carl said, pointing to one of the Sri Lankan squad.

'Well, I wouldn't really know, Carl.'

'Well, why don't you look?'

'At what?'

'The programme. They have numbers on their backs. It will tell you in the programme.'

'Oh.' He looked. 'That's Sanath Jayasuriya.'

'You can just say Sanath. That's what Papa called him.'

'OK.'

'Or you can say just their surnames. That's what people on the radio say.'

'OK.'

The child watched for a while, sipping at the soft drink. 'Mum says I'm not allowed Coke because it makes me hyper.'

'OK.'

'Do you miss Papa? Don't say "OK" again, OK?'

'Er . . . yes. I do miss Papa. Do you?' An announcement – the Sri Lankans had won the toss and were batting first. 'Did you hear that, Carl? Sri Lanka's batting first.'

'Yes. I miss Papa. It's all girls now. Mum, and the two grandmas. I call them that, because they really *are*.' Rohan laughed. 'What would you have called me if I was a girl?'

'We would have called you Smelly, because we wanted a boy.' Carl looked at him with narrowed eyes.

'What other names were you going to call me?'

'I wanted to call you Karl, with a K.'

'Oohhhhhh!' The child was animated. 'You see! I want to be called Karl with a K! I think that would be so *coooooool*.' They watched the batsmen take their places, and the fielders shout to each other. 'When you operate on people, do you cut right down the middle and tear them apart with your bare hands? I mean,' and he turned to Rohan, placing the half-finished drink precariously on the side of the seat, and pushed his hands on Rohan's chest, 'do you take their ribs and pull them apart, one by one, like plink, plink, plink, plink?' and he pulled at Rohan's T-shirt like he was playing the harp, one finger, and then the next. Rohan laughed, taking the boy's hands and kissing them. He saw Carl wipe the backs of his hands down his sides.

'Do you want me to explain how I operate on people?' The boy had turned back to the game, but he nodded. 'I use needles and catheters, which are a type of tube, and I push them through people's skin, and using tiny cameras down the tubes, I can see where I'm going, like I'm a tiny mole going down tunnels in the woods, and . . .' but he didn't think the child was listening, so he stopped. The first batsman took a run, and they clapped.

'We're going to win,' Carl said.

When he was nineteen, Rohan was sent to Sri Lanka for a few months in the summer. Preethi recovering from depression and being near death, his parents wanted him far from her – he and Preethi leant terribly inward, towards each other and away from the world. And in Sri Lanka, there was an unfathomable place of his own identity, a place of such extremities of heat and flavour and dirt and poverty and music and laughter . . . extremes of himself. He found a beauty and a love within himself *for* himself, and his gratitude to his parents was immeasurable.

Nandini's brother and son – his cousin Maitri – took him to the top of Sigiriya, the rock fortress in the middle of the jungle, famed for its lions' feet and its frescoes and fifth-century water gardens. He had been taken there as a child, but his memories of those trips were in photos and feelings: of Gehan crying to be carried, of Preethi skipping far ahead and his mother calling her back, of his father elbowing him saucily and winking at him to close his eyes when they reached the cave of the frescoes of the beautiful bare-chested ladies. When he saw the place again, he fell for it, for the whole of it. He understood its initial impetus in the brain of its creator. He understood that it was a palace of a prideful king, he understood the pride itself, for at the top of the long climb up the winding rock steps, at the summit of the red rock where the palace used to stand, he could breathe in the view across the whole of the island, it seemed, and he sucked it all in, as if he were the king himself, and the beauty of what he saw – an ineffably blue sky (blue was the simplest word for this colour), the rocks beyond, the greenness of the forever threatening jungle below. In this view were gods, and he was a god too, seeing it, and when he breathed out, his shoulders pulled back, and he stood tall. The weight of London had left him, the weight of his family, of everything, and he was himself at last.

On the way down, in the shade of a natural cave, he took Maitri's face and kissed him hard. Maitri kissed him too.

And when they stopped kissing, Rohan saw his Uncle's back walk down the worn stone steps in front of them.

A month later, he went home. In a few weeks he would be leaving for medical school. There were friends to see, his last preparations and drinks and goodbyes, so that his father was easily forgotten – perhaps avoided, when he thought back – until the night before his last night, on his way out again, showered and perfumed, his father stopped him at the door. Victor was a hunched, little man by then, and his anger when it came was shocking.

'When you go,' he said, 'you will not be a bugger,' and this word made Rohan laugh. It was scorching, the shock of it. 'Laughing, ah?' his father said, and his hand, involuntarily it seemed to Rohan, leapt away from the stooped body and slapped Rohan's face.

'Papa!' he whispered.

'Kissing boy,' his father replied, and hit him again. 'I *know*,' he said.

Rohan remembered the kiss: it made him pull himself up, throw back his shoulders.

'You dirty, dirty bugger,' and with each word, Victor hit him again. It had come from nowhere, it seemed. Rohan let him hit, let him say more words, because it didn't hurt. At least, he made himself believe it didn't hurt.

His father stopped when the anger ran out, and Rohan turned, left the house and went to a nightclub with his friends and danced to electronic music until three. When he woke the next day, his father was at work, and that evening, they sat down to a last family meal together as if it had never happened.

Mid-morning, the ground was nearly full. Below them a number of hard-core England fans in white shirts slashed with the red cross of St George had taken their places. Directly below them were a family of four: an English father, a Sri Lankan mother in a blue floppy hat and two browny-gold girls. The younger one read a Roald Dahl book, the older leant against her father, and cheered for every run the Sri Lankans scored. The younger child occasionally put her arm through her mother's arm and squeezed, and the mother took the hat off once and placed it on the child's head. Rohan envied them: there was a grace to their intimacy. Every moment he thought he was closer to Carl was hard striven for, as if their relationship was a piece of work to be got through.

Relax, he said to himself. Let the child lead you. Now you're here, you have all day. And as if Carl had heard, he leant against Rohan.

'Tired?'

'No.' Carl sat up, then slumped back. 'I'm a bit er . . . I'm a bit I don't know-y.'

'OK.' Carl put his fingers on Rohan's lips. 'I'm still not allowed to say OK? But that's *hard*, Carl.'

'You talk American. We *English* say "all right".'

'Oh. O-*K*.'

'Aaahh!' Carl screamed, and Rohan laughed and hushed him. The child with the book turned and smiled. A run was taken and they clapped politely.

After a moment, Carl slumped back against him. 'Shall we go and find an early lunch?' Rohan asked.

'I'm not lunch-y yet. Let's play questions.'

'How do you play that?'

'I ask you questions. Duh. Are you really stupid?'

'*No*,' Rohan said, and wondered if he should be telling the child about respect, or how to talk to adults. It wasn't his place, was it? Even though he was his father, it still wasn't up to him, was it? How easy to manipulate a child, he thought. And then it's a lifetime's work to undo. 'Ask me a question then.'

'You ask *me* a question first.'

'OK. Did you play this with Papa?'

'Not that type of question. Ask me a fact.'

'OK. Let me think of one.'

'No. You have to ask straight away, anything, like this,' and Carl clicked his fingers. 'It's a great game if you play *properly.*' Rohan smiled, because when he said the last word, he had grimaced the way Deirdre would make a face when they were married. He had no fond memories of their few years together, but with Carl in front of him, he felt nothing but affection for his ex-wife.

'You show me first, then. Ask me a question.'

'Do you think green is the best colour for cars?'

'Yes. Definitely. Now do I ask you a question?'

'No. I keep asking you until you can't answer.'

'Go on then.'

'How do aeroplanes fly?'

'They have hundreds of invisible hot-air balloons under their wings that get blown up by elephants farting.' Carl laughed very loudly.

'SIX!' people shouted. There was a cheer, and the mother and father below them clapped loudly, the older child holding up a card with a six on. Rohan clapped, then took Carl's hands and clapped them for him. The child laughed again.

'You ask now,' Carl said.

'Are you happy?'

'Yes.' He paused. 'No. I would like more grandpas and daddies.' Rohan wondered if the child had been primed.

'Did Mum tell you to say that?'

'No. My brain told me to say that.'

'OK. Do you have a girlfriend?'

'Yeurgh. Yuk. Bleugh.'

'Is that a Yes, then?'

'NO!' The child took him by the ears, and put his nose to Rohan's nose, and shouted.

'Ow, Carl, don't!' Rohan's phone vibrated in his pocket. 'Hey, hang on,' and he took the child's hands away from his face, and held one in his hand as he pulled the phone out. 'I bet this is your mum asking how you are.' He looked at the phone. It was Noah. Calling him. 'Hello?' he said.

'Hi. How are you?'

'Noah, I'm in London.'

'I know.'

'Oh. OK. How are you?'

'Well. I'm in London too.' His heart. Stopped. Carl jogged him. 'I'm hungry,' he sighed against his side.

'Wait . . .' he said, juggling his phone.

'Ro? Are you there?'

'Yeah. How? I mean, why? Why are you here?'

'Well, I have an uncle, and there's a conference, but,' Rohan held his breath, 'but mostly, it's you,' Noah said. 'I wanted to spend some time . . .' Carl jogged him. He pressed the wrong button and the line went dead. He pressed and pressed the keys. Squinted at the numbers, tried to call. The signal was gone.

'I'm hungry!' Carl shouted.

'Let's go, then.'

'FOUR!' the speaker shouted, and the girl in front held up her card as Rohan and Carl got to their feet.

'Come on,' Rohan said, and he pulled Carl through the people on their row, stepping over bags and feet. That voice – the way he spoke – it was . . . and as they got to the steps, he slowed. He reminded himself: to give things up was happiness. Noah's voice was simply a test. Just like a bottle of beer in a crowded bar or a steak on a menu when he was away at a conference, say, and no one knew him. Noah's voice was simply a choice not to choose, simply a question to say no to.

It was before they knew how to use Skype. So he did not see for himself how much Victor had diminished. When Rohan called them, it was often when Carl was with them and Carl and he would talk their usual silences. Nandini would prompt and whisper, and then, annoyingly, would say 'Speak to your father,' and put Victor on. He would always be out of breath – and Rohan didn't guess how serious a case his father was.

'Have you seen your GP?' he would ask every so often.

'It's my turn to go, son,' he would say. He had lost his brother in Sri Lanka a few months before his own death. A sister in Australia died a year before.

'Don't be silly,' Rohan would say. His voice lilted in a customary Sri Lankan way, softening tones, teasing his father. 'Just make an appointment, will you?' Then as an afterthought: 'A little less conversation, a little more action, Dad.' He wasn't sure if his father got the reference. He was getting old.

It was only when they talked about cricket that Victor became animated. *His* team, he had called them, *our* boys. He used their first names, their nicknames: Arjuna, Sanath, Aravinda, Mahela and, of course, the special, the unforgettable, Murali. All belonged to the unifying factor in Sri Lanka, piecing together the fractured society into a single beating heart: their team. And Victor was able to hold his head up, able to straighten his back, for he was Sri Lankan, and it was for him that these boys batted and bowled and dived and leapt, causing, in Victor and his friends' minds, colonial edifices to crumble, rubbing away National Front logos daubed on their doors, making the world see beyond their brown skin to the proud, joyful people they were. Rohan knew that to Victor, his team were world players, and Victor and his friends had made their way into that world first, like trusty old soldiers, clearing a path through the jungle territories for their Princes, for their Kings. They had paved the way for the team, testing the empire at its foundations. When Rohan talked to his father about his health, about his worries about his heart, Victor talked of his team, he talked of his boys, he talked of *Sri Lanka*.

There had been a road rage incident: a man driving too fast down a country lane had yelled at Victor to get out of the way. That was all. Nandini said Victor had handled it well – he had waved the man through, smiled even. He hadn't lost his cool, which surprised Nandini. But when they got home, he had sat heavily into the sofa and died.

'Nothing that a little bit of angioplasty couldn't have solved,' Preethi had sobbed into the phone.

How ironic, Rohan had thought. Angioplasty is what I do. But he had cried with her.

Angioplasty is what he does.

Through the skin he punctures, pushing his catheters in, the push against meat, the squeak, the sighs of machines like sighs of many people asleep in unison. The little balloon goes into the vessel, and pump pump it goes, and the fatty cells are pushed, like portly aunts through a corridor. He was renowned for his steady rate of success. He was renowned for the lives he saved.

'Ah! Hello! Hello!' a voice shouted across to them. Rohan and Carl looked around, and then Carl saw Wesley first, and ran to him. He threw his arms around the man, and Wesley hugged him, pulling the child off his feet. Wesley wore pale, dapper jeans and the royal blue and gold Sri Lanka cricket shirt.

'Hello, Uncle!' Rohan said.

'Ro, my darling,' Wesley said, patting Rohan's cheek, although Rohan was a head taller than him. 'You have brought the boy to a great match. We are going to win!' he said to Carl. Carl elbowed Rohan in the groin.

'I told you,' he said, as Rohan winced and turned away from him.

'How are you, how are you?'

'Fine, Uncle. How are you? How's Nil and Ian? How's Mo – how many kids now? And Vita?' and as he questioned, Wesley told him about Nil and Ian and their children, now in their teens, and Mohan's two little girls, and Vita's new job, and her worrying boyfriend, a flashy lawyer in the city.

'Come on, Dad,' Carl said.

'OK. Uncle, this one's hungry. Maybe I can come and see you tomorrow?' He was sizing Wesley up, noticing the hunched-ness, the loose teeth at the front of his mouth. Heart disease was everywhere, in everyone, since Victor died.

'You know, I was thinking of your wedding, just yesterday, Ro.'

'Yes?' He was aware that Carl was listening.

'What a *fine* day that was. It's time,' Wesley said. 'It's time to find someone new.'

He had said *someone*. Rohan noticed the word – it felt like a message. Wesley reminded him so much of his father that as his uncle tiptoed up and smudged both of his cheeks with his lips, tears came to Rohan's eyes, and he was bowled over with love. He let go of Carl and pulled his uncle close into a bear hug, and below he felt Carl hug both of their legs. Wesley did not pull away, but patted Rohan's back gently until Rohan retracted with a sheepish smile. Wesley nodded, and Rohan and Carl strolled towards the burger van.

'What was your wedding like?' Carl asked.

'It was *fine*. What a *fine* day that was,' Rohan said. He wasn't mimicking. It had been magnificent.

Mainly he had danced, with friends and uncles and his father and his sister and brother, and the whole shebang – the whole lot of them, he pulled into his embrace and thrust out again at arm's length, laughing all the while. He drank champagne from the bottle, and toasted his bride drunkenly as she sat quietly and smiled. Earlier she had been told to get out of their car as they were about to drive away, so that the video cameraman could retake her walk up the aisle on her uncle's arm. He had come especially from Sri Lanka for the occasion – it would be a terrible thing for them to have missed it. Shamini had talked sharply to her daughter, and the immense compassion he felt for Deirdre as he waited silently surrounded by the white flowers inside the car was intense: he was struck by the smell of the bitterness of the leaves. They travelled to the reception silently. He wanted to reach over, to hold her hand, but the space between them in the car, a simple seat space, was too far, too wide.

Their wedding had been *fine* for him. He had never asked her how she had liked it. She told him when they were divorcing. She told him when it was too late.

Really, it had been too late before their parents had made the plan.

It wasn't an 'arranged' marriage. It was just that the parents decided and their children turned up. Deirdre had never had a boyfriend. Deirdre was protected, spoilt by her mother. And when he married her, he thought that it was perhaps because Deirdre was a simpleton: perhaps she was educationally challenged, he wondered when they were first alone in his flat. But she was a primary school teacher – how could she be educationally challenged? Then he realised: she was in awe of him. She had no words, and nor had he for her. They had known each other for most of Deirdre's life. In fact, when he was ten, and Deirdre eleven months, he had carried her to her mother after she fell over at a party. There was a picture triumphantly shown at the wedding. It was planned, their wedding, and too late to back out from when he woke up to it, and self-satisfied, and clever as he was, he had thought he could ride it, work through it, build a relationship from nothing. He had tried. But she was an indulged, simple creature, and he – he was too busy, and too arrogant to try.

Now, all he felt was sorrow. Carl said, 'How are we doing?'

'Let's see – Sanath is on 118, Sangakkara on 28. We're doing great, Carl.'

'OK!' Carl shouted loudly.

'OK!' Rohan said. He was fiddling with his phone. No signal, no message. Below them the England fans were getting rowdy. A man in the middle with a tall white and red hat started to shout-sing: 'Everywhere we go-o . . .' and the crowd answered:

'*Everywhere we go-o . . .*'

'People want to know-ow . . .' the man sang.

'*People want to know-ow . . .*' the crowd answered.

'Where we come from . . .'

'*Where we come from . . .*'

They sang out, and as they sang, voices echoed back from across the ground. The man stood on his chair and shouted to all of them.

'WE ARE THE ENGLAND!'

'*WE ARE THE ENGLAND!*'

'THE MIGHTY MIGHTY ENGLAND!'

'*THE MIGHTY MIGHTY ENGLAND!*' and on this line, Rohan joined in, standing up with others in the row.

Carl pulled at his shirt: 'Sit down! Sit! That's not us! That's not us!' He was becoming upset. Rohan laughed down at him, and as the song waned, he clapped with the others around him. The family in front also clapped, the mother waving her Sri Lankan flag.

'It's just a little fun, Carl,' Rohan said.

'But we support Sri Lanka,' he said, and he was near tears.

'But we're for England too, darling,' Rohan said. 'We're for both of them, mate. We're for everyone.' He realised then – the child was *his*. Not his father's, not Shamini's, not Deirdre's alone. Loving him wasn't enough. He had to take this child on. Take him and remould him, and try and straighten him out.

He put his arm around the boy. 'Want to play questions again?'

'All right.'

'I'll start, shall I?' The boy nodded. But at that moment Jayasuriya was out. A roar went up, and Carl jumped. 'Oh dear,' Rohan said. 'It's OK, son. There's more batsmen where he came from.'

'I'll ask questions. Can I come and live with you?'

'Yes. Of course. Do you want to?'

'No. Do you live in a house or a flat?'

'An apartment, we call it in New York.'

'Can we live in Sri Lanka? Papa told me about Sri Lanka.'

'No. I won't ever live in Sri Lanka. But maybe when you're grown you can.'

'Will I ever have a brother?'

'I don't know. Will Mum get married again, do you think?'

'She might marry Phil.'

'Who's Phil?'

'Her boyfriend.' This made Rohan fill with warmth and gladness.

'Do you kiss boys or girls?'

Rohan looked at his son. He did not want to know what Carl had been told. He kissed Carl's head. 'At the moment, I kiss this boy.' This answer was accepted. Sangakkara hit two fours. Rohan stood to clap, and Carl stood too.

The girls in front held up their Four cards. The younger one stooped and picked up a spare card and turned and handed it to Carl. He waved it in the air.

'We are the England!' the Barmy Army sang below them. And Carl and Rohan joined in.

When they sat down again, Carl said 'Can you teach me to dance?'

And Rohan said 'Yes.'

When he took Carl home, he said to Deirdre, 'Carl has changed his name. He's now called Carl, with a K.'

They were ebullient. They had won. 'Er . . . all right . . . Come on, Carly. Come inside,' she said, because he was leaning heavily on Rohan. Through the door, Rohan could see the warm, apricot kitchen at the end of a dark corridor. Music was playing and he could hear someone stirring something in a bowl.

'Is your Ammi here?'

'No,' she said shortly. 'Would you like to come in? For a beer?' She was straining, but, he realised, she was embarrassed, and it wasn't her fault.

He didn't go in. He promised to return tomorrow. I have a date, he said. With my friend Noah. She didn't look surprised. But before she closed the door, she smiled shyly, came out again and put her arms about his neck and kissed his cheek. And he hugged her. He wanted to say – *thank you for Carl.* It would have been crass, stupid. But she had held Carl within her. And Carl now walked in the world, with Rohan's heart replicated, and Victor's smile, and Deirdre's furrowed brow, and Nandini's small hands. He had Rohan's heart, though, and when the child clutched at both their legs, Rohan put one arm down, and scooted him up between them, and there, he held a heart in his hands, his own heart.

HONEY SKIN

It was nearly two years after her Hugo died, that Dorothy began to think about her body's decay. And she started to think about sex, too. He had been her only lover for forty years: in his twenties enthusiastic and overpowering, delighting in her body with whoops and slurps, and when they were married, languid and assured, king and queen of their little world. Only when she had the children and they were tubby and harried, did the sex become secondary to their lasting, kindly friendship full of books and clever talk. When the children left, they resumed more vocally what had been furtive, in fits and starts, obeying the vagaries of the seasons, sometimes in October looking forward to the midsummer madness that always caught them unawares, finding them in bed in the middle of the day, tongue-ing each other frantically.

For Hugo, the sex was centred about *her* and her alone. Her body's changes had only increased his desire, as if each pocket of fat or crease or stretch mark were decorative proofs of his infinite love, as if she were a house, which in its subsidence became safer. How odd, she would think, how odd that you can love me more. For Dorothy, sex was an insular game. When they talked of it, and in their forties and fifties, they talked of it a lot, Hugo would say – but that's all women, isn't it? Women think their way through the process. When he made love to her, he knew she fantasised. Here she lied to him; here, she never told what she really thought of. When he asked, when they talked during the actual moments, she made stories up: stories that would excite smart, funny Hugo. Stories about Hugo as a prince, and Dorothy a slave girl. Stories about Hugo being married to an older woman, and she, Dorothy, being the wife's maid, who fellated him behind a screen. But when she came, the sad truth was that Hugo, in her head, *was* married to an older woman, who Dorothy was in fact making love to behind the screen.

Now she was alone, now he had vanished into death (a future she contemplated with more and more frequency), she could awaken to the reasons she had lied. It was not satisfactory to think – oh, I was a lesbian all along – because she had not been. She had loved Hugo with an intensity and a fire that raged and burnt and nearly destroyed her at times, the bad times when they'd almost parted. She had been fond of him and liked him. She had worshipped his smile, his common touches, his private caresses. There had been no better person for her, and in his death, he had taken her with him, and left in her place a dried rind. Her body, a desiccated, pocked, disfigured old case, which she pulled about, like luggage on an overlong journey.

When she woke in the mornings – late – in the house they had chosen together deep in the Cotswold countryside, near enough to a small, lively town full of things to do (he must have known he would leave her soon, she often thought) – she would walk about naked, looking through the bedroom window at birds, and avoiding mirrors until after her shower. Then she would stand in the steamy bathroom and examine herself. Poor old Tiresias would always spring to mind, with his 'wrinkled dugs'. There she stood, the thin bones of her slumped shoulders jutting like already sprouting angel wings. Her short hair boyish, her belly flat and flaccid, its skin falling like rivulets of candle wax towards her thighs. The breasts she could write an essay about. She had lost weight since Hugo died, and where there had been a fullness still ten years ago, now she was eighty, they stopped being recognisable at all. The gap between the two appendages had widened, the brown skin on the sternum the only part of her chest that was still taut, and this skin was covered in beige, brown, black and red liver spots. When she looked closely, she could see the tiny hairs there, browner now. 'Oh, Hugo,' she would sigh, imagining his hands reaching around her and cradling her body with his own. He would not recognise her now, with the grey hair and the hunch that had arrived back, an old friend from her teenage years before Hugo, before she walked tall.

And once she dressed, pulling on Hugo's old boxers, a pair of Hugo's jeans, and one of his old shirts, she was asexual, as old people become. She was just a shuffler, ambling every day to the library, where she would meet Rosemary, her friend in widowhood, met at the library a few months after Hugo went, and now a comfortable habit. They read the papers in the morning, then used the computers at lunchtime, jumping from subject to subject with clicks, as if they were young and could keep up.

Well, Rosemary liked to do this, bounding through her

genealogy, making visits to great-great-greats like a reverent time-traveller, calling on her long-dead relatives as if they were close friends, telling Dorothy about a front parlour in Birdlip or a rolling journey on oceans which somehow two hundred years later still surged the same waves. Dorothy's family were a mix-up: her father, the son of a British headmaster in Colombo, had never left Sri Lanka, being sickly, and had married a native school teacher, Dorothy's mother Celie. Celie's ambition had sent Dorothy off to university in England. Dorothy's own history was so varied and interesting that she had never required more, and when she had asked, a few names offered up had misdirected and confused her. She wrote to a cousin in Sri Lanka and met her on her only trip back twenty years ago, when she was handed the holiday photos of a maiden aunt from the 1950s. The maiden aunt sitting in the Botanical Gardens at Kandy. This was her genealogy. As Rosemary, woodpecker-like, tapped away at her family tree, Dorothy liked to play Scrabble on Facebook with her grand-children: what she and Hugo had started was genealogy enough. At lunchtime, Dorothy and Rosemary went to the baker's across the road and had soup and a roll. Then a little shopping and Rosemary would walk back up the hill with her as far as the bend, when Rosemary would go her way, and Dorothy would carry on up home. That was weekdays.

At weekends, she stayed in, disturbing her own dust, picking things up, and putting them down again, the way they were when Hugo was there. She would sit in his chair to watch the afternoon movie. On Sunday, after church, she ate a chicken or a small joint, and it would last for two or three meals or more, until she found it in the fridge, or on the side, smelly, and she'd throw it away. This life was enough for her.

Her daughter disapproved. Stella was all for coming to the house and clearing out the bits of Hugo that pervaded every room.

'At least give his clothes to someone who could use them,' she said in their last telephone conversation.

'No,' Dorothy said, but listened to the reasoning. I am eighty, she thought. I am old enough and wise enough to know what is good for me. Her son called once a week, dutiful, and after the painful silences and the too bright chatter about 'the grandchildren' as he referred to his own brood, he would say goodbye. It was only in the inflections he used in that word ('*Good*bye' he would say), mocking himself, that she heard Hugo. She heard Hugo's voice say goodbye, once a week.

Perhaps it was a midsummer madness that caused it. She had no feelings about sex, no longing for it, not even a nostalgia, beforehand. But one early June day, walking down to the library in sandals and a pair of Hugo's gardening shorts, her old sunglasses balanced on her nose like a heavy light-fitting, she suddenly thought of the women that had fuelled her fantasies of old. So many buxom, large-nippled, creamy-coloured plump mistresses of her dreams. It made her stop in her tracks, to think of the photographs she had glimpsed over the shoulders of other people in newsagents, and the one or two magazines she had bought herself when in her twenties, telling the newsagent (an Indian lady, Varma) that she had been asked to buy them for her next-door neighbour, who Varma knew was infirm. These ladies were ideals, glowingly pale goddesses, their fingers trailing along blurred blouses and shiny lips, their legs parted to reveal flesh rarely touched by sunlight. The magazines were 'soft porn' Varma had said, quite enough for the old man, and as it turned out, quite enough for Dorothy too. The porn of today, all over the internet if required, showed girls of all hues and sizes, splayed up towards the camera in much the same way she imagined that sacrificial goats were slit through the gullet and offered up to silent, distant gods.

She had thrown the magazines away, not risking putting them in her own rubbish bags, in case Hugo should tidy the bins for the bin men, as he would sometimes, and find them. She double-bagged them in Sainsbury's bags, tied the top and took them to a park bin. At the last moment, she had felt a sadness for the lovely ladies she had memorised, dressed as French maids and countesses, and had propped the bag against the bin next to a bench, hoping that a lonely man would find them. The ladies were alive to her, they were helpful, kind even. Their bodies, with their warm pink skin, had made her ashamed of her own ugly black, nubby nipples, her beige-brown arms, her servile breasts, which never failed to make Hugo hard. In the middle spread, lying propped on pillows in a state of undress, the ladies' eyes twinkled with warmth, as if the man behind the camera were a friend, as if he were a husband they loved. As if they could spare a little of their wifeliness.

The too-large shorts riffled in the wind, and she looked down to her scrawny, lizard-skin legs, and her toes, such good friends for so long, now irreconcilably worn and wrinkled. The women in the magazines had been ten, twenty years older than her. They were probably all dead now. It was with indefinable sadness that she thought of the games she made up for them in her head. How they would move with bovine grace through her fantasies, their pudgy toes showing through American tan tights, the only pornographic thing about it all.

They would lie languidly on a bed, and she would lie next to them, and as Hugo touched her, she would touch them.

Walking into town tired her, and she was hot. She stopped for a glass of white wine and some olives at the café at the beginning of the high street. She sat at a table for two outside in the shade and wondered if she would see Rosemary marching through. She drank too quickly, perhaps, and did not order a glass of water. At the next table was a woman in her mid-forties, Dorothy supposed, and she was the type of woman Dorothy had been thinking of. It used to happen like this sometimes. A woman would wander into their working life, a therapist of some sort, or someone who had started up a small shop, and Dorothy would become a friend, in the easy way that middle-aged people of shared experience can. She would ask them their names, pat their hands when thanking them. And that would be all, until the night, in the dark, where their clothes would fall from them, and they would kiss her, when her eyes were closed and Hugo kissed her. Dorothy stood up to pay, but the wine had been stronger than she realised, and the sun hotter. She sat back heavily in her chair. The woman looked over and said 'All right?'

'Oh, yes,' Dorothy said brightly, 'I'm fine.' The woman was *honeyed*, Dorothy decided. The freckled skin on her forearms shone with perspiration or glittery cream, the expensive rings on her fingers glinting. Her blonde hair waved about her face as she stood and walked smoothly over, bending towards Dorothy to smile and ask another question. She said something, but Dorothy did not hear because the top button of the woman's blouse had loosened and now came undone to reveal a palely freckled cleavage.

Dorothy thought of the madness of it afterwards, as if it

were someone else. She reached up, and with one hand brought the woman's mouth to hers, and with the other, cupped her plump breast. In order to know how it felt, she thought later. It felt as she thought it would, in fact. It felt as beautiful and warm and soft as she imagined.

When Rosemary picked her up from the police station, she told Dorothy that Stella was on her way to see her.

'You are a *ridiculous* old woman. Imagine kissing a young thing like that? You have no *taste*.' She drove in silence until they entered town again. They drove past the café, now closed up, lights off, a sleeping monument to her folly. From now on it would always be closed off to her. Rosemary stopped her car outside Dorothy's house and left the engine running.

'Will you be all right?'

'Of course. I have no idea what came over me. Ridiculous,' she said, and she gave Rosemary a sad smile.

Rosemary patted her hand. 'We're all lonely in our own way, darling,' she said. She beeped as she drove away.

Stella was waiting in the sitting room. She had been crying.

'Oh, please don't make a drama of it,' Dorothy said wearily.

'I've made you a gin and tonic and some fish.'

'All in the same glass? How kind.'

'Hair of the dog, by the sounds of it.'

'Who have you been talking to?'

'Well, you were drinking?'

'I had a glass! One glass of white.'

'And look what happened . . .' Stella stood, went to the kitchen to see to the fish. On the coffee table, next to the gin, was a photograph album Stella had left open. There was Dorothy's maiden aunt Megan, sitting on the grass in the Botanical Gardens, next to three friends, all wearing saris, white blouses and pearls. Their legs curled beneath them, they sat straight-backed, smiling in black and white, the fronds of a palm tree invading the picture on the side, exotic plants she had forgotten the name of swaying above their heads. She positioned the album on her lap and looked closer. Megan's arm was placed gently around the girl next to her in the picture. Oh, genealogy and genetics are peculiar sciences, she thought, and I hold no truck with them. And yet, Stella? She took her drink to the kitchen.

'Stella? Why did you never get married?'

'Why are you asking me today? Why have you never asked before?'

'Well . . . because I thought that one day, you would tell me. I didn't want to pry . . .'

'I would stick to that if I were you.'

Stella turned to the sink where she was washing a pan. The water arced out and splashed the surface, and Dorothy had to stop herself from saying the things she said – *why do you put the tap on full* or *can't you be more careful*? It would lead to the inevitable snapping and bickering, the tired nonsense they always spoke to each other, a couple of old maids.

'She thought I was a man,' she said instead.

Stella looked around, appraising her. She nodded. 'You do look like a man in Papa's clothes.' She turned back to the sink, wiped down the surfaces with the drying-up cloth.

'Shall we eat?' she said. Then: 'Would you like me to stay? I could move in for a while, if you want.'

They sat at the table and the things Dorothy never said wanted to come: *I am like you*, she wanted to say. *I loved your father . . . but* – but she nibbled at the plaice and garlicky potatoes, and kept her counsel.

'It's a very kind offer,' she said eventually, taking her daughter's hand, 'but I think I am fine on my own. I think I will be fine, I mean.' And Stella nodded and after they had drunk some coffee, she walked out into the night, on her way back to a life that Dorothy had no inkling of, could not even guess at. She had no right to know, she thought. It was Stella's life. Private.

When she lay down that night, keeping the curtains open to the moon, she remembered Hugo kissing the back of her neck. 'What I love most about you is your smell,' he said. 'You smell of honey, you look like honey, I could eat up every part of you.' 'What are you doing?' she remembered saying, in one of those reveries before she let herself sink into him. 'I'm licking your honey skin,' he said. Your honey skin, he said.

In the middle of that night, she woke to a noise, and she was sweating and she realised that she had been dreaming of the woman in the café and she was near orgasm. After, she listened for the noise again, but it had been her own laughter, and in the dream, Hugo had been laughing with her.

META GENERAL

And here is Preethi, off to Sri Lanka, and Simon in the house, not going to work today, unsteady in his mind. Preethi pulling a suitcase downstairs, her mind on other things. The children, all grown up and in their different places: will they be safe without her, she wonders. But they are safe every day, going about their business, one in her last year at university, the other with a lucrative role in advertising. She does not think, 'Will Simon be OK,' because she wills him *not* to be OK. She stops on the stairs, remembers once, at a work dinner, Simon's managing director saying quietly, 'And how do you handle the girls?'

'Girls?' she had asked, startled. The man smiled salaciously. She looked at Simon then. Looked at his devastating lean towards the director's wife. Looked at his taking in of the breasts, the juicy, gravy-ed lips. 'They're welcome to try,' she had said. 'He's nothing without me.' And she'd turned away.

It was sad to think that that might be true. Preethi, on the stairs, sees his feet in bedroom slippers, sheepskin, bought by her. Was it true? The case bumps each stair, and the day shines in on her, quietly, balancing its rays on her head. She waits a moment, as if waiting to be blessed. Simon sits in the kitchen – look, *my* kitchen, she thinks. But it is alien to her, this place she created for them both. Alien because someone came in and touched her things. Someone came here, when she was away, and used her cooking knives. Used the fruit knife, and didn't wash it up. She found it under the corner cupboard. A woman sat in her kitchen, ate in her kitchen – who knows, she thinks wildly, sucked him off in my kitchen. She thinks of excited hands tugging at his clothes. And look at him, in his slippers, his hand round a cup. His curls are receding from his forehead, greyness invading the honey brown. At the bottom of the stairs she inspects herself in the mirror, glances towards him, compares them both. As separate entities, they are fading, their powers less because they are parting. Together, they are still a force, she thinks. Together, when they arrive in their expensive coats, with their smart smiles, they are formidable.

'When's the taxi booked for?' he calls.

She doesn't reply, and he's used to that. But then she says: 'Eleven.'

'Do you want a coffee?'

'If I want a drink, I'll make it.'

But since he has admitted that *she* was here, Preethi has stopped using the kitchen. She drinks water from the tap in her bathroom. She buys cold food. Has coffees in cafés. Goes to friends' houses and admits nothing. Nothing about Simon.

'Do you remember the barn dance?' she asks him from the corridor. He is silent. She knows he thinks this is another opening to anger. 'Do you remember the tall guy I introduced you to?'

'His name was Freddie. You were at school together.'

'Yes.' She stops. What use is this? 'I should have married *him*.' As she says this, she sees the photographs in the hall. The boy who is now a man. The girl-child, so warm, so funny. She imagines them as Freddie's. Imagines them the same, with Simon's eyes and the curly brown hair that knots across their scalps. He says nothing.

Passport and ticket check again. Handbag zipped shut then opened, then shut. And here is Preethi, she thinks, as she looks into the mirror. Here is Preethi, a single woman. Here is Preethi, on her way to Sri Lanka. She looks at her smartly bobbed hair, her still full lips, the cheekbones high in her middle-aged face.

She hears him stand, and flinches away. He will want to say goodbye, perhaps put his arms around her, and it repels her, the thought of him near her. It scares her. She abruptly turns towards the back door, walks out into the fresh, cold air. It has rained in the night, but the sunshine glosses over everything, making it all seem new and tempting. Stay here, in your garden, work it all out, she thinks. And in the past, she would have. Her duty, powered by fear; her ability to think over anger, to not acknowledge pain, all perfectly convenient for Simon. Just keep walking forward with the smile on your face. Don't bow to it, just throw your shoulders back and *smile*. She feels the tears in her stomach, pushed there for safety, churning at her gut like a disease.

The doorbell rings. Let him get it. He calls. He still calls her darling. Does he call *her* darling too, so there are no mistakes? She hears him talk to the driver, and she panics, worried that Simon will touch her bag, and then it will have him on it, and all the way to the airport she will worry about his hand print on the handle, and if she takes the bag out of the car, will the hand print transfer to her hand – and she knows any amount of washing will not wash him away.

Here is Preethi. She sees herself in the mirror take the handbag and the coat-wrap from the hall table. She pulls the front-door key from her bunch and leaves it pointedly there. She has no intention of coming back. When she returns, she will find somewhere new to live. But she has months to think about it. Here she is politely nodding her thanks as the driver takes her bag with his rough, huge hand. And when they are alone, she watches Simon approach her, watches him attempt to move towards her. She skips away, and quicker than a cat, she is through the front door and away from her marriage. And she never looks back, never sees Simon with the tears in his eyes. But she does see the slippers as she passes him, and his hands, his lovely hands, fall as they reach for her. She will remember his hands, as she will only remember the good times, when they loved irrevocably.

It is the madness of love gone that takes her there – to the sad little paradise island, its understanding lost to itself, the way her own sense of self is lost. Victor, her father, is long dead: she wishes to visit a semblance of him, the old relatives, gnarled like trees in a fairytale. And the last of them towards the north are travelling away from homes that have been a part of her family for generations. The war is finally defeating them, and just as her anger for Simon is abating and moving towards sadness, so her anger towards the Sinhalese government is becoming stronger, braver. She will travel towards the war, daring it to strike her, knowing her passport is British and untouchable. Maybe she could get a story into a national newspaper? Get a book out of it.

She stays a few nights in an air-conditioned hotel in Colombo. She has savings in Sri Lanka, the rent from some property of her mother's. She contacts the people in her little notebook, still puzzling over the pronunciation of names, at times, quite happily corrected by sharp receptionists at various offices. She tries to hire a driver, knowing there are few people who will drive to the belt outside the war zone. She makes discreet enquiries. Phones a cousin and then her cousin's friend who has contacts in the military. No. She doesn't want to go that way – the Western way, wearing a flak jacket and looking on from the inside of an air-conditioned vehicle. If she is to go to her father's village, she will go herself, by bus, train, car.

Preethi has withdrawn a few million rupees. She has a last dinner in the marble-floored restaurant overlooking Galle Face, and the sea. She has ordered an arrack cocktail: arrack, passion fruit cordial and ice. As the sun sets, she sips and allows the taste to permeate, allows the alcohol to throb into her head: she is Preethi, the woman who has run away. Out there, on Galle Face, boys sail kites, throw balls. They play cricket into the sunset, and she enjoys their show. She realises tomorrow she is travelling into the unknown.

It is the little boy running who makes her realise: here is Preethi, making her biggest mistake. The boy's flip-flop comes off as he runs ahead of the bus, and then he falls. He does not get up. As the bus drives past him, the dust clouds over his body, so she cannot see if he is dead. She stands. 'Stop!' she shouts. The man at the front has heard, but ignores her. 'Stop! I want to get down.' The man shakes his head vigorously at her – the driver, his eyes red-rimmed, looks at her in the rear-view mirror.

'No stop,' the man at the front says. He is young, maybe the same age as her son. She remains standing.

'Stop. *Now*,' she says. They are fifty yards away from the boy. It was the way he carried himself, holding his arm before him. She pulls her bag from the seat next to her. The bus stops in the middle of the road, and she jumps from it. They are near to Vavuniya, the woman on the opposite seats had told her. Her father's family will live near enough, she thinks. Everything she has passed is familiar, and not familiar. She has no idea what she will face. LTTE soldiers everywhere, perhaps. As she jumps from the step of the bus, it pulls away, and her bag is still on it. She yells – 'Hey!' and the bus stops again, lets her pull the bag down. She stands in the middle of the street, pulls the handle up on the bag, walks towards the boy, who is prostrate still. She notices the silence as the bus pulls away. Sees houses in ruins around her. She is scared, so scared that she thinks she may wet herself. She reaches the boy. Crouches down. And then she hears the crack in the distance – gunfire? It is the first time she has heard gunfire – ever? No, she heard people shooting pheasant once on a visit to a university friend in the country. It didn't sound like this – like American war movies, an unreal, make-believe sound.

The boy is not bleeding, and not dead. His eyes are closed, but he is breathing. The gunfire again, and nearer. She gets low, and his good hand comes up, pulls her over, so that she lies sprawled on top of his legs and in a ditch below him. She feels liquid drench into her blouse, smells the stench of it. Sees its blood redness seep.

'Fuck!' she says. The boy holds her down.

'You wait,' he says.

'Fuck,' she says, because she has wet herself.

They lie for half an hour, maybe an hour. The gunfire abates, sounds further away. He sits up, pulls her up.

'Come,' he says. When he stands, she sees she was right: his arm is misshapen, the elbow pointing inward towards his body, the forearm is wasted, the fingers thin and bent backwards. He takes her hand with his good hand, and leads her quickly to a side alley. Everywhere there are red puddles, some still wet, some dried, holes in the walls, a shoe, a slipper. Further away, she can see a leg, single and forlorn.

'LTTE,' he explains. 'Tiger, tiger,' he says. He pulls at her. He is taking her to his home, she thinks.

'No,' she says. 'No go this way.' Why speak in this pidgin English, she wonders. Look at Preethi, she thinks scornfully, the posh English lady.

Eventually they were picked up and taken to a camp. They ran for two days, three nights, hiding in empty houses, trying disused cars. Thanks to the government shut-down of the media, she had had no idea the war zone had widened this far. She thinks of the journey here, passing normal towns, rural places where people marketed and girls washed clothes in the river. Here, people are only fleeing, running with their belongings wrapped in ripped sarongs, babies on their hips:

and sometimes, the baby is dead, and there is nothing to do but leave it there, on the side of the road, for all to see as they run past.

The boy, Swami, has become hers. She holds his good hand at all times, covers his head with her hand instinctively when she hears gunfire or shelling. As they have been gathered up by soldiers, she has chosen not to speak. She keeps her passport in her knickers, her money she has distributed to others who walked with them. If they are to buy their way out, she thinks they should have equal chances.

And now, here she is, old, good-time Preethi, sitting in a tent she shares with three women and two old men, three children and Swami. She looks alien, of course, and people have asked her questions in English, because they have guessed she must be from elsewhere. One of the older women touches her arm, strokes the skin, and she is ashamed of its fairness, its refinement. There is little to eat, and she does not want food in case she needs to shit: there are only a few latrines, and they are overflowing and stink in the heat. It reminds her of Glastonbury – if only there were Glastonbury rain. She is always thirsty, but gives half her water to Swami when they get it. She sometimes thinks of holidays with her children and Simon, when the bottle of water would run low before the car journey ended, and she would tell them to ration it, to take small sips, and she would forego her share, thinking that this is what mothers in tight situations should do. This is what mothers do. She worries about the terror she must be causing her children. She thinks of their lives, torn open by her: like a family photo that she has been cut from.

When she and Swami were on the run, he told her the LTTE wanted him for a soldier. His friends had been taken to fight on the front-line. She has told him to say nothing. She is hoping his arm will save him. She has started to teach him her own mutism – talking with her eyes and little nods, shakes of her head. As her fear of being separated from him grows, she becomes stronger. Her other life is no longer real. Her son, her daughter, now seem to be the inhabitants of a glossy magazine; her house in London, Simon – all are dreams. When she sits in the tent, she thinks of her kitchen; its lustrous black marble worktop, its cherrywood cupboard doors and its gadgetry are now like little fairytales she tells herself. The Philippe Starck juicer on its three prong-like legs gleaming in the mid-afternoon sunshine. She thinks of the knife block, takes each knife out and sees the glint of their sharpness. She forgives Simon's mistress, whoever she is, for not washing the fruit knife. She forgives her for using the knife and the kitchen and her bed, and her husband. For here Preethi is, in this camp, not using it all, and it seems like a waste. If she were to ever get home, she would take everything out and chop and strain and squeeze and dirty – no, not dirty. For she has had enough of dirt, enough of blood. She would take out the fruit knife, cut a lemon cleanly in half, Sabatier after all, are the sharpest, are they not? Before she squeezed it on her space-age juicer, she would take the knife to the sink and drop on to it a smidgen of the grapefruit and ginger washing-up liquid and run it under the gas-heated hot water that always steamed from her shiny kitchen mixer tap, like a miracle.

She would tell her co-habitants: but she cannot speak. Her trousers are so loose now, after five weeks, that she has had to use some rope Swami found for her, to hold them up. She doesn't mind. When they sleep at night, she and Swami sleep on the same mat, and he snuggles to her, and she only feels safe if a part of him touches her. It is presumed by the people in her tent that she is his mother. Or aunt. It doesn't matter to them. They are all family now, and Preethi wonders if in reality they could be related. Who is to know? She cannot speak to find out.

There is a peace in the camp: they are aimless, dirty, disabled by soldiers who hold guns. Most there mourn losses that Preethi finds difficult to fathom. She is scared, desperate to be released, and yet, here there is a sort of home, under the torn tent, with Swami, and the old women. She can be busy and helpful: in the makeshift hospital she helps a midwife as she turns a breech baby, she mops at the child when it is born and exhausted, wiping it with a torn-up sarong. She helps to cook, sloshing rice and lentils together over an open fire. It is exciting, like playing home when she was a child. Here, she realises one day, reduced to nothing, she has achieved a purity of happiness. And she is ashamed, because all around her is death. All around her people wait to die as the war comes closer, like a menacing animal.

One day, she sees a man she recognises. He is beyond the fence, inspecting the camp. She knows him: it is Gertie's brother, who argued with her father at her parents' New Year's Eve party. His stomach is fat, but the rest of him is still lean, his face foxy and clever. He wears the dark green uniform, short-sleeved, but incongruously there are many ribbons on his left chest, and his general's hat makes him seem taller. Everything about him seems big, robust. He is an anomaly in the camp, so clean and ironed, as if one of the gadgets from her kitchen had journeyed to her, as if it had personified itself – one of her knives – like a Disney cartoon. And she: she would be the princess. She cannot help herself, and moves forward to see better. Swami is with the other children, roaming about. The old man in her tent is asleep, the women crouch with family members under a tree further away. So no one sees the general spot Preethi, leaning against the barbed wire. No one can tell Swami where she has gone.

○

Six months later, she realises that Simon is telling the truth: their house is to be sold. The kitchen, the bedrooms, the bathrooms, all places of infinite comfort and beauty are to be swept out from under her, and soon another family will be there, as if Preethi and Simon's twenty-five years were make-believe. He has lost his job, the downturn ending his false success: his pride is gone. She realises that everything rides on the selling of her book.

The first agent's letter said, '. . . *you write beautifully, but the actual story itself wasn't quite persuasive enough.*' The publisher who had got back to her was worried that the war in Sri Lanka would simply not interest an audience: it is a small island, its infighting only interesting to those connected to it, and perhaps some pinko-Marxist *Guardian* readers. As an afterthought, they said, '*The storyline with the general is compelling.*' Every day, she thinks of them, the family in the tent with her. Every day, when she wakes, she imagines Swami's eight-year-old head resting on her arm, imagines kissing the tufty hair. She does not allow herself the memory of his broken body, lying under a tree.

Simon has busied himself with the sorting of things, putting books into boxes marked S or P. They are to separate because he cannot stand his own guilt. There is no one else. The lover was finished with before Preethi went to Sri Lanka. He is eaten with guilt and anguish, and although Preethi wants things to go along the way they did before, they cannot, because *he* cannot . . . be for her . . . never mind, she thinks. She won't think of what Simon cannot do: she will simply save herself, and save him in the process. There were people, a person, she could not save, and, for ever, she will try to save him, in whatever she does.

Sri Lanka is ruled by a president who brutalises one race, while saving his own. He has a moustache and a mass, flag-waving, loyal following. It doesn't take her long to make the very small leap from fact into fiction. She thinks maybe Zimbabwe? The oppressed there were white – that should appeal? Iraq is discounted (too fresh), Gaza too. She takes her laptop to a coffee shop, and one afternoon, so desperate for money she forgets the existence of her moral compass, and her general is German, Swami a Jewish boy. She, too, is Jewish, and all the inmates of the camp are white. They don't live in a tent but in muddy barracks in a cold winter in the 1940s. It is fun, easy to rename Deva – David, Ranjini – Ruth. And Swami becomes Daniel: for that was the source of her passion for him, his arm.

She retells the story of the general:

Across the barbed wire, Sebastian saw a beautiful woman. She was thin, and careworn. Her clothing was sparse, like the others who stood around the edges of the camp, but she held herself with dignity: he sensed she was from a background of refinement. Sebastian said to the commander of the camp: 'Bring that woman to me,' and when she arrived, when he saw her closer, he knew her.

'Who are you?' he asked her. She shook her head.

'This one does not speak,' the commanding officer said.

'Leave us. She will speak to me.'

In the dark office, he walked around her, inspecting the tears in her dress, the lice in her hair. He looked at her scrawny arms and legs. He stood behind her, and reached forward and touched her arm. She jumped away.

'Don't be scared,' he said. But he could see she was petrified. 'Tell me who you are.'

'I . . .' the voice creaked.

'Yes,' he encouraged, 'go on.'

'I met you once,' she whispered, 'at a party.'

'Really?' He laughed loudly, sat down in a chair behind the desk.

'At my parents' house. My father was Jewish – but my mother – she is a friend of your sister's.'

'Enough. I am fascinated. Did we meet recently?' he asked, as if they were at a social function.

'No. When I was young. When I was a teenager. I must have been sixteen or seventeen,' she whispered. He found her intoxicating. Only half a Jew. It was rumoured that even the Führer was a quarter. He stood.

'What will you do for me?' he said.

'Please,' she said. 'for your sister, please save my son,' and he laughed, and reached forward to touch her. He felt hungry.

'I could take you with me.'

'No. Please no, not me.'

'Why?'

'Take my son. He is in the camp. He is disabled,' she said. She said no more.

'He is your child?'

'Yes. No.'

That *no*, she shuddered in the coffee shop. That *no* that killed Swami.

Throughout their marriage, when they argued, Simon would say, 'You think in black and white – in your world, there are no shades of grey,' and this has defined her: she believed him. When the book was finished, sent off under a male pseudonym, and bought after a bidding war, she had time to think. Her viewpoint was the same as all people in a foreign country, she imagined. Either you are rich, and belong to the class who rule, or you are not. Either you are seen to belong, or there is always the question behind people's eyes: who are you, why do you speak with that perfect English accent? Are your motives completely clear? Are you *for* us? And when she was in Sri Lanka, in the camp, she saw this too in black and white: no colours in between, just alive or dead.

She wins awards for the book, but refuses to partake in the circus of publicity. The more cut off from the world she becomes, the more curiosity is generated. The house is saved, though. Simon and she start to live again, hermit-like, of course, but together. Their children don't know of her success. They think it is a lottery win that has created this new world for their parents – where everything in the house is renewed, apart from the kitchen. They are glad of it for her: their anguish, when she was lost, turned to anxiety for her health, and constant checking on her safety now she was home.

Finally, someone who read the slush-pile at an agent's at the beginning of her process tweets: '*This book came through my hands, but was set in an entirely different country*'. And Preethi is found out.

Six months before, the general asked for Preethi a third time. The women in the tent instinctively protect her. She understands Tamil now, says a few words – *I'll be all right, feed Swami*. They are getting better rations thanks to the general's fascination with her. He gave her chocolate after he fucked her – she took it to Swami. The general told the camp commander to feed her well. He has offered to get her out – her passport fell out when he pulled at her clothes.

'British passport, after all,' he says.

'But I need to bring my little boy.'

'What little boy? One of these?' He indicates the children leaning against the fence through the window of the commander's hut. 'Vermin! They are trained – brainwashed! Why take one of *these*?You are Sinhala too. Take a poor Sinhala child, if you want. Not one of these *rats*.'

'He is my cousin's child,' she lies. 'I have to take him home.'

'What? To England?' His laughter comes from his shaking belly. She hates him, wants to be sick. His ooze trickles down her leg. But she stands straight and looks him in the eye.

'Yes, to England. I am a British citizen, married to an English man. You will contact the British consulate and . . .'

'Yes, yes,' he dismisses her with a shake of his hand. He has lost interest now. She does not leave. 'Go, go,' he says. He plays with the stud on the leather revolver holster. It is beginning to swelter in the hut. She doesn't know what time it is – her watch was bartered weeks ago.

'Please. For Gertie,' she says softly. 'Call the consulate, tell them I'm here. Please?' He looks at her. She remembers the young man he was, at her parents' house in London. 'What happened to you?' she said.

'Get out,' he says wearily. And she goes. As she leaves the

hut, she looks towards the children, and she sees Swami clearly, his wonky arm held before him as he runs.

○

Someone comes to the house and knocks on the door. Through the glass, she can see a face: she thinks it is brown. Sri Lankan maybe. Simon is out. She should call the police. She is worried. She is down the corridor, peering around her kitchen door. She watches the outline. She knows it, it is *him*. She sees clearly what will happen when she opens the door. She is afraid, the way she was when Swami first pulled her on top of him. She is still, frozen, her mouth dry, her instincts clear. He has come to rape her again, come to kill her. All her wealth means nothing. She has bought her husband, bought her home, but this man at her door has more power. She is petrified. When she was small, she was scared of monsters on the stairs, saw people's faces in the paintwork, and it is this primeval dread that comes upon her now, the fear of the darkest night.

'Who is it?' she shouts. And hearing her voice, hearing the anguish as if it were apart from her, she remembers Swami's little body on the ground, the eight-year-old head seeping its purple puddle into the red earth, she remembers his eyes, still open, looking to her, and the women in the tent rushing towards her, pulling her away as from somewhere came a clamour: her heart tore in two, and its noise loudly screamed into the white sky.

No answer. Here is Preethi walking backwards into the kitchen, but the knocking is more insistent. She runs to the knife block and takes the fruit knife. Holding it in front of her, she walks unsteadily to the door. If it is him, she will kill him.

She hates him: yes, he brought her to Colombo, getting the glory and the thanks from Simon and her children, but he exacted his revenge. She saw him order the child shot. She saw him point at Swami, and the young soldier pull the boy with his bad arm, swing him, and in a synchronized movement, bring his pistol up and shoot. That soldier was the general's gun. She sees it backwards and forwards even now as she walks to the door, as she opens it, holding the knife behind her.

It is Simon. His face had merged with the stained glass of the door. She drops the knife. 'What is it?' he says, and his tenderness, his kindness, his ordinariness makes her cry. She does not stop crying for weeks, and eventually, after a visit to an exclusive rehab unit, she is allowed home, into Simon's care, and she is finally, irrevocably broken.

AT THE FUNERAL

Preethi looks around the cemetery chapel. There are a number of faces she recognises, but cannot place. She is trying to spot Nandini. Near to the front, she sees her grey hair, and notices she wears a nice green blouse and a brown skirt. Preethi and Simon are in black suits, sunglasses still on, though the chapel is dark. Nandini has not turned. Preethi whispers loudly, 'Mum!' and Simon takes her by the elbow and guides her down the aisle. She trips on a piece of carpet, but she is not drunk. It was only a nip in the car. Simon slips into the pew next to her, and leans over her to kiss Nandini on both cheeks. God, she hates Simon. What a weak, feeble man she married, she thinks. She hates his simpering smile as he retracts. Her mother studies the side of her face.

'What?' Preethi asks loudly. Nil is on the other side of Nandini, and leans forward to say hello. Preethi smiles at her, but says nothing. She picks up her handbag and ruffles in it, looking for a tissue and a mirror. She looks at herself, brushing hair back from her made-up face, bares her teeth to check for lipstick, adjusts the sunglasses, but doesn't take them off. Nandini stares straight ahead. 'You all right, Mum?' she asks, loudly. The chapel is hushed, and she is aware that around her, people are staring, and some are deliberately looking away.

'Preethi,' Simon whispers, 'why don't we go and take a walk around the block?'

'Why?' Then she looks at her mother. 'What?' Nandini's jaw sets hard, downward. She leans into her and whispers 'Whatever I do, it's just . . .' but Simon takes her arm, and almost yanks her up. 'All right, all right,' she says, and they walk quickly out into the sunshine, her feet moving faster than they should. She feels like a child being lifted.

A few people go by, as Simon lights a cigarette in his mouth and passes it to her. He doesn't smoke, hates it in fact. But he knows it calms her. She didn't see the general there. This time, it wouldn't be her imagination. It is Gertie's funeral, her brother should come.

'I didn't see him, did you?' she says to Simon.

'No. Well, no one in uniform.'

'He's not going to be in uniform, idiot. Is he?'

'No. Well, maybe. It is a funeral. But do you think he would come? With the elections in Sri Lanka?'

She smokes her cigarette.

'Let's not go back in there, Preethi.'

'But we're here now.'

'If we go in, let's sit at the back.'

'Tell you what – let's go to the pub instead. We can catch everyone afterwards.'

'No. No more drinking.' He is firm with her these days, and it is what she longs for, a steady hand. She longs for strength in all things: her foundations, the places inside where thought used to be, are crumbling. Without Simon, she would be little pieces.

⭘

Mumtaz has come. He wears a suit, he is clean-shaven, his hair short. He lives in London now, in halls of residence. He is reading English Literature, in his second term. He loves his course, loves his life. He met Gertie for a coffee at 'their' café near Marble Arch, twice. The first time, a year after, on July 7th, and they talked about that day, and about their lives. The second time, he was there for his interview, so texted her, and she turned up. When she died, Nandini got in touch, told him when the funeral was. They were friends in adversity, that was all. But he wanted to come, pay his respects.

⭘

They hear a car approaching, and soon enough the hearse drives very slowly to the door of the chapel.

'Shall we go in?' Simon says.

'All right. Come on then.' Preethi stands, wipes her skirt down at the back and front. It is a Chanel suit. Cost a huge amount, but what the hell. Money is the only problem she doesn't have any more.

They slip past the undertakers and go in. Simon holds her arm tightly and tugs and pushes her into the first pew they come to. He passes her some gum, and as she sits he takes her sunglasses from her face. She is about to shout 'Hey,' but the devil is out of her. She no longer feels disruptive and afraid. There is simply tiredness: she is small; she would like to curl up and sleep. She reads the order of service, and sighs quietly.

The casket is walked down to the front where trestle legs stand waiting for it. The men gently place it, taking flower arrangements and putting them artfully about the coffin. They unscrew the top, and remove it, so that from where she sits Preethi can see Gertie's soft fat hands clasped together. She stands half up in order to see the face more clearly. There she is, old Gertie, the customary frown and smile resting on her face in that puzzlement she looked upon life with. Preethi would like to laugh out loud at her, in her pale blue sari, but she sits down again, with a bump, knocking her elbow against the carved wood knot of the pew. The words of a song come to mind, and she has to swallow the urge to sing them out loud.

✿

'Oh, this is my *favourite* hymn,' Dorothy whispers to Rosemary. 'And the right tune too,' she says, before chiming in with the congregation: '*Dear Lord and Father of mankind, forgive our foolish ways.*' She looks around her, at all the lonely people, all the women left behind by husbands dead. Some have been dead for years, like Hugo. Like Gertie's Reggie. Dorothy looks tenderly at Gertie, lying there in front of them, and wonders if all the others feel as she does – a small envy. After all, Gertie is with Reggie now, in heaven. Tears well up and she has the good grace to let them fall: she loves a funeral. Rosemary links her arm into Dorothy's, and they sing together, their weak sopranos getting stronger as their voices warm to the tune.

✿

After the service, Nandini has invited everyone to her house for the wake. Gertie's little home would be too small, for all the people who would want to pay their respects. She was well known in the community, for her charity work for orphanages back home, and for her welfare work with refugee families in London. She has kept it hidden, flitting here and there on buses, so that only at the wake do people start to piece together her importance to so many. It is typical of Gertie, Nandini thinks, as she helps to serve the fish-balls and samosas, that as people stop her to talk, they all have a story to tell of Gertie, sometimes a whispered joke. Only Shamini says something bitter, but people know her as difficult, resentful of a life lived well. She pulls Nandini to one side, says, 'All these people! How can you afford?' But Nandini tosses her head, pulls her wrist away. Shamini takes the opportunity to ask, 'Is Preethi very upset? She *seems* very upset.' Nandini follows her gaze to where Preethi sits, legs splayed apart, her black suit skirt riding up to reveal her thighs. Her hair is messy, her lipstick blurred: she looks like a broken doll, Nandini thinks. It is a shame, for Nandini is proud of Preethi's wealth, her intellectual prowess, the power her novel has given her. Poor little Preethi, Victor's favourite, his little girl. Nandini goes to her, stands in front of her daughter with the plate of food offered. It is only when she stands with her knees touching Preethi's, that she realises, behind the sunglasses, Preethi is asleep.

Preethi wakes because her mother kicks her foot. She is startled to find herself in her family's home. For a moment, she is disorientated and doesn't know who is alive and who dead. She thinks she awakes into a different party, and that her father is in the dining room, and Gertie and Mrs Chatterjee are sitting with their backs to her. She looks around: there, in the corner, is Chitra, on her own, in a high-necked black blouse and smart trousers. She is very much alone, and Preethi thinks how beautiful she is, how glacial in her beauty. Gertie is not here, she has to remind herself. Gertie is dead. She fumbles her feet into her shoes. Is Simon there? Did Simon come with her? She looks into the garden, and outside, men stand and smoke. Among them, Simon laughs with Mohan who carries a little girl on his arm. She will go out to them: she wants to talk to Mo, wants to throw her arm around his shoulders and hold on to his steady assurance. Mo is not changed, the way her family have changed, the way *she* has changed. Rohan dead, Gehan in New Zealand, as far from here as possible. Only she and Ma now, Dad gone five years ago. She wants to see someone from her childhood, she wants to say 'What has become of me?'

As she stands, she stumbles forwards and catches herself just in time, against a chair. Dorothy comes to her side. 'Come with me, sweetheart,' she says gently, and takes Preethi's hand.

'I was thinking about Gertie, Dorothy. I was thinking it was like the song: do you remember that song about the corpse?'

'No, darling. Come on, let's get you a drink of water in the kitchen.' As they walk through the crowd, she starts to hum. She can see Simon stand on tiptoe and register that she is not where he left her. He will come for her in a minute, and she'll be safe.

Her voice is loud, but in tune, and clear. She likes the sound of it, likes the noise in her head. It is not her *own* voice, not the voice of crying or grief or fear. She begins to sing.

Dorothy hushes her, takes her firmly into the kitchen. She walks past the photographs in their frames on the wall. There is her wedding photo, her parents' in Sri Lanka, Rohan and Victor on Ro's graduation day, Gehan in New Zealand with his family, Gertie with her foster child, Chitra and her ex-husband Roy, Dorothy and Hugo, Siro and Wesley, Mohan, Nil and Vita. She sees that they have dust on them, she sees the dust, not the faces, sees the appalling age of the photos, the creeping bleed of moisture trapped. She sees the dust only.

Mumtaz is on his own at the wake. He doesn't know why he accepted a lift, why he is standing with his orange juice and samosa in a corner. People smile at him, and he at them, but no one talks to him. He looks around at the house, at the mainly Sri Lankan people, worries that he looks out of place, wonders how to get out soon. A woman brings more food on a plate. She is in her late forties, and has that arched-brow type of face that reminds him of Anna Karenina – kind, funny, ironic. She says, 'I'm Nil. Are you a friend of Gertie?'

Mumtaz chokes. He has yet to get used to the sudden thrust of a conversation on to his thoughts. After all these years, his comfort is still in silence. He makes an overplay of his coughing, to give him time to formulate the words, then says: 'We met on a bus,' gasping words quietly out.

'Oh! I know about you. We used to tease Gertie about you. You're her 7/7 boyfriend.' He grimaces. 'Oh, I'm sorry, I didn't mean to offend you,' she said, 'but Gertie was very proud of her friendship with you. We all thought it very touching – how you met up in your café.'

He smiles and looks away. Tears have taken him unawares. She sees them, he knows, and he is mortified. 'I . . . really liked her,' he whispers. 'We were friends. We talked about things.'

'Yes,' she says. She offers the plate of food, and he takes a fish-ball. She looks about for others to offer the food to. Then, she says, 'We have an album of photos, you know. Over there, on the coffee table. Nandini Aunty is clearing up Gertie's house, and we found boxes and boxes of photographs.'

He is grateful for the diversion. He lifts his hand, says, 'I'll just go and wash my fingers,' and walks away. He has to creep behind and around groups of people standing in the hallway and the corridor, and as he gets nearer to the door, he realises the people in the corridor have stopped speaking and are listening to a commotion coming from the kitchen. He pauses, starts to walk back, but stops abruptly, still. The photographs on the wall have arrested him. It is a photo he recognises: Gertie, her hair only greying, holding a child on her lap, and the child is his mother.

Preethi is surrounded by women: her mother, Dorothy, Shamini, Chitra. Nandini stands behind her, not daring to look at her, Preethi thinks. When Simon pushes his way into the kitchen, Preethi feels him, more than sees him, feels the aura of calm about him, the way that he wraps her, as if from him emanate rays of trust and warmth. She goes to stand, but Nandini's hand comes to her shoulder, pushes her down.

'Hey,' she says. Simon walks to her and takes her hand to pull her up.

Nandini says, 'No, Simon,' and amazingly, he leaves, as if by prior agreement.

They sit in silence. Then, of all people, Shamini says, 'You shouldn't have written that book,' as if it is her business.

Dorothy says sharply, 'Enough. It is not up to us to tell a writer what to write.' Shamini stands, and is quickly gone. 'But,' Dorothy says quietly, watching Shamini leave, 'she is right. It made trouble for you, for all of us. Look now: Sri Lanka is rid of terrorism. Everyone has the flag flying – they are all nationalists. It is a peaceful place.'

'Peaceful, my arse,' Preethi says. The women pull in air sharply, tsk tsk at her. 'For goodness' sake, it's a dictatorship and he kills anyone who doesn't agree with him: even his closest friends! Editors of newspapers! Can't you see? It's a mad place, and no one really cares about the dead, not here, not there. Of course I should have written the book.'

'Yes,' Chitra says. 'Yes, of course you should. It was a brave book, a wonderful book. I read it and I loved it and loved it more when I knew it was about Sri Lanka.' Preethi smiles at her across the table, and Chitra takes her advantage. 'So, why not be brave and stand up for it? Why fall apart? Why are you drinking so much? It is time to stop being so . . . I'm sorry . . . so *weak*.'

Nil comes in. 'Weak?' she asks with a smile, 'who is weak?'

Preethi looks toward her desperately. 'Me. They say I'm weak,' but as she says it, she makes a sudden movement, of arms waving in front of her, her wrists feeble and tumbling. Dorothy and Chitra wince, and Nandini turns away.

Nil laughs. 'Oh, leave her alone,' she says. 'Let her be herself.'

'What, a drunk? Not *my* daughter,' Nandini suddenly explodes.

'Yes, *your* daughter,' Preethi says.

'Not *a* drunk,' Nil says. 'Just drunk sometimes. We're all upset today, aren't we? We all loved Gertie, and . . .'

'It's not that, Nil. That's not why I'm upset.'

'Why then?'

'I don't know. Don't ask me. I . . . I just want it all over with. I want to stop feeling this way.'

'What way?' Dorothy says more tenderly now.

Preethi wakes up. Why would she share her innermost thoughts with these old women? They have no understanding: only judgement. 'Where's Simon?' She stands up. None of them stop her. 'I think we'll go, Mum.' She looks around for her sunglasses, walks unsteadily to the door, where Nil puts her arms around her.

'No one is judging you,' Nil says, and then to the rest of them, 'no one has the right.' Preethi hugs Nil, holds her close. 'But Preethi, you know, in a way they're right.'

Preethi pulls herself away. 'But *you* of all people would know how I feel, Nil. *You* know how it's always been – here we are, in England, and we're different, and there we are in Sri Lanka, and we're different. Nowhere is home, nowhere! And it makes me *so angry*! I want to feel I *belong*. I want to feel . . .'

'But, you do belong,' Nil says, pulling her close. 'Here. You belong here, with *us*. You belong with Simon, with your children. Why have a meltdown about something like that, for goodness' sake?'

'I'm not. It's not just *that*. It's everything,' she says in despair. She throws her hands in the air, tries to pass Nil. But Nil stops her.

'You're not allowed to break down. Simple as that, Preethi,' Nil says, laughing.

'Why? Because I'm a dutiful daughter? Because it would be letting the side down? Me being depressed is not about winning or losing, you know. It's not about how it looks, or who else it affects.'

And then Nil is angry. 'Yes. Yes it *is*. You have to deal with it. Stop being so bloody selfish. You think none of us feel the way you feel? You think you're the only one? This is not about being white or being brown, or belonging or not belonging or winning or losing. You're not allowed – *I'm* telling you now, Preethi,' and Nil turns Preethi's face to her own. '*I* won't allow it. *We*,' she juts her chin at the women at the table, 'won't allow it. Because that's life, baby. Either you struggle and survive, or you go under. And we're not going to let you go under.' Preethi sees the fire in Nil's eyes, sees the reflection of herself there, but behind her, there is her mother, Dorothy, Chitra, all in Nil's eyes.

As dusk gives way to night, Nil's son Max finds Rohan's old guitar and Victor's small Thammattama drum safely stored in the dining room. He takes them out and between them, he and his uncle Mo start to play quietly. Nandini walks into the sitting room and as she passes Max, she tussles his glorious long black locks. She switches the floor lamp on so that everyone is bathed in the warm glow of the here and now. She thinks of other parties, she thinks of glorious times when Victor's voice soared above the rest of them: his laughter echoes still, in Mo's easy taps of the drum's skins.

'Aunty, what was that song Uncle used to love?'

'Which one, which one?'

'You know, the sweet one,' but Nandini cannot remember straight away.

Preethi sits with her arm hooked into Simon's, and watches her mother. She wonders whether her mother is getting old, that she can't remember the song. So much left unsaid between them, she thinks, and that is a good thing. She watches Nandini settle herself into her corner of the sofa. Then quietly Preethi says, 'It was *Ma Bale Kale*,' and they all nod, smile. Nandini claps her hands in a sliding motion. There is no sense of estrangement or sadness directed towards Preethi. She is simply there with them.

Next to Simon, on a low leather footstool, Mumtaz sits with the photo album held close to his chest. He is simply there too.

'*Ma bale kale, Ammage Ukule*,' they all sing. Nandini has no memories of her life with Victor before this room, this house. Here they had all grown up. Here, their life had happened.

ACKNOWLEDGEMENTS

I would like to thank the following people for their guidance, help and often, love: Tom Saul, Stevie Davies, Ira Fernando, Edward Saul, Isobel Saul, Miranda Saul, Spiky Saul, Nigel Jenkins, Mali Fernando, Ishani O'Connor. Thanks to Elisabeth Bennett, chief Archivist at the University of Swansea for her invaluable help with the research for 'Research'. Thank you, Su Chard, for the photo. Thank you to John Tams for permission to use 'Rolling Home' in 'At the Barn Dance'. Thank you, Euan Thorneycroft, for everything. Thanks to Richard Willis, Colin Morgan, Julie Swales and Celeste Fine. And many thanks to Alexandra Pringle and Lexy Bloom for all their advice and help.

A NOTE ON THE TYPE

ITC Galliard is an adaptation of Matthew Carter's 1978 phototype design for Mergenthaler. Galliard was modeled on the work of Robert Granjon, a sixteenth-century letter cutter, whose typefaces are renowned for their beauty and legibility. Matthew Carter combined his design skills with computer-aided technology to produce this elegant revival.